UNDERTONES

MICHELE'S STORY

MAGGIE LYNCH

Windtree
Press

Windtree Press
Hillsboro, OR 97124
Visit us at https://windtreepress.com

Publisher's Note: This is a work of fiction. Names, characters, places, and incidents are a product of the author's imagination. Locales and public names are sometimes used for atmospheric purposes. Any resemblance to actual people, living or dead, or to businesses, companies, events, institutions, or locales is completely coincidental.

Cover Art by Christy Caughie, Gilded Heart Design

Undertones / Maggie Lynch. – 2nd ed.

Print ISBN 978-19479834-7-2

Ebook ISBN 978-1-9423686-2-5

✿ Created with Vellum

This one is for Michele Templer, who has read my creative writing for years, remained my friend through love and loss, and offered sunshine to my life just by being herself. No matter how close or far we live from each other, I know she cares. Michele, you rock!

$\mathcal{M}$ichele Scott's fingers flew over the strings as she plucked the last eight bars of "Black Mountain Rag" on her bass. The vigorous applause from the twenty or thirty people in the audience washed over her and she bowed with the rest of the band. The smell of beef barbecue wafted from the grill making her mouth water and her stomach grumble. Ten hours since that piece of toast and coffee was a long time. No wonder she was hungry.

The announcer bounded up the short flight of stairs to the stage. "Great set, everybody!" he whispered, then grabbed a microphone and turned to face the audience. "Ladies and gentleman, let's hear it for the Ad Hoc Bluegrass Band. I hope they'll come back and play again in Sandy real soon!"

Michele waved to the cheering crowd, her smile as tight as the knot in her stomach. She could make it through this. Just one more time to wave at the crowd. Just one more time to thank her band-mates. Just one more time to pack up her bass and forget about her dreams. Then she could curl up at home with a triple scoop of Umpqua Chocolate Brownie Thunder and cry her eyes out watching Demi Moore try to reconnect with Patrick Swayze's ghost.

As the crowd dispersed, Michele picked up her bass and followed the other players behind the stage where they'd stacked their instrument cases. A tight grip on the bass, she hurried to her gig bag and laid it inside. She flexed her hands, staring at them as if they weren't her own.

This had been a good performance, definitely one to remember. The vocals and instrumental breaks had been tight and the sound system, thank God, had been high quality —always an unknown factor for a pick-up band.

She sighed. Time was up.

Five years gone with nothing to show for it except harder calluses and a lot of miles on her car. Oh, but how she loved it. Maybe… No. She shook her head hard. A promise was a promise. Her time was up. She'd given herself exactly five years to make it in bluegrass and swore she'd find a "real job" if she couldn't support herself by then. And here she was. Flat broke. It was time to face the truth. She dug her fingernails into her fist as she choked back tears. She could get through this. It's not like she'd never play again, it would just become a hobby.

She forced herself to stand tall and paste on a smile as the other musicians exchanged praises and headed out. She shook hands with the mandolin player and wished him well, her eyes misting as he sauntered toward his family.

"Great playing with you again, Michele." The lead guitarist barely got the words out before her boyfriend grabbed her around the waist. Her surprised squeal cut off when he dipped her dramatically for a passionate kiss. The banjo player rolled his eyes and waved goodbye as he strode off with his case. Michele discreetly turned back to her bass and finished zipping it in. She hadn't told anyone her plans. She figured it was best to quietly slip away from playing professionally. It would be easier that way.

"We're headin' out for a beer," her friend said when she finally came up for air. "Wanna come along?"

"No thanks. I think I'll hang here at the festival." She waved them off as they turned hand-in-hand, giggling at some intimate joke.

The last thing she needed was to be the third wheel with those two lovebirds. It would only remind her of her own nonexistent love life—another thing she'd given up while pursuing this ridiculous dream. She reattached the strap to the case with a resounding snap, then held her waist-length hair out of the way as she hefted the bass over her shoulder. All she wanted was to get home before she ran into anyone she knew and lost her emotional wall.

"Excuse me," a voice behind her said.

Michele swallowed hard as she turned. A friendly face smiled at her, the grey-frosted, shoulder-length bob hinting at her age. Her light-brown eyes twinkled with approval as she held out her hand to Michele.

"Hi, I'm Theresa Mosier, and I just want to say 'Wow!' You not only play a mean bass but you can sing, too. You really belt it out! The timbre of your voice is definitely distinctive."

"Thanks." Michele smiled. Audiences were without fail surprised by the rich, husky voice booming from her slender, five-foot two-inch frame. Apparently, most people expected her to sound like Shirley Temple.

"You sparkle up there, so full of energy. And you're not timid about involving yourself in the between-song banter. It was very entertaining."

A fan's praise was usually music to the soul, but not today. She wasn't sure she could smile and be nice for long, knowing this was the last time she'd play professionally.

Theresa cleared her throat. "Uh...am I to understand from the name Ad Hoc Bluegrass Band that you're not a full-time, fixed group of musicians?"

"That's right," Michele answered, her voice straining against the stone in her throat. She took a deep breath. "We're a circle of friends, mostly fellow music majors I know from my days at Portland State. It's pretty informal. The band members change from gig to gig, depending on who's available."

"And... is that your goal—as a musician?" Theresa asked, her head cocked to one side.

"Well, no...not really. I've always wanted to do this...as a career," Michele stammered. "But I've recently decided..."

"Great! Here." Theresa handed her a cream-colored business card with the name Sweetwater Canyon emblazoned in burgundy-red ink above an artistic rendition of Mt. Hood and a winding river. Below the drawing it read *Music Americana*. At the bottom right in smaller print were Theresa's name, a phone number, website, an email and a P.O. Box address.

"There are five of us in the band—all women. We play a fusion of traditional music—bluegrass, country, folk, Celtic, and anything else that strikes our fancy. On occasion will take on a rock or jazz tune and mold it to our acoustic sound. We do covers of songs by artists we like, whatever the style—Mary Chapin Carpenter, Keb' Mo', Ry Cooder, Dr. John, it doesn't matter—and each of us writes a little of our own music."

Oh, man, was this for real? Playing with this type of band would be a dream come true. As much as she loved bluegrass, having the opportunity to work in related styles would be a joy and a challenge. She clasped her hands together, afraid she might be caught silently fingering the bass part to a Keb' Mo' tune.

"Most of our gigs are at smaller venues around Portland, down to Eugene, up as far as Seattle, sometimes across the mountains to Spokane, Yakima or Bend. We're hoping to release our first CD toward the end of the year after a summer and early fall road trip. We're looking to build our fan base."

Michele didn't trust herself to speak. Could be one of those waking dreams where everything seemed real but eventually she would realize she was still asleep in bed?

"We have a tour set to begin in six weeks, all across the Midwest with additional stops in Idaho, North Carolina, and Arizona." Theresa paused and put her hands on her hips. "There's only one problem."

Michele's fingers tightened on the card.

"We've lost our bass player."

"You...you've lost your bass player?"

"Well, no...I guess that's not literally true," Theresa said with a laugh. "We know exactly where Denise is. It's just that she's no longer available."

Michele held her breath. Could it be? She didn't dare hope.

"Denise's husband is a marketing executive for Nike. He was just offered a promotion and a transfer to Hong Kong. She'll be gone for at least two years."

"Oh, I'm sorry," Michele blurted as the breath escaped from her lungs all at once. "That is, I mean I'm sorry for you...but happy for her...I mean, if that's what she wants...or if...oh, hell!" She trailed off, thoroughly mortified. Way to make a great first impression.

Theresa's lipped quirked up in a half smile as though she heard such jumbled thoughts and fractured sentences every day. "Let me get right to the point. We're looking for a replacement to tour and record with us. You can certainly carry your weight on bass, and I assume someone with your talent can sing *a cappella* and harmonize in the lower ranges. The question is if you're a good fit, personality-wise, with the rest of the band. Also if you're cut out for life on the road—some people simply aren't. It's not the same as local gigs where you meet up for a couple of hours and then go your own way. On the road we're together 24/7. You *have* to be able to get along when you're on tour."

Michele's chest tightened as it filled with a breath she didn't dare let go.

"One more thing, you'd have to give up your day job. This is a full-time commitment. If you're at all interested, give me a call." Theresa pointed at the number on the bottom of the card. "We'll set up an audition and get-acquainted session with the rest of the band to see how it feels."

The air rushed out all at once. "Of course I'm interested. I would love to audition."

Theresa patted Michele's hand. "No rush. Think it over a few days. I gave you a lot to take in. If you still want to do it, call me and I'll give you directions to my house—that's where we practice. I live up the mountain."

~

MICHELE TUCKED a wayward strand of hair behind her right ear as she drove the last couple miles up Mt. Hood to Zig Zag. She sang several scales and arpeggios until she felt more relaxed. Then, just for fun she jumped into a couple of bawdy Irish drinking songs at the top of her lungs. They always lifted her spirits. She wondered what Theresa would think about that.

When she traveled this route in winter to reach the ski areas on the upper slopes, the mountain almost always hid behind a thick curtain of clouds. But on this delightful spring afternoon she had "lifted her skirts," as the locals say, and was revealed in all her glory. She took it as a good omen.

Michele glanced over her shoulder for the twentieth time since leaving home to inspect her prized possession. Taking up most of the cargo space, even with the rear seat folded down, the outsized, ungainly case was still strapped down. Inside rested the Kay upright bass that had consumed every penny of Michele's meager savings, plus two years of monthly payments, and had generated countless arguments with Jon—her ex. Her bass was her best friend, and Jon had said it was the only thing she truly loved. At least she could count on it to never judge her. That was more than she could say for any man.

She spotted the bright red mailbox and checked her watch. Right on time. Turning into the driveway, she could see nothing beyond the towering evergreens that lined the narrow track. Their interlocking branches created a green tunnel leading deeper into the forest. Michele emerged from the semi-darkness into a clearing shaded only by a scattering of massive Douglas Firs. Their lower limbs, starting perhaps fifty feet up the bare trunks, admitted plenty of filtered sunlight and gave the setting an airy feel quite different from the claustrophobic entrance.

The driveway terminated in a circular gravel parking area rimmed with large stones. Off to the left stood an open-sided carport under which rested a green, four-door sedan and a large RV. But her attention quickly focused on the house nestled among the old-growth trees.

The two-story log cabin was obviously old but solid. The dark brown logs matched the standing trees in color, and the cedar shake roof was weathered to a silvery grey and half-hidden under a pillowy blanket of green moss. A deep, covered porch, scattered with cushioned wicker furniture, wrapped around the front and sides. Sword ferns, trillium, lupine and rhododendron grew in profusion under the trees and around the cabin's river rock foundation.

It didn't look like it was built, but rather like it sprang from the earth. Beside the front door she noticed a carved wooden sign mounted on the wall. *Abhainn fàrdach,* it read. She had no idea what it meant, or even what the language was. She chuckled. Maybe elvish. Just another surreal touch in this mystical place.

Michele moved to the back of the car, lifted the cargo hatch and, with practiced motions, gently extracted the heavy case and lugged it up onto the porch to rest against a pillar. Squaring her shoulders, she took a deep breath, rang the doorbell and waited for her life to begin anew.

"No, Earl!" A teenaged girl in faded jeans and a baggy orange t-shirt balanced on one leg with her left hip against the frame while her right foot held back a grey-and-white cat poised to spring. She shook her leg at the cat. "Back up." The cat meowed and still hunched in anticipation of escape. The girl stomped her bare foot directly in front of the cat's face. He jumped straight up, turned one hundred eighty degrees in mid-air and scampered back to the darkened interior.

The girl giggled, showing a pronounced dimple on her left cheek. With a swing of her hip she pushed the door open wider. The loose posture, smooth healthy skin and voice indicated the girl might be about 14 or 15, but Michele wasn't sure. Her height and brimming self-confidence suited someone a bit older. She held a red apple in her right hand with several bites missing.

"Hi, sorry about Earl," the girl said, brushing the bangs of her shoulder length blond hair. "He's our free spirit. Even though he's a house cat, he still has a wild desire to explore. We have coyotes poking around up here, so it wouldn't be good for his health." The girl switched the apple to her left hand and began to offer her right to shake, then withdrew it. "Oops. Sorry. Snacking. All sticky. I'm always snacking," she giggled again. "Just can't seem to get enough to eat."

Michele smiled. "Hi I'm…"

"I know. Michele," the girl interrupted without taking a breath. "I'm Kathryn, but I go by Kat. My Mom is Theresa. I think you met her. Right? Yeah, right. That darn cat. I wonder where Doc…Oh, I play accordion…mostly. Also pick up on percussion…but then I'm trying to learn fiddle but it's not cooperating."

"Did you say accordion?" Michele asked.

"How long did it take you to grow your hair to your waist? Gosh, I hope Doc isn't hiding. Hey," Kat pointed to Michele's case on the porch. "Do you like Kays? Or is that German?"

"Why yes, it's a— "

"Geez, where's my manners? Mom always says I forget them. Come in, come in." Kat gestured for Michele to enter. "Just watch your step. We have two more besides Earl, but they're usually scaredy cats. I'll show you where we set up. I think the others are coming…or is that later, I'm not sure." She spread her fingers in front of her. "Darn! Why can't I grow my nails like other girls?"

A little dazed, Michele lifted her bass over the threshold and followed Kat inside. Did the girl ever take a breath?

Kat continued her nonstop, one-sided conversation about the house, the cats, the members of the band, high school events, her current boyfriend, and countless other non-sequiturs as Michele tried to absorb as much of the interior as possible.

Most of the main floor seemed to consist of one large room. She noticed wood everywhere. Over the entryway, dining room and kitchen, square-cut fir beams supported a ceiling of unstained pine planks. The ceiling stopped short of the living room and Michele's eye followed the vaulted space upward perhaps twenty feet to the steeply pitched roofline.

A sliding glass door in the exposed-log wall on the far side of the living room opened and Theresa appeared, laughing and holding out her hand. "Welcome. I see you've met my daughter. I hope she didn't scare you away already."

"Mom!" Kat drew out the word and let out a big sigh as she slumped with her hand on a hip.

Theresa pulled Kat to her side, with a warm one-armed hug. "You know we love you and we can't survive without you. But you do talk and talk."

"I know. I talk, talk, talk and eat, eat, eat." Kat giggled. "But it's important to be friendly. Hey, do you know ..." and she was off again, walking toward the refrigerator in the kitchen while talking to the cat.

"Go ahead and take your bass in there," Theresa pointed through the door. "The rest of the group will be here shortly. Kat, while you're in there, turn the burner on under that pot on the stove. Be sure to set it on low."

"Okay." Kat waved fingers at Michele. "See ya later, don't forget that I ..." and she turned her, the rest of her sentence trailing behind her.

Michele drew in a breath as she saw the view from the bright, spacious room that was obviously an addition to the original cabin. The opposite wall consisted entirely of large picture windows. About a hundred yards from the house, an untamed river hurtled along its tree-lined channel, plunging over small cataracts and crashing against jumbled boulders. It mimicked the feeling in her stomach.

"It's the Sandy—you crossed it just down the road," Theresa said.

"It's so beautiful! How can you ever leave?"

"Well, I don't like to ... but I've got to make a living. When I come home from a long week of traveling and gigs, I appreciate it all the more. You'll see."

"You can set up over there." Theresa pointed to a space fitted like a stage—boom microphones, monitors, instrument stands, straight-backed chairs and a mixing board. The rest of the sparse furnishings crowded against one wall.

"Is the newbie here yet? I have some tricks up my sleeve." An accented voice from inside the main house asked. What was it? Irish? Scottish? Definitely a soprano.

Theresa rolled her eyes. "That's Rachel. Don't worry, she doesn't bite." She turned toward the door. "I'm sure Sarah isn't far behind. Go ahead and warm up. I'll try to calm the hordes before they descend on you."

Now that the moment was almost upon her, Michele's case of the jitters returned with a vengeance. Would she measure up? What if she wasn't good enough? What if they just didn't like her?

With shaking hands Michele stood her bass on its endpin and plucked each of the strings, listening carefully. She fingered the harmonics and tuned by ear, followed by practicing a couple of the more difficult riffs she'd worked out to play for one of the songs. She shook out her left hand after making the same mistake three times. *Please, not now. I know this. I can do this.* Her hours of practice would pay off as long as she didn't let her nerves get the best of her.

She closed her eyes and plucked each note of the errant riff at a slower speed, concentrating on the deep tones. Her breathing slowed and she increased the speed back to the required time signature. Now, her fingers moved with ease and confidence up and down the neck as she let the resonance wash over her fear.

As she finished the piece for the second time, she heard a cacophony of voices coming from the front of the house, then Theresa, Kat and two other women swept into the room with a burst of color and talking. Theresa waved her arms in a palms-down motion. "Let me start the introductions. Michele, this is Rachel Cullen, our fiddler."

"And mandolin virtuoso," Kat added.

Rachel took Michele's hand in a firm grip. "So, you're the fresh meat...I mean talent," she said in a charming brogue. Her face flashed a huge smile, but her deep-blue eyes flashed to the side, as though she were withholding judgment for the time being.

Stunning to behold, Rachel stood three to four inches taller than Michele, probably no older than thirty and built lean. She exuded confidence, as evidenced by her attire: tight white shorts and a lime-green, sleeveless tank top that rode just above her navel. Michele noted admiringly that she wore them very well. She also noticed the well-defined biceps as they shook hands.

Michele took pains to keep herself in shape but whereas she had the elfin body of a gymnast, Rachel looked more like a track and field athlete. Her most striking feature, however, had to be her long platinum blonde hair. Not dyed, Michele wagered, because her skin was also very pale. It certainly suited her confidence and slight rebellious streak.

"And this," Theresa said, "is Sarah Cosgrave. She plays guitar, flute, and assorted other instruments." Michele looked up into friendly, olive-green eyes.

"Welcome, Michele. Theresa has already raved about your singing," Sarah said, both of her hands warmly covering Michele's. Sarah's melodious voice was as lithe as her physique. She moved with the willowy grace of a dancer. Thick, straight, chestnut-brown hair fell casually over and below her shoulders, perfectly complementing an elegant heart-shaped face. She suspected that Sarah easily held the attention of all the male audience members wherever Sweetwater Canyon played.

"What do you say we play a little first and chat later?" Theresa said, shepherding the group toward the stage. "Michele, you take the outside mike." She pointed mid stage left where there were two mikes —one lower for her bass and another higher for her voice.

Her heart fluttering, Michele picked up her bass and stretched her fingers over the strings. She took a deep, calming breath as the four other women took their accustomed positions: Kat and Rachel stood to Michele's right, and Sarah and Theresa stood to her left and slightly in front of the others. Like Michele, they each had two microphones. Sarah turned on the soundboard, activating the mikes. Then each adjusted her own stage monitor.

"Okay, Kat, give us an 'A' on your accordion," Theresa directed. When they were all satisfactorily tuned, Theresa said, "Let's warm up our fingers to start with, then we'll stretch our vocal chords. How about *County Clare?*

Michele nodded as she moved her fingers to the first position for the song, thankful to be starting with something she knew well before getting to the more difficult pieces.

Kat put down her accordion and stood ready with the *bohdran*—a Celtic drum.

Theresa kicked it off with an eight-measure banjo solo in the tempo of a classic Irish jig and then Rachel joined in for the next eight, matching her note-for-note on the fiddle. Sarah came in next, strumming chords on her dreadnought guitar and letting them ring while the banjo-fiddle duet continued to build.

Wow! They're really tight. Michele noticed they were taking a New Grass Revival turn with this instrumental tune. It gave her a chance to show her stuff right off the bat.

At measure thirty-two, Michele added her bass line to the mix and Kat interwove a simple but persuasive beat on her *bohdran*. Michele recognized the break halfway through where the melody changed and the tempo accelerated to a lightning pace. Here, she really cut loose, her left hand flying up and down the neck while her right slapped the strings with controlled abandon. The tune concluded with the banjo and fiddle again matching licks and all the instruments sustaining a long, final note. She half expected to hear a spontaneous burst of applause.

"Not bad, everybody," Theresa said. "Michele, you've got that bass line down pat."

"Yeah, I think that was at least as good, if not better, than Denise," Kat added, and the other two women voiced their agreement.

Michele warmed with pride.

Theresa leafed through several pages, then tapped one on her stand. "Okay, let's try one of the vocal numbers I e-mailed to Michele. *If I Needed You* will give us a chance to use all five voices. Michele, would you prefer first or second tenor on this one?"

"I think second tenor would be the best fit," Michele responded.

"Good." Theresa rested her banjo on its stand and reached for a small-bodied nylon string guitar. "Kat, time to strap on the squeeze-box." She turned to Michele. "Sarah and I will do a four-bar intro on the guitars then we'll all come in on vocals. Michele, you start laying down your bass line at the pickup to nine—the same time Kat comes in on the accordion."

Michele knew this song by heart; the bass part was easy so she could concentrate on merging her voice into the blend.

Sarah sang solo lead on the verses in her sweet alto and Rachel put down a wistful fiddle break so silky that the bow seemed to float over the strings. Even Kat's accordion added a nice smoothness to the instruments and the voices. They ended with all five women repeating the opening refrain by softly humming the melody.

"That sounded pretty seamless to me," Sarah said in her soft voice.

Rachel nodded and turned to Michele. "Hey, not bad."

Michele suspected that, coming from Rachel, this constituted high praise indeed.

"Way cool," Kat said.

"Thanks." Michele's body pulsed with the rhythm and the notes still swirled in her head.

They ran through six more songs, mixing the tempos and alternating instrumentals with vocal numbers. Michele kept up, but just barely. The group was very, very tight. She could tell they'd spent many years together.

Finally, after the last song, Theresa said, "That's enough for today."

Michele took her time moving her bass to pack up. She still felt the flush of a great session. Whether they asked her to join them or not, she knew she had just done the best audition of her life—and she'd enjoyed every minute of it.

Theresa touched Michele's shoulder. "Let's go into the kitchen and chat. I've got a pot of chili on the stove."

"I'll get the bowls and spoons," Kat piped up, practically dancing from one foot to the other. "Who wants what to drink? I think we're out of..." and she disappeared through the door. The others followed at a much less frenzied pace.

Sarah, Rachel and Michele perched on high swivel chairs around the kitchen island while Theresa stirred the chili and Kat busied herself in the cupboards, chattering to herself all the while.

"You're good," Sarah said, turning to Michele. "So tell me, why the bass? It's pretty rare to find a woman playing bass."

"Yeah, why not something a little…smaller?" Rachel smiled, looking her up and down.

"Well," Michele paused determining how much to share. *Ah, go for it.* "That bass is probably my best friend. It's stayed with me longer than any other relationship. It has the power to make me cry, to make me laugh and to warm my soul. In the last six years, it has shown me how to work hard and enjoy my path no matter what anyone else thinks of my choices. It has simply become the best part of me."

Silence. Everyone looked down at their bowls, even Kat. Michele lifted a hand to cover her heart. Her breath stuttered. *Whoa! Too deep… too heavy.*

"Eerie…but cool," Kat said. "Do, do, do, do," she hummed the opening bars of the Twilight Zone theme and everyone laughed.

Smiling, Michele joined in the light hearted banter. She learned that Rachel came from Dunoon, a small town near Glasgow, and had immigrated to the States four years ago. Sarah had been a history teacher at Sandy High School until budget cuts and a lack of seniority forced her layoff. Since then she had worked the front desk at Timberline Lodge to make ends meet. Theresa mentioned a divorce and a mostly unsuccessful career as a real estate agent.

Michele loved the easy-going camaraderie of this group. She felt comfortable. They made it easy to talk, to share opinions and she now knew the teasing was without malice. "You know, I never would have pictured an accordion in a band like this," she said, "or that it could possibly sound so good with this kind of music. In fact, the only time I've even heard one was at my grandparents' house back in Montana where every…Sunday… afternoon" —she drew out each word dramatically—"they would play these old Lawrence Welk records on their phonograph." Michele sighed. "Much as I loved my grandparents, I always felt that those visits qualified as cruel and unusual punishment."

A dead quiet sucked out every bit of air. Each member of the band stared at her in disbelief with eyes wide and mouths agape.

Michele froze. Her heart beat so loud in her ears she was sure even the neighbors could hear it over the river. She panicked in silence, trying to think of a way to undo the damage. She'd been having such a good time. After things were going so well she had now completely blown her chance. Too shocked to even cry, Michele held her breath as the seconds of her life ticked away.

Then the room erupted in gales of laughter, startling the cats not half as much as Michele.

"Consider yourself initiated, newbie," Rachel said, patting her on the back. Her voice was mischievous, but her eyes finally showed genuine acceptance.

The others got up from their chairs and gathered around Michele. "Sorry about that," Sarah said sympathetically, "we just couldn't resist. The whole accordion thing always comes up."

Kat held her sides, almost doubled over. "We love to pull that on people, and you stepped right into the trap."

Still laughing, Theresa gave her a hug. "Welcome to Sweetwater Canyon."

"Do you mean?" Michele began, her eyes misting in surprise.

"Yes," Theresa said, hugging her again. "You're in." She looked her straight in the eyes. "You're talented, sweet, and a good sport. We'd love to have you join us."

CHAPTER 2

$\mathcal{M}$ichele stood and stepped away from the keyboard. With a heavy sigh she tore up the sheet of music she'd been trying to compose. The song just wasn't coming together. Lifting her hands toward the ceiling, she stretched as tall as she could, then slowly twisted to the left and then to the right until she heard the comforting, crackling sound of her spine readjusting.

The past few weeks had been a heady blur as she worked hard to catch up with the other members of Sweetwater Canyon. She needed two original songs to include in their tour set. During a rehearsal last week she'd debuted Breaking the Bonds to a very enthusiastic reception. One down, but the second one was going nowhere. How could she possibly write a love song when her only experience with the subject had been the ruinous relationship with Jon? Perhaps she should start from scratch with a different theme.

Michele retrieved a half-finished glass of tomato juice from the fridge. Sipping it slowly, she stood in the middle of her tiny studio apartment and basked in the mid-day sunshine pouring in from the four large, east-facing windows. She rolled her head in a circle, working out the kinks in her neck. She needed a break. Thinking about her non-existent love life wasn't helping at all.

Turning in a slow circle, she finished her tomato juice and took only a few steps to the kitchen—actually kitchen, living room, dining room, bedroom, all in one. "Well, Michele," she said with a touch of resignation, "you sure don't have much to show for your twenty-eight years."

Most of her friends were married and already had at least one child, a house in the burbs, and a career that was definitely on the upswing. But Michele had never been "most" people. From the day that Jon had walked out five years ago, no man had spent the night in her bed. Both sex and romance eluded her. Love? She figured that just wasn't in the cards. And she was fine with that. Really. Now that her career dreams were coming to fruition, she had no time for a relationship anyway.

The antique clock on the credenza—an heirloom from her mother's family—bonged twice and she looked up. She still had plenty of time to get the tickets. Rehearsal didn't start until four today, and it was an hour's drive up the mountain. She grabbed two twenty dollar bills from her wallet and stuffed them in the right front pocket of her jeans and ran out the door, locking it solidly behind her.

Sweetwater Canyon practiced six days a week, taking only Sundays off—and Michele had special plans for a concert next Sunday. Alison Krauss would be at the amphitheater in Bend. Even though Bend was a three-hour drive from Portland over the Cascades, it was Union Station's only concert date in the Northwest and she wasn't going to miss it.

Michele jogged the four blocks to the Ticketmaster office at Portland State and took her place at the end of a long line. Several teenage girls were ahead of her buying tickets six months in advance for a Brittany Spears concert at the Rose Garden. The line dwindled and Michele perked her ears listening to the middle-aged woman asking about symphony tickets for the upcoming season. Yes! No one was asking for Alison Kraus tickets. Just one more person to go—the tall man directly in front of her. His stylish Polo shirt and slightly mussed hair gave her confidence he wouldn't want her tickets. Certainly not the Alison Krauss type. He looked more like an opera or Cirque du Soleil fan.

Standing behind him Michele came only to the top of his shoulder blades. Her eyes traveled down his broad back. Powerful, but not overly pumped like those muscle-bound types who live in the weight room. Hmmm…nice butt! It looked like he was poured into that pair of jeans. Embarrassed by her train of thought, she blushed and quickly looked away. Then the line moved forward and he bent to the window to order, his butt again sustaining her attention.

"I'd like two tickets for Alison Krauss," he said.

"You're very lucky, sir," the woman behind the counter said. "The reserved seats are sold out. I'm afraid there's only lawn seating, and I've got just two tickets left."

Michele couldn't believe her ears! She squeezed next to him, her face cheek to cheek with his as she tried to talk through the same small speaker hole in the window.

"No! Wait! These can't be the last two tickets. I have to go. This is my only chance to see her."

The woman gave her a blank stare while the man turned toward her. The left corner of his mouth quirked up to form a bemused smile. Michele felt the heat rise to her cheeks as she blushed once again.

"I'm soooooooooo sorry," she apologized to both of them. "I don't know what got into me. I'm…oh gosh…" She quickly turned to leave, but the man reached out and laid a hand gently on her forearm.

"Wait. I'll happily give up my tickets to someone who wants to go that badly." His eyes followed hers as she looked down at her arm. "Sorry," he said in a gentle tone, releasing his grip.

"Thank you, but I really couldn't take yours." She stared at her arm, wondering why it stayed stuck in midair as if it was no longer under her control. She forced it down to her side, focusing on letting it hang casually against her thigh.

"Please?" He held up his index finger. "Hold just a moment? Maybe we can work something out."

She turned her face upward. His eyes. His blue-green eyes held her transfixed.

"Give me one minute," he said, reaching for the wallet in his back pocket.

Unable to find any words or to move, Michele simply stared.

He turned to complete his transaction, his voice a distinct, rich baritone. He talked easily with the woman at the window, thanking her as he put the receipt and credit card back in his wallet. Michele studied his profile. A pronounced chin led to a chiseled cheekbone. Not a thin face, but well defined and strong. The thick hair was cut just above the collar of his shirt, the style neat along the back with a natural curl that created waves. The muss she'd noticed earlier was closer to the crown, where it appeared he had deliberately made sure there was no part. The jet-black hair color captivated her almost as much as those mesmerizing eyes. She tried to guess his age, maybe twenty-eight or thirty. He definitely didn't look older than thirty.

Then he turned to face her, a roguish smile lit up those deep-set eyes.

"Maybe there's a way we can both come out ahead. How many tickets were you looking to buy?"

"Just one," she barely choked out a whisper. Damn! Should I have told him that? I should have said two. Why didn't I say two? She was too dazed to think straight.

"Excellent! Then you get what you want," he said, holding out a ticket, "and I get what I want."

"Which is…?"

"To take you to the concert."

"No, no…I couldn't," she said, struggling to recover a semblance of self-control. "I don't even know you."

"Well, we can easily fix that. Let me buy you a cup of coffee?"

"No!" Michele blurted as panic set in. This was not at all what she wanted. She wanted nothing to do with men. She had a new career. She'd be traveling. She'd be unavailable. It didn't matter that he was charming, gorgeous… maybe even nice. She'd sworn off men and she was going to keep her promise.

"No, thank you," she repeated with more confidence. "I'm not in the habit of going off with strange men."

"I'm not so strange, once you get to know me." Those twinkling eyes chipped away at her resolve. "Just give me five minutes to make my case."

She sighed and looked away. She'd hear him out and then that would be the end of it. She could be polite and then be on her way.

"Okay, five minutes. I'm heading down the Park Blocks. You'll have to talk while I walk." She started toward the main entrance of the student union building, not looking back to see if he followed. He reached the door first and held it open for her, still smiling broadly.

They emerged onto the busy sidewalk and she turned right toward her apartment then hesitated. She certainly didn't want to lead him to her building.

"There's an empty bench," he said pointing to a shaded spot near a raised flower bed in the center of the park blocks. "Could we sit for just a couple of minutes?"

"Good idea." She hurried toward the bench and took a seat, but he continued to stand, pacing up and down in front of her. He seemed to be gathering his thoughts. She didn't dare look up and give those eyes power over her again. Instead, she focused on the low circular brick wall that outlined a bed of multi-colored pansies just behind him.

"Let me try this again," he began in a serious tone augmented by his rich, deep voice. "Would you do me the honor of being my date for the Alison Krauss concert?"

Michele giggled. "You've got to be kidding. Who are you?" She tilted her face up to meet his gaze. "'Do me the honor?' No one talks like that anymore."

"Okay. So, the chivalrous approach doesn't work with you." He sighed and rubbed the back of his neck, then smiled and took a deep breath.

"How about this?" He put both hands in his front pockets, leaned back and thrust his hips forward slightly like a clichéd cowboy. Michele almost grinned, but held it back.

"Howdy, Miss," he drawled. "I've got two tickets to this rip-snortin' concert and I've heard tell you wanna go. I think you're kinda decent lookin' and it don't seem that you got cooties, so I thought to myself 'What the heck, I might could spend a day with this purty little filly.'"

He placed his hand over his heart. "I promise to shower and brush my teeth 'forehand, and I swear I won't put any moves on you...that is, unless you want me to." He exaggerated a wink.

She couldn't hold back her smile any longer. "I don't know that your pick-up lines are getting any better. But at least you're sounding more truthful."

"Truth is stranger than fiction, Ma'am," he replied, pursing his lips, furrowing his brow and rubbing his chin melodramatically in a passable Lieutenant Columbo impersonation.

Her smile widened.

"Or, how about 'The truth shall set you free!'" he cried, raising his arms skyward in an exaggerated gesture. "Or," he bent close to her and screwed up his face into a maniacal grin, "how about, 'You want the truth? You can't handle the truth!'"

She laughed. "That was the worst Jack Nicholson I've ever seen."

"Well, I do have other talents." He paused and tilted his head as if waiting for her to ask about them.

She swallowed as her imagination filled in the blanks of all kinds of talents he might have. She couldn't form a coherent thought beyond that.

"So? How about it?" he asked, sitting next to her on the bench, his voice back to normal.

"Look, you don't have to do this," she stammered. "It's nice of you to be polite and all, but— " Then she stood abruptly, feeling uncomfortable sitting so close to him. She walked over to the flower bed a few feet away. "It's obvious you already had someone in mind. After all, you bought two tickets." She took a deep breath and wondered if he was really single—really available. Stop it. It doesn't matter if he's single. You. Are. Not. Interested.

He didn't say anything right away. Then he stood and let out a deep breath. The skin around his eyes crinkled as his mouth formed a half smile.

God, he's tall! She wondered what it might be like to be with someone so tall. Geez, get your mind out of his pants, Michele. Is this what happens when you don't get any for five years? The first guy who is nice to you has you ready to jump his bones?

She shook her head and pushed back her shoulders. He approached closer. She stepped up on the brick wall to extend her height and face him. Now eye-to-eye she could look directly at him. That was better. Maybe.

He raised an eyebrow, acknowledging her new height, and stepped forward again, now within inches of her face. He took her hands in his. She could have withdrawn them; he wasn't holding tight, but she didn't want to acknowledge how acutely he affected her.

Michele swallowed hard. At this distance she could see his long dark eyelashes. What would they feel like against her cheek? A spark kindled in her belly and moved a warming heat upward to her head. What's the matter with me? Not even Jon, with all his sophisticated charm, had gotten to her so quickly and so dramatically. And she didn't even know this guy's name.

The smile started with a twitch at his mouth, then slowly went up his cheekbones and finally reached his eyes. Michele stared back at him, her chin slightly tilted.

His eyes fixed on hers. "Knowing how much you want to go, you are now the only person I have in mind."

She pulled her gaze away from his lips. "I couldn't possibly...I...I don't even know you."

He pulled out his wallet and handed her his driver's license. "I'm David. See?" He moved to Michele's side, standing shoulder-to-shoulder with her, barely touching as he pointed to his photograph. "It's not my best picture, but at least you can see where I live."

She noted the name exactly: David Michael Blackstone. The license listed an address only ten blocks from her in the Pearl District —definitely a part of town she loved but way out of her price range for renting, dining, or anything other than window shopping. She imagined him in a swanky loft in one of those refurbished warehouse buildings with windows overlooking the city. Maybe he lived above an upscale art gallery or antique store.

She drew her attention back to the license. Six-foot-one and 195 pounds. Hmmm. Hard to imagine dating someone almost a head taller. And she had guessed his age fairly well after all. He was thirty-two.

"Have you memorized it yet?" He smiled and stepped back in front of her.

She looked at him and smiled back. "Still working on it."

"You can write it all down if you want."

Michele lowered her head as the desire to attend the concert warred with her trepidation about going on an out-of-town first date with a man she had met just ten minutes ago. Especially a man who generated such unnatural lust in her. She handed the license back to him. "I'm sorry to have started all this. I can't. I just can't."

He put it back in his wallet. "Why not? You now have my name and my address. Give the information to a friend and tell her exactly where you're going and when. You can even include my license number. Tell her you'll check in as soon as we get to Bend and when you get home."

"I just don't know. It's really kind of you but—"

"At the very least you get to see Alison Krauss for free. At best, who knows? You might actually enjoy my company."

She felt the heat rising to her face again.

"You do that a lot, don't you?"

"What?"

"Blush."

"I do not blush!" she said, gritting her teeth and raising her chin in defiance.

"Oh yes, you do," he countered. "Either that or the sun has decided to set at three in the afternoon and the brilliant shades of pink are reflected on your skin."

"Three o'clock? Oh, my god, I'm going to be late." She took a step forward, forgetting the wall, and tumbled forward. Her arms automatically wrapped around him to stop her momentum.

David caught her with a strong arm around her waist, and slowly lowered her to the ground. She stood frozen, pressed against his chest, a little stunned. Neither of them spoke. She could feel his heart beating. A low, quiet, but steady beat—like the way she would set the tempo for a ballad on her bass.

"Thank you," she barely whispered. She consciously removed her arms from around his waist and took a step back. "I...forgot...where I was standing."

David gave her a little more space. "So, what time shall I pick you up Sunday? I thought we could get an early start, maybe take a picnic and stop somewhere for lunch along the way. If we leave in the morning, we can still get to the amphitheater with plenty of time to get a good spot on the lawn for the concert."

Michele shook her head. "Look. I can't be dating now. I'm sorry. I shouldn't have said anything. I just didn't think before. I'm late for an appointment. I'm..."

He stared straight at her, as if she were making it all up.

"All right. I get it. I'm not that dense. " He clenched his teeth, which made his jawline more pronounced. He looked down to the ground. "You're just not attracted to me." Then he looked straight at Michele. "That's okay. No problem. Nice meeting you." He turned to leave.

"No, it's not that. I find you very attrac...No. I mean..." She blushed again. David turned his face back toward her with renewed hope in his eyes. What was she thinking? She was about to admit how attracted she really was.

She heard the beginnings of his chuckle choke off. She really did want to see Alison Krauss and she had to admit David Blackstone intrigued her.

"How about we meet in Bend," she offered. "There's a deli with a striped awning on that street downtown that runs along the river and overlooks Mirror Pond. Do you know it?"

"You mean Freeman's?"

"Yes, that's the one. Oh, and my treat, since you bought the tickets."

"Are you afraid you'll feel beholden to me?" his voice elicited that teasing drawl again.

"Just want to keep everything in the right perspective."

"And what perspective would that be?"

"I'm not interested in a relationship right now," she said, making sure her voice sounded confident, matter-of-fact. "I'm far too busy and … well…I just can't invest the time and energy a relationship takes."

"Fine by me," he answered without hesitation. "So, casual sex and no snuggling afterward works for you?"

"No! That's not what I meant." The heat rushed to her face before she heard his chuckle and knew he was teasing her again.

"Okay. We'll do it your way then. I'll meet you at Freeman's. Just one more important detail we need to settle."

"Oh?"

"What's your name?"

"Oh, god, what was I thinking? I just made a date and … oh my god!" She shifted her weight back and forth. "I'm just not used to agreeing to go somewhere with someone I just met. Okay. Let's start over." She stood tall and formally held out her right hand. "I'm Michele Scott."

He shook her hand with a warm, affectionate grip, then said in a husky whisper, "I'm afraid that just won't do, Michele." He gently drew her to him and bent low as if to brush her lips with his. But then he hesitated. "Michele, I …"

She looked into those blue-green eyes and found her lips opening in invitation as her hand snaked around his neck and she stood on tiptoe to meet him.

He sighed and pulled her softly against him, his fingers working through her long, dark hair as he deepened the kiss, his mouth alternatively teasing and ravishing her lips. She held his head tight to hers not wanting him to stop.

Before she fully realized what had happened, he pulled away with a moan. He took a step back, brushing both hands through his hair and clearing his throat.

Michele looked down to get her balance, surprised she could still stand at all given that her legs had turned to rubber. Half expecting to find pieces of her clothing missing, she fingered each of the buttons on her shirt to make sure they hadn't come open.

No man had ever gotten to her like this. She didn't even know herself anymore. She had never been the one to make the first move—and in the middle of the Park Blocks, no less.

She looked at David, her eyes slowly lifting from his chest to his broad shoulders, to his face. He looked at her without shame—not smiling, but taking her all in, as if he couldn't get enough of her.

Oh, yes. David Michael Blackstone was definitely trouble. And she had just promised to meet him in Bend for what would be at least six hours together. She would have to be very careful.

David smiled, then bent and whispered into her ear. "I guess we're beyond shaking hands."

He brushed his lips against her ear and stepped back with confidence. "See you at noon, Sunday, at Freeman's. I'll bring a blanket for us to sit on and a little snack to get us through the evening. You bring the entertainment."

"What exactly do you mean by that?" she huffed, certain he now had the wrong idea about her.

He laughed heartily. "Something to do while we're waiting for the concert to start. Cards? Checkers?"

Then he turned and strode away, his long legs moving him quickly down the Park Blocks as if he hadn't a care in the world. Michele stared after him, trying to stop the deep flush she knew stained her face. She looked at her watch.

"Damn! I'm going to be really late for rehearsal."

CHAPTER 3

*D*avid walked for close to a mile before he realized he had passed his car at least six blocks ago. He swore and turned around, hiking back up the street. He needed to cool down before attempting to drive. That kiss had set every nerve ending in his body on sizzle.

Yes, Michele was cute—those dark-brown eyes set in a girlish face framed by her impossibly thick, long, wavy hair—and that blushing practically undid him. But she wasn't drop dead gorgeous and she definitely wasn't his type. He preferred older, experienced women— and taller, more glamorous, like Danielle.

Now there was a good fit. Danielle, a flight attendant based in Seattle, had been his only partner for the past two years, even if it was only once a month or whenever their schedules meshed. They knew the relationship would never progress beyond the occasional social outing topped off with a little wild, passionate sex. No complications and definitely no promises of everlasting love that could never be kept.

David's parents' divorce, after 26 years of marriage, had taught him that nothing lasts forever. That's why relationships like the one with Danielle worked for him—no promises, no long-term expectations—no hurt feelings when he moved on.

Danielle and Michele were like women from two different planets. Danielle would have put up with an Alison Krauss concert because she would enjoy the ride in his car, the fancy dinner and the raging sex afterward. But the truth was that a band like Coldplay was really more her style. Danielle epitomized what he fancied—tall, slender, with long fingers that knew what he wanted. She usually liked it hard and fast, and she didn't expect conversation afterward. When did that combination start to bore him? Did that make him shallow?

Finally at his car, David rested his hip on the hood and stared into space. When Michele had pushed her face up right next to his at the ticket window, demanding to get a ticket, all he could think of was how to get to know her better. He'd planned to get two tickets and ask his friend, Bill, to go with him. He laughed. Michele would obviously be a much more interesting companion for this concert. She had a good sense of humor, or at least she had the graciousness to laugh at his cornball clowning around. And her strength intrigued him. David had felt it when he caught her as she tripped off the wall. He could imagine her sturdy legs wrapped around him.

He'd never experienced such pure chemistry with a woman before. No, it was more than chemistry...it was passion. The way she went after those tickets. The demur way she rebuffed his attempts to hand over one of his tickets before finally giving in—on her terms. And then the exhilarating pleasure he'd felt as her mouth pressed against his. He hadn't expected that a woman could give so completely just with a kiss. When she'd fallen off the wall into his arms, her breasts pressed tightly against his chest—not especially large, but firm and oh so...

Damn! His body reacted immediately to the memory. David quickly turned toward his car, leaning against the door. He glanced up and down the street. No one too close at least. He stepped back, thumbed the unlock button on his key fob and heard the locks snap open and the alarm beep once as it disengaged. Then the gull-wing door popped up to let him in. He folded himself into the driver's seat of the Bristol and pulled the door shut with a soft click.

Too much fantasy. And now he had an itch he couldn't scratch. He turned the key in the ignition and checked for traffic behind him before pulling onto 10th Street. Damnit! Michele was already causing complications and they hadn't even had their first date.

Sweetwater Canyon ran through one of their playlists of eight songs. At the end, Theresa bent down and checked the stopwatch. "Not bad. Forty-eight and a…almost forty-nine minutes." She stood and looked at Michele. "You seemed a little fast on the pickup to the opening number, but then you calmed down. Do we need to do that one again?"

"No. Sorry." Michele laid the bass on its side. "I just needed to settle after pushing the speed limit to get here."

"I'm starving!" Kat slid open the door and held it in invitation. "Anyone?" When they all shook their heads, she closed it.

Theresa sighed. "That girl can eat morning, noon, and night. I'm pretty certain she eats in her sleep too. But she doesn't gain an ounce."

"It's that teenage metabolism," Rachel said. "I remember being like that once. But never again."

"Yeah, like you have a problem," Theresa replied, regarding her wistfully.

"Everything okay?" Sarah asked Michele as she settled her guitar in its case and offered her Dasani water.

A part of Michele yearned to describe her extraordinary encounter with David Blackstone. But another part urged her to hold back. But why? For fear of looking too impetuous? Or too irresponsible? Too easy? Yeah, all of those.

She unscrewed the cap and took a long swallow. The past few weeks had brought her so much closer to her band mates, but they weren't all fast friends yet. Motherly and forgiving, Theresa wouldn't judge Michele for what had happened. Sarah, cautious and private, was a willing listener, but she'd probably never done anything like that in her life and wouldn't even consider it. Rachel, the wild woman of the group, would understand—could probably identify with the immediate infatuation Michele had felt and advise her to jump head-first and bring another guy along for Rachel. Either that or she'd turn the whole episode into a bawdy joke.

Michele sighed and made up her mind. She kept one eye on the door in case Kat should suddenly reappear. There were parts of the story she didn't think a 15-year-old should hear, at least not without Theresa's prior approval.

"I was running late because I had to get Alison Krauss tickets."

"Alison Krauss? When, where?" All three voices were asking simultaneously, as they each grabbed their own bottles. "Did you get enough for all of us?"

"It's in Bend. This Sunday. No. In fact, the guy in front of me got the last two."

"Oh, that's a shame," Sarah said. "Any of us would have loved to go with you."

"But I'm going," Michele forged ahead, determined to get it all out before she lost her nerve. "I kind of ...made a scene. Then he asked me to go with him...and I refused....and then I gave in...but I'm meeting him there...for lunch and then the concert." She let out her breath in one swoop, unaware how tightly she held it.

"Hmmm...interesting way to get a date," Rachel said. "You've got spong. At least you got what you wanted."

Michele blushed. "Spong?"

"Uh, chutzpah...spunk," Sarah offered. "After awhile you'll get used to Rachel interspersing Gaelic phrases with English."

"I'm not sure it was spunk," Michele said. "I just didn't think. I wanted to go so badly. It was kind of strange...but ..."

"But what?" Rachel looked her directly in the eyes, her platinum hair framed in a halo of light from the windows behind her. "Come on, I can tell you're bursting with something."

"Oh, I don't know, I..."

"Oh. My. God." Rachel jumped in. "I've seen that look on myself. You are madly in lust, aren't you? He must be some looker." She punched her shoulder. "Ooooo, do tell all. Don't leave out any details. Measurements are nice too, if you have them."

Michele blushed again as all three women gathered around her. She recounted the whole incident, from her brash interruption at the ticket window to his varied and comical attempts to get her to say yes to the tumble from the wall into his arms and, finally, to the impassioned kiss.

"He's way too tall for me...but he's soooo good looking! I was stumbling over my words, and I couldn't think straight."

"Definitely lust," Rachel pronounced. "Any bets on whether she sleeps with him on the first date?" She held out her hand as if expecting Sarah and Theresa to hand over money.

Michele stood tall. "I am not sleeping with him on the first date, or any date. I made sure he understood that nothing could come of this. That a relationship was out of the question, what with our tour about to start."

"But casual sex is not a relationship...just fun," Rachel poked her arm again and laughed as Michele blushed deeply, remembering that David had said pretty much the same thing.

"So, what does he do?" Theresa asked.

"Huh?" Michele squinted her eyes, surprised by the question.

"What does he do? What's his occupation? How does he make his bucks?" Rachel said.

"Uh...I don't know."

"You mean you kissed him and made a date but you don't know anything about him?" Sarah asked, her eyes wide.

"Of course she doesn't." Theresa put a comforting arm around Michele's shoulder and squeezed. "And that's what makes it so exciting." She gave her a private wink. "You're smart to meet him there instead of having him pick you up and know where you live. Who knows, he may be something really special or just a way to see Alison Krauss. You'll have plenty of time over lunch and during the concert to find out everything you want to know."

"Right." Rachel drew out the word. "If you get scared, let me know. I'll be happy to stand in for you."

Michele held her lips tight together. For a moment she was completely and unreasonably jealous. Rachel was actually a better fit for David. Confident, ready to take on a new adventure at a moment's notice, and there was no doubt Rachel definitely had more experience in love and sex than Michele.

Rachel's bright blue eyes twinkled as she threw back her head and laughed. "Ooooooooooooo, if looks could kill."

"What do you mean?" Michele tipped up her chin just enough to be a challenge. "If you want to meet him, it's fine with me but you're not getting my Alison Krauss ticket."

Theresa and Sarah backed a couple steps away and laughed. "Cat fight," they said simultaneously and giggled.

"Nah, long and tall is definitely not my type. I like 'em about 5'10". Well… they can be long in one area." Rachel laughed over her shoulder as she walked back to her fiddle, drawing it out of the case and tuning again. "Be sure to tell us all about the concert and take lots of pictures—especially of Mr. Handsome."

Theresa turned back to her chair and lifted her guitar from the stand. "Let's get this practice on the road again. Sarah, would you let Kat know her snack time is over?"

Michele picked up her base and mentally berated herself as she tuned and practiced a couple of riffs for the next few numbers. Where did that jealousy come from? She didn't even know the guy. What was wrong with her?

Sarah's sandals flapped as she bustled to her position. Kat's quick steps tripped behind her. She placed a glass of soda on a table in front of the stage set and picked up the bohdran.

"Well, what's everyone waiting for?" Kat asked.

Theresa rolled her eyes.

"1 and 2 and 1 and 2…" Rachel began the count with her voice and heel taps for an original reel that she had composed. As she launched herself into the fiddle's intricate melody line, her eyes closed in concentration and her whole body started rocking back and forth. Everyone else joined in after eight bars. Kat's bohdran kept the quick beat and Michele's bass provided the rock-solid foundation. Sarah had switched to her recorder to provide counterpoint to Rachel's driving fiddle while Theresa strummed the accompaniment with her large-body, steel-string guitar to give the proper resonance.

The reel concluded with a final flourish from Rachel and everyone smiled as Rachel practiced her between song patter. A great opener for the second set, the number would draw the audience back to their seats and get them up on their feet. Then it was time to change the tempo to something slower and more serious.

Michele stepped up to her mike. Theresa switched back to her nylon-string guitar and picked out the first measures of a haunting melody as everyone else stood quietly. Michele closed her eyes and began to sing her original composition, Breaking the Bonds.

> *I am not Eve. I am not temptation.*
> *I am not grace. I am not salvation.*
> *I will not take your guilt. I will not take your praise.*
> *I will be what I am. I will make my own way.*
> *I am breaking the bonds.*
> *Breaking the bonds of centuries.*
> *I am breaking the bonds.*

After the first verse, the fiddle and guitar played a musical interlude, then Michele and Theresa joined voices in the second verse—a verse about the struggle between a culture left behind and the culture ahead.

Michele had written the song to reflect her experience volunteering with a domestic violence hotline. Affected by the plight of many of Portland's immigrant women—women who were caught between the patriarchal culture of their homeland and the western vision of women's self-fulfillment—she had been heartbroken by the stories she heard from women who accepted abuse as their due and were shamed into silence by their partners and often their own families. From her time with Jon, Michele had some understanding of that fear, of that abuse—though not as horrible as some of those women had endured.

Sarah's recorder added soft, breathy background notes during the instrumental interlude before the third verse. Then she joined in on the vocals as the song embraced a middle road—a road where each woman finds her own way and revels in the strength of individuality. As each voice grew stronger, Kat reinforced the rhythm with the bohdran. It now took on the quality of a Native American drumming circle—strong and proud.

On the final verse the five women set down their instruments and stood together at center stage, arms around each other. "We are breaking the bonds. Breaking the bonds of centuries. We are breaking the bonds." Their a cappella voices brought out harmonies that emphasized the power of molding diversity into a whole greater than its individual parts.

Quietly, each voice dropped away and each musician turned her back as she returned to her position. Finally, Michele completed the song as it had begun, alone but this time imbuing the words with the force and assurance of a woman who has found her way.

The set continued with a ballad written by Sarah, then back to an up-tempo bluegrass number with Rachel picking an energetic mandolin solo. The rest of the 45 minutes went quickly as each of the women took a turn doing an original composition in between instru-mentals and cover songs.

Theresa looked at the stopwatch. "We are right on target. Five minutes to spare. Just enough for your second composition, Michele. How is that coming?"

"Uh…not so well, at least for the moment. I'm kind of blocked."

"Maybe we better have an alternative then," Sarah said. "Just in case you don't have it finished by the tour."

"I'm sure she'll be fine," Theresa countered.

"Once I wrote something only a day before a concert," Kat said. "Remember? Last fall when we played Pendleton? Everyone learned it and it went great. Nothing like a deadline." She smiled and then downed half her soda in one gulp.

"I don't mind if we plan some alternates," Michele said. "I do think I'll have something in the next week or so, but it would be safer to make other arrangements. Besides, you might not like it when I'm done."

"Doubt that." Rachel closed her fiddle case with a snap. "Your Breaking the Bonds tune is solid, and I'm sure whatever else you do will be just as good." Then she packed her mandolin, and quickly picked up both cases. "I've gotta get goin'. A lot to get settled. See ya Monday."

"Okay," Theresa responded in a tone that drew out the second syllable with a slight question at the end.

Rachel promptly slipped through the sliding door before Michele could even say goodbye. Seconds later they all heard the front door slam and she was gone.

"Did I say something?" Michele wondered.

"About what?" Kat asked.

"It's nothing," Theresa said.

Michele shook her head. "I don't know. It seemed that Rachel was in a hurry to get going. Is it because of before?"

"Before what? What did I miss?" Kat's eyes widened and she leaned forward. "Did you two have a fight? Was it about…"

"Nothing," Theresa repeated firmly. "She's just having a rough time. Today's her anniversary…well, would have been her anniversary if that jerk hadn't left her." Michele knew that Rachel had been married for four years before being unceremoniously dumped by her husband shortly after he'd moved them both to Oregon from Scotland.

"She's still pining for him after two years?" Michele asked. She couldn't imagine hanging on that long. She'd been able to put aside all that had happened between Jon and her after a couple of months. Or had she? Did she still carry emotional baggage from that disastrous relationship? Is that why there had been no one else? She shook her head at the thought. Well, she definitely didn't want him back.

"Not pining," Theresa said. "It's just that she's not involved—not with anyone who wants more than…" She glanced in Kat's direction.

"Sex, Mom. I know what it is. You can say it in front of me."

"Okay, okay." Theresa shrugged and looked back to Michele.

"Rachel gives every appearance of being spirited and adventurous but deep down, behind that confident façade, she wants the same thing we all want, love—the kind that gives back and that lasts. Instead, she seems to find a lot of men who only want sex. She makes it sound like that's fine and good, but it's not. And we all know it."

Michele knew exactly what she was talking about. Maybe all of their expectations were hopelessly flawed. She really did think that kind of love could exist. For her. It did for her parents. They clearly had a happy marriage that still brimmed with romance. In fact, her father had proposed to her mother on Valentine's Day and they were married the next month. Just two months ago they had celebrated their thirtieth anniversary. How much more romantic could you get than that? They still held hands when they went out; and they still kissed—maybe not as passionately as she had with David... She stopped herself. No, not David Blackstone. That wasn't passion. That was...well, she didn't know what it was. Lust, maybe. Pheromones. Who knew?

She looked around at the remaining members of Sweetwater Canyon. They were professional musicians and they had chosen not to get involved in other relationships, right? Who had time with a tour coming up, anyway?

Maybe they hadn't chosen after all. Theresa was right on one thing. Everyone was looking for love. Michele tried to tell herself she didn't have time—but the truth was she wanted to have it all, and to have it all right now.

Living to the eastern side of the Cascades was always a revelation. Oregon may be typecast as a land of fir-clad peaks dripping with moss and ferns under a perpetual downpour, but Michele knew better. As she crossed the southern shoulder of Mt. Hood the rain first got heavier, then began to diminish. After Clear Lake it stopped completely as the highway began its long eastward descent through open forests of Ponderosa pine that eventually gave way to scrub oak and spindly juniper and finally to the arid high desert of central Oregon. Just fifty miles east of Theresa's house in the rain forest and here she was in sagebrush country. Another hour or so through the desert would bring her to Bend.

To the west loomed the Cascade Range, deep green and tree clad, broken at intervals by soaring, white-tipped volcanoes. As Mt. Hood receded in her rear-view mirror, the triangular outline of Mt. Jefferson filled the view out her passenger window. And on the far horizon stood the unmistakable silhouette of the Three Sisters. Bend lay directly to the east of these imposing peaks. The tops of the rain clouds piled up behind the crest of the mountains trying vainly to force their way over the divide. But none succeeded, and the sky on this side remained an unbroken sweep of cerulean blue.

An hour later she was on Brooks Street, which fronted the Deschutes River at Mirror Pond. She found a space right near the striped awning that identified the restaurant. Bend seemed so different from Portland, she mused—traffic was manageable and parking was a snap. And yet she guessed it was about the same size as Missoula, which had always been "The Big Apple" to her when she was growing up.

She sat in the car for a moment with her eyes closed and took a deep breath. She flipped down the visor and checked her hair in the mirror. Already a few stray strands had escaped and were curling around her face. She spread them back again and adjusted a couple of pins in her chignon.

The queasy feeling in the pit of her stomach returned. Was it anxiety about spending an entire day with a man she didn't even know? The possibility that she might discover in the first hour that they had nothing in common? Or something else? Fear, perhaps, that he might decide she wasn't his type and that he'd made a big mistake in asking her?

"It's not a real date," Michele shouted into the mirror. "Get over it. You're going to see a great concert, and your time with David will be fine." She pasted on a smile, grabbed her handbag and slid out of the car.

Outside Freeman's front door, she alternated between examining the menu posted on an easel next to it with trying to peek through the window to see if David had already arrived. The reflection from the midday sun made that impossible. Gathering her courage, she put her face right up to the glass, cupped both hands to her forehead and peered inside.

⁓

DAVID STOPPED in his tracks as he noticed the petite woman peering in the glass ahead of him. How he'd like to walk right up to her and cup that cute little behind. Nope. That wouldn't be a proper greeting. And, as jumpy as she was about this date, he wasn't going to push his luck.

Instead he brushed against her shoulder and whispered close to her ear, "See anything you like?"

She jumped back with a start, then recognizing him she blushed. He stepped forward to claim a kiss, but she placed a hand against his chest to stop him.

"Hello, David. It's nice to see you again." She formally extended her hand to him.

His chest tightened. So it's back to formal.

"I thought we were beyond that…but, okay, if you prefer…" He took her hand warmly but politely in his. "Hello, Michele. I'm very glad you could make it. Would you allow me to escort you into this dining establishment so that you may buy me lunch?"

She smiled, her brown eyes sparkling. She still held his right hand. Taking advantage of the situation, he reversed his grip without letting go, opened the door with his left hand and led her inside.

A portly woman, with short dark hair and a big smile reached for menus from the stack in front of her. "Two?"

"Yes," he answered, "and something by the windows, please, if you have it."

The woman glanced at a busboy as he cleared the last plates from a table at the front of the deli. "Looks like one just opened up. This way.

She led them to the table. "Thank you," Michele said. He stood behind her, holding the chair while she sat down.

"You're quite welcome," the woman replied brightly, handing them each a menu. "And your husband is a real gentleman. You see less and less of that these days."

"Oh, we're not— "

"That's very kind of you," he interrupted, placing his right hand over Michele's left. "You know, it really takes so little effort to be courteous. I don't see why it's falling out of favor." He turned his smile from the woman to Michele and back.

"Let me guess. Newlyweds?"

"You don't under—"

"Actually," he broke in again, squeezing Michele's hand, "a great romance always feel new, don't you agree." He turned up the wattage and the woman beamed in return.

The waitress pointed out the board next to the kitchen where the daily specials were listed, told them their waitress would be there shortly and withdrew, still smiling.

Michele pulled her hand from under his and placed it in her lap. "Why did you do that?" Her tone and expression were stern but not angry.

He regarded her closely. "What did it hurt? Didn't you see how happy she looked?"

"But you let her think we were married," she said in a low voice while leaning over the table, "or at least engaged."

"The lady doth protest too much, methinks," he replied in an exaggerated Shakespearean intonation.

She sighed and sat back in her chair, but the hint of a smile played on her lips. "Your Olivier is even worse than your Nicholson."

"Forsooth! Your remark has cut me deeply, madam," he said, still in character. Then dropping the accent, he added, "But at least you could give me credit for knowing Hamlet. And as I told you before I do have other talents."

"Well, we'll see about that." The waitress appeared at their table. "You could start," Michele said teasingly, "by demonstrating your talent for picking out a good local brew while I have a look at the menu."

"Hey, I'm from Oregon. If there's one thing I know it's good beer." Turning to the waitress David asked, "Do you have a Porter on tap?"

"I'm sorry, sir, but I'm afraid we're out. We do have Obsidian Stout, though."

He looked at Michele inquiringly, "You do like dark beer?" She nodded. "Heavy beer? The very antithesis of 'lite' beer?" She kept nodding. "Beer so rich you can stand a straw up in the glass…so rich you can scrape the head with a putty knife?" She was grinning now. "Beer so thick you have to drink it with a spoon…a veritable loaf of beer?" Michele laughed out loud and his heart flickered with pleasure.

"Two pints, please," he told the waitress, and she walked away smiling.

David leaned forward conspiratorially, "I'll bet she thinks we're married, too."

Michele groaned. "Oh, let's not start that again." But she continued to regard him with merriment.

"I've been thinking about you all week, looking forward to today. I couldn't even concentrate on work."

"Hmmmm. Not a good worker." Michele feigned writing down a note, as if it was a performance evaluation. She pantomimed closing the notebook then cocked her head to the left and smiled. "So, what exactly is it that you do? That is, besides picking up helpless young women?" Her smug smile accentuated the tilt of her chin.

"You're anything but helpless," he answered quickly. "In fact, if I recall correctly it was you who barged into my life, not the other way around."

Michele didn't say anything. She rested her chin on her clasped hands and exuded a smile filled with promise.

He cleared his throat. "Okay, short answer. I'm a computer consultant, self-employed, have been for five years now. After I got my degree from Oregon State I went to work for a software company, but I didn't like the bureaucracy, office politics, or cutthroat competition, so rather than stick around for twenty years just to get a pension and a gold watch I went off on my own. I work on contract, get to travel all over the world. Been doing all right for myself…and I lived happily ever after. The end." He sat back and waited for Michele to speak.

She dropped a hand to the table. "You forgot the clown school, Shakespearean work at The Globe, and understudy for several movie stars."

He softly covered her hand with his. "Well, I didn't want to overwhelm you on the first date."

She smiled. "I knew some computer geeks at PSU. When they got together it was like they had their own secret language."

"Oh we do." He turned her hand palm up and traced her fingers. "We have a secret handshake too."

She swallowed and her withdrew her hand. "You'll have to teach me at least the handshake then. Actually, I'm afraid that I'm just barely computer literate myself. I know how to surf the net, do email, and use word processing programs, but that's about it."

"That puts you in a very large majority of the human race."

"Computers are like cars in today's world," she continued. "Everyone uses them and depends on them every day, but very few of us understand how they work—or how to make them work. You have a skill that requires creativity and determination to develop. I admire that."

David stared straight into her eyes, checking for truth in her statement. None of the women he had dated over the years had cared about his career, only what the money he made from it could buy. Danielle had squealed with delight when she first saw his shiny new Bristol. She didn't ask how he could afford such a car. He might have been a drug dealer for all she knew—or cared.

"So who do you do your consulting for?" Michele asked. She leaned forward and looked straight at him.

"Well, I work with large corporations, mostly. I troubleshoot their websites. I make sure their clients can reach them and do business with them via computer. I teach them the ins and outs of inventory management, ordering and customer service over the Internet. And one of my biggest moneymakers is putting their employee training programs online."

"I guess you do alright for yourself, then," Michele said.

David realized with alarm how cold and mercenary his description must have sounded. His job was good. He admitted it made a great income. But that wasn't why he did it. Did it really matter if she knew why? This wasn't anything long term. He didn't want a relationship. He just wanted another Danielle—kind of.

The waitress appeared out of the blue with their beers. "Are you ready to order?" They looked at each other and laughed, realizing simultaneously that they hadn't even glanced at the menu.

Michele looked over at the chalkboard. "How does the turkey wrap special sound?" He nodded. "Two please." The waitress wrote it down and walked away.

"Look," he said, staring intently into her eyes, "I don't want you to think I'm just in this for the money." It suddenly seemed the most important thing in the world that she understood what really mattered to him. "Sure, I do well for myself, but I also have the opportunity to do good for others."

Michele raised her eyebrows, but said nothing.

"Remember the story of Robin Hood? I guess that's how I see myself. I take from the rich—these large companies—and I give to the poor, namely local school districts that don't have the funds to purchase computers for their classrooms. I get the companies to donate equipment and then I install it and show the staff how to use it. Everybody wins."

Michele pursed her lips and regarded him solemnly. What were those dark-brown eyes saying? Acceptance? Understanding? Or thinking he was an idiot, wasting his money on a cause that really needed a lot more investment to solve?

The waitress returned and set their plates in front of them.

Michele said in a soft voice, "You are a good man, David Blackstone." Then the corner of her mouth turned up in an impish smile. "Even if you do harass helpless young women."

He laughed out loud. "Okay, I've spilled my guts enough for one date. Your turn."

"What do you want to know?"

"Everything." And he suddenly realized he meant it. He wanted to know all about Michele Scott. What she did. What she ate. What was important to her. What she liked in bed. He swallowed. Down Boy. Plenty of time to work up to that.

Michele took a deep breath. "I'm afraid it's pretty mundane compared to your globe-trotting and philanthropy." She paused, debating whether she wanted to hear the criticism or dead silence about her choice career. "I'm a professional musician." God, it felt good to be able to say that.

David's face lit up and he slapped his forehead. "Of course! I should have known. The calluses."

She balled her left hand into a fist and moved it away from him. Jon had hated her calluses, saying there were too manly.

"Wait! Don't do that," David reached out and uncurled her fingers as he brought them back to the center of the table. He brushed his palm softly over the hardened fingertips. "You've earned these. You should be proud of them."

Michele's stomach flip-flopped.

"So, what do you play?"

"Bass," her voice quavered. She cleared her throat. "Not electric, acoustic."

"Now I see why you wanted to go to the concert. I bet you'll be watching the bass player, Barry Bales."

Her mouth dropped. She consciously closed it. "You know Barry Bales?"

"Only that he has at least seven Grammy's to his credit. He's one of the best. Right?"

She couldn't believe it. Not only was he not turned off by the fact she played, but he actually knew something about bluegrass. Of course he does, she berated herself. He bought tickets to Alison Kraus. Not all men are bluegrass idiots like Jon.

"How did you come to like Alison Krauss?" she asked.

"Actually, I'm a Jerry Douglas fan and that's how I got to know about Alison Krauss. Even when he's not playing with the band, I still like to see Union Station though." He squeezed her hand. "It's a bit unusual to see a woman playing acoustic bass, but I love unusual. Tell me all about you, how you chose it, why you love it."

Michele briefly outlined the last six years, but David kept asking for more details, probing for insight into her motivation and her goals. She left out any mention of Jon. That story wasn't important for a one-time date—rather shared concert. When she got to the part about the audition and her membership in Sweetwater Canyon his grin was so wide and accepting that her eyes misted.

"So you've made it. You're living your dream." He squeezed her hand.

Michele's heart raced and her head seemed to be separated from her body, like watching a romantic movie. Entirely different from the giddy rush of passion that had overwhelmed her at their first meeting. David seemed genuinely happy for her. Darn! Why did she have to meet him now, when she was about to go on tour? She didn't have time for a relationship. She couldn't get involved. She just couldn't.

"We'd better eat our sandwiches before they get cold…or warm. I forget what we ordered."

Michele looked down, when did the food arrive? "Turkey wraps. Cold. They look pretty good." She took a bite and concentrated on chewing instead of what she couldn't have.

"You know, I asked for a table by the window in case we ran out of things to talk about, thinking at least we could admire the view of Mirror Pond. But somehow, I don't think that's going to be a problem."

She smiled. "No, I don't think it will."

When the waitress came by to clear the plates, Michele asked for the check. David didn't say anything about her threatening his manhood, and the waitress accepted her request without batting an eye. Another point in his favor.

As she signed the credit card slip, David looked at his watch. "We still have plenty of time. Would you like to walk around downtown before we head out to the amphitheater?"

"That sounds wonderful."

They walked out into the sunshine and turned south down Brooks

Street. There were plenty of interesting boutiques to window-shop along this scenic stretch of Bend's waterfront. They held hands easily and comfortably while sharing ooohs and ahhhhs over antiques, woodcarvings and hand-painted pottery. She worked on accepting this was the one and only date. She worked on enjoying the moment and not having any expectations.

David found himself staring at her figure for the second time that day, intoxicated by the sight of her dancing down the sidewalk, trim and taut in her sleeveless top and green shorts. God, she was beautiful.

Michele suddenly squealed with delight and bounded across the street to a playground in the riverfront park. "Come here, you have to see this." He hurried after her.

She dashed to a circle of painted metal hobby horses anchored to the ground by strong, thick springs so that children could rock back and forth. "Oh, to be five or six again!" Her hand traced the back of one of the horses. "They remind me of the merry-go-round I used to ride when I was a little girl." She mounted the horse and closed her eyes as if she were feeling it move up and down in its never-ending circuit.

Mesmerized by her pleasure in the moment, he couldn't speak.

"I can still remember the county fair back home. It was a long drive from the ranch but it was the highlight of my year. I usually entered a sheep through the 4-H Club and Mom and Dad were always proud when I brought home a ribbon—any color, it didn't matter. But the best part was the midway with all the rides, especially the carousel."

She grabbed the horse's head, pulled herself into a kneeling position on the saddle and put her arms out to each side for balance. David moved a little closer, ready to catch her.

"I would try all sorts of things to see how far I could lean out while turning," she continued. "Mom would yell at me to sit back down, but Dad would just laugh and wave."

She kicked off her sandals and stood on the saddle. Her arms extended to both sides for balance and she lifted her left foot about six inches. David started forward, watching her right foot wobble, but then she found her balance. She lifted her foot further, bringing her knee up at a ninety-degree angle from her hip. Very slowly she extended her leg behind her, arched her back and pointed her toes in some kind of ballet move.

David sucked in a breath. The line from her shoulders across the bent waist to her extended bare leg was magnificent. It took every bit of willpower not to put his hands on her and trace that line himself. He could see the muscles as she balanced on the saddle, yet the position seemed to streamline her entire body, showcasing an alluring blend of athleticism and grace.

Michele smiled broadly and slowly brought her foot back to rest on the saddle. "Ten years of ballet. From age four to fourteen ballet and music were my mother's contribution to my feminine side. Finally, my teacher told me my body type was not ideal for a professional ballerina and to find some other artistic pursuit. So I spent my high school years mostly with my dad, learning how to be a ranch hand. Thank God I didn't give up the music."

She turned toward David while still standing on the saddle. "Catch me?"

Before he could answer she launched herself into an arc, executing a half-twist in mid-air. He caught her easily, one arm under both her legs and the other across her back.

She placed both hands around his neck and face toward him, rolling into his chest. "Thank you. You can now add hero prince to your repertoire of characters."

Then she kissed him. At first it was a very light brush against his lips, but then she nipped at his lower lip and held tighter as she kissed him thoroughly. When she pulled away, she simply smiled and said, "You can put me down now."

At a loss for words, he slowly lowered her to the ground.

She slipped out of his embrace to place her bare feet back into her sandals, then returned to him and slipped her arms around his waist, locking her hands behind his back. Her face lowered, placing her cheek directly against his chest.

David placed his arms around her shoulders and gazed down at the top of her head. From this vantage point he could see a few strands of hair had escaped the pins. The long tresses caressed the side of her neck and brushed against her collarbone. He took a deep breath to slow his heart. All he could think about was how he could keep her holding on to him.

"I really like you, David," she began in a voice so low he had to strain to hear. "I didn't want to." A heavy sigh escaped her lips. "I really, really don't have time to get involved with anyone right now, but…I can't deny the way I feel. So…I'm trying to just enjoy today… with you."

Time seemed to stand still as her chest pressed against him, rising and falling with every breath.

Still not looking up, she said, "So let's just take things slow and see what happens." She turned her head to look up at him again, her eyes held a longing and a trust he'd never seen from a woman before. "Is that okay with you?"

"Yes," was all he could manage.

"I'm so glad," she said, slowly unlocking her embrace. She threaded her arm through his and guided him back up the street. "I, um, think it's time we got ourselves to the concert."

"Why don't we take my car and I can drive you back to yours after the concert?"

"Sounds good to me. I just need to get my bag out of the trunk. I'm parked right there." Michele pointed to the six-year-old Toyota Corolla two spaces down the block. She still had his arm locked up in hers with her face snuggled gently against his shoulder. "Which one's yours?"

"Right over there across the street," he said, waving his hand.

Michele's mouth fell open as she realized which car David was pointing out. She couldn't help but run over to it and stroke the sleek, impossibly low-slung frame. "Oh my!" Her fingertips followed the line from the hood to the door. "I've never seen a car like this...except in movies. What is it?"

"It's a Bristol Fighter. There aren't many around, especially in the Northwest. They're sort of hand-made in the U.K., one at a time."

Michele noticed that his tone lacked any trace of pretension, but he was clearly proud of his car. She could understand that. Wasn't she proud of her handcrafted prized bass?

Without removing the key fob from his pocket, David thumbed the unlock button and the gull-wing doors popped open.

"Ooooooooooo. It's like a 007 car." Michele couldn't help but clap her hands. "Computer consultant, my foot! You're really a secret agent, aren't you? No, don't tell me." She held up her palm. "I know then you'd have to kill me."

He laughed and shook his head. "Shall we go?"

He held her hand while she climbed through the unfamiliar vertical door and settled herself gracefully into the leather seat.

As he slid behind the steering wheel, Michele blurted out, "This is the sexiest car I've ever seen!"

"I'm glad you think so. I really couldn't afford it, but…" He paused and looked at her with a question in his eye that she couldn't read.

"But?" she coaxed. "Please don't tell me you stole it or used to be a drug dealer or something awful."

His shoulders dropped as he let out a sigh and chuckled. "Nothing so exciting. A couple years ago I was working on contract for a very wealthy client in London. He had one of these and I fell in love with it during my three months there. I'd never owned a fancy car before, or even a sports car. But I decided it was now or never; so I ordered one from the factory and had it shipped here. It cost me all the money from that contract, plus the next two." He looked over at Michele. His hand found hers and squeezed. "Did you ever buy something you really couldn't afford but knew you had to have?"

"Yes," she replied immediately, "my bass."

"Ah, but that's different. You needed that for your career. I didn't need this. It's just a…"

"The difference between men and boys," she said, fixing him with a warm smile, "is the price of their toys."

"I guess so."

"Besides, I'll bet this little beauty has gotten you lots of dates."

He chuckled. "Yes, it has." He turned toward her and placed a finger under her chin, his eyes holding hers for a moment. "But it didn't get me this one, did it?"

"No, it didn't."

"Good." He turned the key and the engine roared to life.

"So, just how fast will this baby go?"

"Faster than a lot of small airplanes, but don't worry, I went to flight school as part of my secret agent training."

Michele laughed. She couldn't take her eyes off him as he drove. Kind, funny, attentive, rich—but not pompous. Man, she was in really deep trouble. She snuggled into the leather seat and closed her eyes. The breeze flowing through her open window felt cool and dry against her warm skin although it played havoc with her hair. She reached up and unfastened the chignon, letting her hair fly. This was not a day for being in control.

DAVID GLANCED over and sucked in a breath, undone by the sight of her long, wavy tresses blowing free. He couldn't help himself. "You are so beautiful."

"Thank you." She reached over and laid her left hand on his forearm, her fingertips tracing the muscle from the inside of his elbow to the wrist. She stopped abruptly and withdrew her hand. "My calluses don't gross you out? Really?"

"Not at all." He took her hand back and caressed the callused ends as he drove toward the amphitheater. "They're a part of who you are —a part of what makes you so fascinating." He brought her hand to his lips and kissed the tips of each finger.

Michele burrowed against the soft, luxurious leather.

"Oh damn, I missed it." He hit the brakes, dropped her hand, checked the traffic, and made a u-turn then a quick right into the parking lot.

When they got out of the car, she rearranged her hair in the chignon.

He reached for the neat bun. "Hmmm…I liked it down, wild and free. But this is nice too. Shows off your neckline." He trailed his fingers along one side of her neck.

Michele stopped his hand when it reached her collarbone and cleared her throat. "The…uh…picnic." She blushed, then twirled out of reach taking two quick steps to the back of the car.

David opened the trunk and retrieved her carry bag along with a square wicker picnic basket with a Hudson's Bay blanket laid across the top.

She raised an eyebrow as she took her bag from him. "You came prepared, I see."

David chuckled as he closed the trunk. "Just a little wine and cheese for later." He draped the blanket over his arm, picked up the basket and took her hand in his as they walked toward the entrance.

They were early enough that the lawn wasn't crowded yet. David looked around the amphitheater and then up at the cloudless sky.

"Well, even up front we'd still be behind all those rows of seats which would put us a good distance from the stage. And that would mean sitting in the direct sun for a couple more hours. Or...we could find a spot back there in the shade." With a nod he indicated the tall oaks that edged the rear of the lawn seating.

"I vote for shade," Michele said. "And it's high enough we'll see over everyone's head."

They selected a level spot at the base of one of the largest trees. David unfolded the blanket and spread it over the grass. He set the picnic basket off to one side and then, using both hands, slowly eased himself down until his back rested comfortably against the thick trunk.

In one nimble motion Michele flipped off her shoes, swung her right foot over the left and lowered herself into a cross-legged sitting position facing him. She thrust her arms out from her sides with the palms up and grinned as if to say 'ta da!'

He let out an admiring whistle. "How in the world did you do that? If I tried something like that I'd break my nose...or my ass. Or maybe something else."

She laughed. "It's the ballet, I tell ya. I gave it up fourteen years ago but I still work out and do a lot of the exercises I learned as a girl to keep limber."

"Well, it really shows."

His eyes raked her up and down, noticing her erect posture, the smooth creamy skin on her thighs that he wanted to touch, and the delicate unpainted toes. He immediately thought of what he would like those toes to do to him.

Hold on, bud. It's not even dark and you already have her laid out on your bed without clothes. He wrenched his eyes back to her face.

"If I remember correctly, you were in charge of the entertainment," he said.

"And I didn't forget." Michele leaned over and stretched toward her bag, revealing a patch of skin along her back as her shirt rode up. David twitched involuntarily as he saw how her shorts gaped slightly.

Michele drew out a pen and a folded sheet of newspaper, which she quickly spread out, on the blanket between them.

"The New York Times Sunday crossword. Did you already do it?" She paused. "You do like crosswords, right?"

 "It so happens I work them in the paper every day, and when I travel I buy a book of crosswords to pass the time in airports and during flights." His brows scrunched. "How did you know? Did I mention it when we met last week?"

"No, just a lucky guess," she answered. "Or," she tapped a finger against his forehead, "maybe I can read your mind."

"Uh oh. Now, that could be dangerous. Can you tell what I'm thinking right now?"

She looked straight into his eyes. He imagined she could probably see only all the lust that had built up since lunch.

Michele blushed and looked down at the paper. "Let's do the crossword."

Without standing she turned herself around on the blanket and scooted back until she rested comfortably against David's chest. Looking back at him over her right shoulder she asked, "Is that okay? Now we can both see the page. No one has to read upside down."

David wrapped his arms loosely around her waist. He bent down and kissed her softly on the cheek. "Do you like to start across or down?"

"Definitely down."

Over the next hour they read clues, brainstormed possible answers and playfully bickered over whether educated guesses—or only sure things—should be written in the squares. They had filled in about two thirds of the puzzle when the announcer came on stage to introduce the warm-up act, a solo female singer neither Michele nor David had heard before.

Michele put down the newspaper and laid her head comfortably against his shoulder. The singer, accompanying herself on an acoustic guitar, began a set of folk songs in a rich soprano that carried easily to the back of the lawn.

"She has a beautiful voice."

"I'll bet yours is even more beautiful." He nuzzled her ear. "Though probably not so high."

Michele blushed and smiled. "You're right about the second part, anyway. As for the first, you've never heard me sing."

"But I will…and soon I hope. And someday I'll hear you sing in this very amphitheater."

Michele sighed. "I'll make sure you get a front row seat and a back-stage pass." She placed her forearms along his thighs and rested her hands on his knees.

"Is it okay if I undo your hair?"

"Sure, if you want to." She leaned forward slightly so he could unfasten the bun.

He swept her long hair from her back to trail down one side of her front. It hung almost to her elbows. His fingers combed through her hair, from the roots to the ends. He let it lay across his arm as his hand traced along her shoulder and arm all the way to the elbow. He could imagine himself enveloped in that hair. He wanted to feel it all around him. With her hair blocking a view of her clothing, he could easily imagine her naked sitting right here in the park.

Michele sighed and leaned further into him. He wrapped his arms around her and she turned her face up and stretched her neck toward him. Though her lips barely touched his, he felt a sizzle all the way to his groin. He groaned and pulled back, hugging her back against him. How would he ever last the entire concert without tearing her clothes off?

The concert continued in a blur of romance, music, and a lust that grew throughout the evening. They stood and clapped together to Choctaw Hayride and danced in the moonlight. Later, he held Michele to him, kissing away the trail of tears that escaped when the band did Sitting at the Window of my Room. She was smart, confident, vulnerable, and sexy as hell. He could already feel his heart begin to slip.

~

AFTER TWO ENCORES, the concert ended with a song Michele knew she would hold in her memory of this evening, Let Me Touch You for Awhile. As they stood, she leaned into him, the back of her head resting against his chest as they swayed to the music. David's arms wrapped tightly around her waist, a warm blanket enveloped both of them. He surprised her by singing the lyrics softly into her ear.

"Why didn't you tell me you could sing?" she asked as they swayed together.

"I don't. Not professionally."

"You could. Your baritone is silky smooth. You could have women swooning."

He chuckled and brushed her lips. "You are the only one I want swooning right now."

She returned his kiss with more fervor. She was doing much more than swooning. She was falling, in spite of all her self-talk otherwise.

Even when the music ended, Michele barely registered the other concert patrons moving past them back to their cars.

She didn't want the evening to end. The final melody continued to play in her mind, as if it demanded her to follow through with more. No, she couldn't. It was getting late and she knew they both had a long drive back. Reluctant, she turned to face him, burying her head in his chest. She could hear his steady heartbeat as he held her tight against him and stroked her hair.

"I think it's time we..."

"Don't think." He interrupted, leading her to the back side of the large cedar, blocking them from view. "Let everyone else go first. We're not in a hurry."

He held her eyes as his hands continued to massage her shoulders and back. She relaxed again and melted into his embrace. He drew her back to the ground and gathered her into his lap, pulling the blanket tighter around them, trapping the ends between his back and the tree. She eagerly straddled him and snuggled closer, enjoying the heat they shared.

His hand slowly traced a path from the nape of her neck to the front of her collarbone. She could feel the heat rising to his touch. She gasped when his fingers dipped into the vee of her shirt and lightly brushed across the tops of her breasts. She arched into his touch, finding his mouth and taking control.

Michele tasted the raspberry and wine flavors still lingering on his tongue. She sucked, savoring the texture and flavor. She hummed low in her throat as the scent of him filled her head. He smelled like musky cedar and he felt like a strongly rooted fir—one that she could climb and feel secure in the nook of a branch for hours on end.

Threading one hand through his hair, she splayed the other across the back of his neck, then locked her ankles firmly behind him and held on, opening her kiss to invite him deeper.

He took full advantage and thrust his tongue, taking possession. It wasn't slow this time. She could taste the snaps of frustration as his hand fisted on the back of her shirt and she felt the hot surge of need that pumped from his body. It was as elemental as the drumming of the bohdran, calling the need from each of them.

"Oh, no!" she yelped as the entire situation became perfectly clear. Her breath came out in short staccato. She pulled herself away and tried to regain her senses, as the heat continued to wash over her. She placed her hand against his chest, struggling to catch her breath.

"Back off, David."

"Look..."

Michele swallowed seeing the hunger in his eyes—a hunger stronger than she had ever engendered in anyone before. She began to shake. He put his arms around her and drew her close, his lips lowering to hers again, but she stiffened.

"Just…" She blew out a breath. "Back off a minute."

"Okay." He dropped his hands and leaned against the tree.

She leaned away from him, unclasping her ankles and scooted off his lap. She closed her arms around her, surprised at the coolness after breaking that body-to-body contact.

He stood. "Is this far enough?"

"Yeah, that's fine."

Michele looked into his eyes, confused. She never had sex on the first date, and here they were obviously heading in that direction. She closed her eyes and shook her head. Actually, she didn't have a rule. The only person she'd ever had sex with was Jon. She sighed and opened her eyes. David's mouth crooked up and he arched a brow. Crap! He was so sensual, her body had never responded like this with Jon.

Michele took a deep breath. Her friend, Kim, had told her men just thought differently about sex—and that didn't mean it was bad. Maybe that's what she needed to do. Just admit to what was happening, and go from there. She could be more straightforward—businesslike. Isn't that how men did it?

"Look," she finally said. "I'm not going to pretend I didn't participate in that. I obviously have some kind of elemental attraction to you. I just didn't intend to act on it."

"Why?"

"Because it's not smart."

"Seemed smart to me."

"Yeah, well, it's my decision."

"Seemed to me you had decided already."

"No, I didn't decide. That's the problem. I didn't think, I didn't decide. I just let it take over. That's not right. I have to decide."

"Sex isn't something you think about, it's something that happens when it's right. It sure felt right to me."

"No, it's a definite decision. And right now, for me, it would be a stupid one."

He raised a brow. "Hmmm. So, you don't like sex."

"Look, I'm not against sex, it's fine as things go, I guess…It's just that I didn't want to complicate things before leaving on tour. On the other hand, I must have some need that I wasn't even aware of, and… well… I think you'd be pretty good at fulfilling it."

He opened his mouth, shut it again. Cleared his throat. "Excuse me while I replay this movie. Somehow the lines aren't matching the script I thought we were following earlier. Let me get this right. You're considering being stupid and having sex with me."

"That's right." Good, she was in control now. She was handling it. "That is where you were heading with all this, right? That was your plan from the beginning."

"Man, you don't beat around the bush, do you?"

"I'm just trying to get things in the open, so there are no misunderstandings.

"I guess I was kind of inept in my approach. Sorry," he said.

"Your approach was fine. There was nothing inept about that kiss."

He rubbed a hand over the back of his neck. "Uh, I've never played this scene before. I'm totally lost. Should I beg and plead, pretend we're in love? I'm not sure of the game you are playing here."

"No game, David, I'm just trying to give you the facts as I see them. I don't want to hear promises you can't keep, so why play games?"

Why was he making this so hard? Isn't this what all guys wanted? She was trying to be business like. What was wrong with him?

"Look," Michele continued, her voice not quite as confident as before. "I don't indulge in sex very often – actually it's been about five years. But not because I don't like it. I'm just, well, I'm busy … and I'm picky. But I do consider it natural, and given nothing can be permanent here …well, I guess I'd like to approach it like a man."

"A man?" He chuckled, and pulled her against him again—his arm tight around her back as he lifted her lips to his. "I don't have an interest in having two men in this relationship."

Presumptuous and dominant, he kissed her again with potent male heat. He branded her with the strength and depth of his passion, and she could feel the promise of forbidden pleasures to come. Then, just as easily he drew the kiss into softness and patience, as if he had all the time in the world to explore her mouth. After what seemed like an eternity he stopped and looked directly into her eyes.

"You'll never approach it like a man," he said softly. "I'm not sure what you really want, but I know it's not casual sex. And I want more than that too. But we need time, Michele. We need time to discover each other, to learn what we like and don't like about being together— not only sexually but emotionally. But right now, tonight, we both want each other. Let's find a motel here in Bend, spend the night together and begin to discover how deep the relationship should be."

She looked into his eyes and saw only a powerful lust. Fear slammed into her chest and her legs almost buckled. Her body shook. Her heart beat in double time. She was doing it again. She'd promised never again. Jon had warned her and here she was. Oh God, would it ever stop? Would she ever know what was true—what was the difference between desire and love?

David wrapped his arms tighter. "What's wrong? What did I say?"

She couldn't stop the shaking if she went further. She pushed away from him.

"I'm so sorry. I just can't be with you right now." It really was her fault she had led him on. Toward the end of their relationship, Jon had warned her about how she did that, how she would act like a whore when she allowed desire to take over. "I'm so sorry," she repeated.

Tears came unbidden to her eyes as she looked up at him and wondered if she had made a mistake, but she bit her lip willing herself not to let them fall. She would find a way to make this right. She turned and busied herself with packing up her carry bag. When she had all her belongings safely stored, she faced him again; her arms braced the carry bag in front of her like a shield.

"No one has ever made me want to say yes this badly before."

David didn't respond. He continued to stare at her. Her resolve began to waver and she stepped toward him, holding his eyes.

"You could change my mind so easily. I can barely think even now."

"Don't think, Michele. Why not simply feel and see where it leads us?" He reached to caress her cheek with his thumb, then traced her jaw line to the pulse in her neck and trailed it down the vee in her shirt.

She sucked in her breath, her hand closing over his, stopping its downward path.

"I know. But that's what I do. I think. I've learned, the hard way, not to allow my emotions to rule me...usually anyway." She paused, unsure how to explain her feelings to him. "I can't go forward without thinking of the consequences—of the misunderstandings and the hurt that will inevitably come."

He kept silent, but his fingers were busy working through her hair.

She smiled wistfully. "I know I've never felt this way about another man. But I haven't had all that much experience. Just one guy. Jon. That's it. And...I ...I wasn't very good. He had to teach me. He had to tell me what to do. It just wasn't great. That's all. Just one guy, David— it's not a lot of experience. It would be so easy to say yes. I really do want to ... but I just can't. Believe me, you're better off this way."

He took the bag from her and set it down. "Please, look at me. What are you afraid of? I won't hurt you. I would never hurt you." He reached for her, but she turned her back as tears threatened again.

"Michele..." He slowly turned her back to face him. Tears fell as she realized maybe he was the one—the one who could erase the fear, erase all that she had experienced with Jon.

He carefully drew her back against him, and she burrowed into his chest. "My God. What did he do to you?" She shook her head against his chest. "Look, I'm not Jon. I don't tear a woman down. I don't take just for myself. Whatever he told you, it was his problem, not yours. You don't need anyone to tell you what to do. You know what to do naturally. Did you hear me telling you what to do just a few moments ago?"

"No."

"That's right, I didn't tell you anything. But you gave freely, Michele."

"I didn't give. I took," she mumbled against his chest. "I selfishly took for myself." She was ashamed of what she did. Ashamed that she had taken so much and now stopped him. "That's what I do. I take. I lose control. It's… It's…"

"Michele, look at me." Her lashes lifted but her head didn't. "Look at me," he repeated so softly she had to look up. "Do I look like I didn't want to give to you? Do I look hurt?"

She studied him a long time. Finally, she shook her head.

"Seeing the pleasure in your eyes and knowing I gave that to you is the biggest turn on I could have. Don't you see that?"

She looked steadily into his eyes. "That makes it even harder to go with you."

"What?"

"You're very dangerous for me, David. The truth is I want more than a one-night stand. I thought I could play the game before, but I can't. I can't sleep with someone just once knowing I want more. I want a long-term relationship, and I know you don't."

"Michele, what I meant was—"

"No, you don't have to say anything. I do understand, and the truth is I don't have the time. What if we took this next step and … well …"

"Liked it?"

"Oh, there's no doubt we'll both like it." She smiled again and trailed her hand across his chest. "I don't doubt it will be great. I already had a taste of how great." She paused, not sure if she should go on, but then made a decision. "I know we'd both like it very much. But…"

"But what?"

She continued to hold his eyes in hers, wanting to judge his reaction at close range.

"What if we didn't want it to end? What if we changed our mind about the whole relationship thing? How could we manage that? The tour is starting in three weeks. I'll be gone for four months. How would we manage that?"

"Why not cross that bridge when we come to it?"

Oh, how she wished it were that easy. Her mouth turned down. "That's not who I am. Tonight I tried not to be a thinker, and I almost succeeded. But in the end, I have to weigh things. I can't go into this without having considered the ramifications and made my peace with them."

She could see the frustration in his eyes. "So, no romance?"

She shook her head.

"No nookie?"

She giggled and lifted her hand to follow the line of his jaw. "And after you did such a good job putting the idea in my mind." She winked at him.

He clasped his fingers around her wrist and brought her hand to his lips, grazing the knuckles softly. "I did, didn't I?"

"It was an amazing seduction, David."

"Thank you."

She cocked her head and studied him.

"I know that when I go to bed tonight…"

"Yes?" he prodded.

"My dreams will be filled with you."

"Yeah?" He leered teasingly. "What specifically?"

She paused for a moment and then laughed. Could she? It was an out. But could she really do it? She turned away and dug in her purse until she found a piece of paper and a pen. She quickly scribbled something on the paper, chuckled and stood on her tiptoes.

Drawing his head to her level, she whispered in his ear. "Why don't you call me after you get home, and I'll share my thoughts with you?" She pressed the piece of paper into his hand.

David swallowed as he looked at the number. He cocked an eyebrow in question.

She smiled. "Not as good as the real thing, but it would take the edge off for both of us."

He laughed long and hard. "Yes, I guess it would."

Then he ravished her lips once more, making sure she knew exactly what she was giving up tonight.

CHAPTER 5

Tired, Michele pulled down the Murphy bed. She immediately saw her grandmother's quilt hung in the interior space above the headboard and illuminated by a small light. She was home. Safe. With the shelves rolled out, the other side of the bookcase held four small alcoves where she could keep personal items and bed linens. At night, she often read in bed just before falling asleep. With only the small reading lamp casting a warm glow on her pillow, she really did feel insulated from the rest of the apartment, with the other spaces as hazy shapes in the dark. Also, the opened bookcases provided two short walls near the headboard that helped to give that secure and enclosed feeling in her bed space.

She shed her clothes, debated about putting on her long t-shirt and decided it might be better not to have to deal with it and the phone too. Michele snuggled deep in the sheets, drawing the comforter to her chin. Was she really going to do this? What had she been thinking when she made the suggestion. She wasn't thinking. Again. She was trying to compromise, with herself more than him. Argh!

The bedside clock read 2:00am. She watched the numbers click over one by one as the minutes passed. The phone remained silent in the cubbyhole near her pillow. It had been at least 45 minutes since she got home. Surely he was home by now.

Maybe he forgot. She should feel relieved. She didn't know what she would say anyway. Now that she was in her own bed and her own apartment, all the mesmerizing lust of the evening seemed to be just a dream—not something she had really been caught up in.

2:15. He's obviously not calling. She turned off her lamp, closed her eyes, and drifted into a light sleep.

DAVID WANDERED around his loft trying to settle down. He finished off his third glass of beer and headed to his bedroom. He knew he probably should have called an hour ago, but he was still worked up over her hesitation to spend the night. He'd never before wanted someone so badly. He'd followed her all the way to Portland to make sure she didn't fall asleep while driving. Once they approached the city, however, she took I-5 south while he continued into City Center. He knew she lived somewhere near the university but he still didn't know where.

Fine thing, he thought to himself. You want to get her in bed and you don't even know where she lives. That made him angry all over again. How had he let this little slip of a woman get under his skin so quick? Well, he would just have to work harder.

He stripped off his clothes and grabbed his cell before getting into his king-size bed. It suddenly seemed far too big and empty when all he could think of was Michele filling the vacant spot next to him.

Whoa! Now that's really stupid. I never bring women to my bed. No one in my house. No one in my bed. That's the rule. No matter how cute she is there will be no serious relationship. Glad to have his head on straight again, he set three pillows against the headboard to cushion his back and then pulled the sheet to his waist.

He'd never had someone offer to seduce him over the phone. He wasn't even sure she knew what she offered. Damnit! He still wanted to finish what they'd started tonight. He wanted to erase whatever that jerk, Jon, had led her to believe. He'd work hard to build her a fantasy over the phone. In fact, he'd make sure she was satisfied. It's just too bad he couldn't be there to watch the surprise in her eyes as she brought herself to orgasm.

Punching in the phone number he had memorized during the drive home, he settled himself against the pillows more than prepared to seduce and be seduced.

The phone jangled and Michele came immediately awake. She glanced at the clock in a confused haze. 3:05. Fumbling, she finally picked it up on the third ring.

"Hello?"

"Make it home okay?"

She sucked in a breath. David's voice immediately filled her with warmth from her toes to her heart.

"Did I wake you?"

"Uh, kind of…"

"Good, then you're relaxed."

"I got home fine," she offered.

"Good."

"I guess you're calling to collect on my offer."

"It crossed my mind. But if you're too tired…"

"I don't welch on a bargain."

"Look. I had a great time tonight. I wanted to make sure everything was still okay between us. I understand you were uncomfortable with where things going. You don't have to do this.

Michele paused for a moment. Okay, so her idea was a spur of the moment crazy offer. But the truth is she was interested in him and this seemed…safe…kind of. No way was she backing out now. She would give him the best damn phone sex ever—if she could only figure out how to start.

She switched on her bedside lamp and sat straight up. Fluffing her pillows with one hand to make herself more comfortable, she scooted back against the headboard. She pulled the sheet and comforter up to her chin, making sure she was completely covered.

"You're not scared are you?" she challenged.

David chuckled low, all male and pure seduction. She drew her knees up to provide better balance as she leaned against the headboard. If she was going to do this, she needed to concentrate. She couldn't be lounging casually.

"Where are you?" she asked, purposefully lowering her voice and drawing out the cadence in what she hoped sounded sexy.

"In my bed," he said.

Michele swallowed. She imagined him stretched out, totally naked, not at all concerned about covering himself. "Um...what are you wearing?"

She had read an article in Cosmo once that said this was how phone sex calls always started—talking about seductive clothing and then using that clothing to do things. She looked at her unclothed body. Hmmm...should she make up something or be honest? She decided on honesty. She wasn't sure she had an imagination for anything else.

"I'm wearing my birthday suit," he said.

She gulped.

Unbidden, mental images appeared of David stretched out looking into mirrors on the ceiling reflecting a feral look that bore straight into her eyes. She'd seen a model posed like that once in a magazine. She couldn't remember which one.

She could picture a whole lot of sleek, naked skin showing around a silk sheet draped strategically over one thigh and the bulge between his legs. The delicious, arousing fantasy caused her breasts to swell and her nipples to tingle. She could easily imagine herself responding to that look and slinking into the room to join him.

Her breathing became more rapid. Afraid he could hear her heart palpitating, she placed her hand over the microphone part of the phone.

"And what are you wearing?" he asked.

"A cool cotton sheet," she barely squeaked out. Now what was she supposed to do? Both of them were wearing nothing. Where did she go from here?

His lazy laughter drifted through the phone line. "Good, we're both even then. I don't have to worry about undressing you."

"David, I…" she didn't know what to say next. The magazine article hadn't gone beyond the first few lines of set up. It then suggested you talk about your sexual fantasies. The problem was Michele didn't really have any sexual fantasies—at least none that went past the kissing after getting naked part.

With Jon it had always been the same every time—same positions, same progression to their coupling. In fact, she could almost tell to the minute when he was ready to release whether she was close or not. The two times she had tried to spice things up, he quickly put her in her place, letting her know it was the man's job to call the shots in the bedroom.

"I have an idea," David said, after her long pause. "Let me talk and you do. That will make it good for me."

"Are you sure?" she asked. "I feel like I'm letting you down."

"Is this only for me?" he asked. "If it is, we should stop now. It's not fun if both of us can't enjoy it."

"Yes, of course you're right. It's just that I…well the truth is I've never done this before and I don't know what I'm supposed to do next."

"Ah, I see."

"I'm sorry. It's stupid. I should have never suggested it."

"Don't be sorry. It's the most turned on I've been in a very long time. I'm flattered I'm your first."

Michele giggled. "I guess that makes me a virgin then."

David laughed. After a pause he said. "I'm a virgin too, but I have a great imagination. If you're comfortable let me take the lead. I promise my imagination can do the work for both of us."

Michele sighed with relief. "Thanks," she whispered. She promised herself she would definitely do whatever he said. She wouldn't cheat. Maybe she couldn't be there in person, but she could do this for him.

"Are you sitting against pillows?" he asked.

"Yes."

"Do you have a light on?"

"Yes, my bed lamp."

"Do you have any candles?"

"Yes, in the kitchen."

"Go get them. Light them and put them around your bed."

"OK, just a minute."

Her feet padded on the floor as she ran to the kitchen naked. Geez, if anything happened to her now, her mother would always wonder what she was doing skulking around her kitchen in the dark with no clothes. She fumbled through two cupboards until she found three votive candles and some matches. She placed them quickly and climbed back into bed. Pulling the blanket up to her chin again she grasped the phone to her ear.

"OK. I have one on either side of my bed in little cubby holes and one larger one at the foot of the bed near my window on a small table."

"Did you light them?"

"Oh. Just a minute."

Again, she hopped out of bed and lit each candle. At this rate it would be dawn before either of them actually touched anything. Back in bed she reported her success.

"Now turn off your lamp. How does it look?"

"Kind of romantic, I guess."

"Good." He drew out the word on a sigh and she could picture him relaxing against his own headboard. She wondered what his room looked like, if he had a view.

His voice interrupted her thoughts. "Now, I want you to lie back on your pillows, your back to the mattress and just allow yourself to relax. Get used to the candlelight as it wraps your bed in a warm and safe cocoon."

Michele snuggled deeper under the comforter and let the candlelight fill her vision. On a deep sigh she expelled a breath.

"Oh yes," he whispered, his voice gravelly and low.

"I just hope I don't fall asleep while we're on the phone."

David chuckled. "Oh, I don't think you'll fall back to sleep. Are you feeling warm and comfortable and safe?"

"Yes, I'm feeling nice."

"Good. Now, look around your bed and describe everything you see. Describe your bed and the bedding. Tell me what is within immediate reach of your bed as you are lying down. Don't reach for them, just describe them. And be sure to especially mention all the things that are meaningful to you that you can see with just the candlelight. Don't leave out any details."

Michele sighed and moved one hand above her head then back down to her side, as the other hand cradled the phone against her ear. She loved the feeling of her fresh flannel sheets. She had washed them this morning and the light lavender scent from the dryer sheet still clung to them.

Her voice low and intimate, Michele began her description. "Well, it's a Murphy bed. When I turn my head to the right, I can see the cradle for my cell phone in a little cubbyhole. Above that is one of the candles I lit. To the left is a small glass of water I keep by me, just in case I get thirsty in the middle of the night. Above that is the other candle."

"Your sheets and pillows, describe your sheets and pillows," he said gruffly.

"Uh…they're flannel. I keep flannel sheets on even during the summer."

"Color?"

"Hunter green. Green is my favorite color."

"Perfect," he whispered in her ear. "I can see your fair skin and dark hair against the dark background."

She could hear a rustling of material through the phone, but couldn't make out what was happening.

"I have four pillows—two are flat on the bed so I can roll to any side and still have a pillow. The other two are stacked off to the side. Sometimes I like to sleep with my arms around them, like a person."

She stopped. What made her admit that?

"I mean…about the pillows…"

"I understand," he said softly. "Go on with your description."

"I don't know, what else?"

"Jewelry? Books? Trinkets? Anything else in reaching distance?"

Michele looked closely. Everything was immediate in this apartment. None of her things seemed sexy. "Um…I don't really have much jewelry. Just one long fake gold bead necklace I got at a High School Mardi Gras party. I don't wear it, but I keep it because it has happy memories. What else should I look for?"

"Don't worry about it. Just relax now. Stretch your hands above your head and point your toes to the other wall."

"It's hard to stretch and hold the phone at the same time."

"Ummm. Can you put the phone right next to your ear and still hear me?"

She tested it and that worked nicely.

"OK," he continued. "When you feel like you've stretched as hard as you can, release and just let your entire body luxuriate in your nice warm sheets."

She stretched as he asked and when she let go, she really did relax into the sheets. She could feel them along her sides, caressing her bottom and her calves.

"Now, push the comforter off you to the foot of the bed and move the sheet down to your waist."

"How did you know…" She sat up immediately, searching her room, wondering if he were somehow standing there watching her every move.

David chuckled. "A good guess. I'm in tune with you. I have an idea how you think and react to these things. Now do it, Michele. Remember, you promised."

She peered around her room. She didn't know why she was being shy. It wasn't like anyone could see her. Satisfied she wasn't being watched she flattened against the mattress once again and did as he asked.

"Okay."

"Good, now we are going to use things to help both of us feel good, and I want you to believe that it is my hand guiding you. It is my hand moving over your body and doing everything I'm going to suggest to you."

His voice was positively wicked, impenitently so, and husky with promise. She already started to feel the warmth rising from her belly.

"Run your finger, very slowly, from your chin, down your throat."

She did as he asked and, feeling silly, she let out a giggle.

"Michele," he said a little harshly. "Remember, this is my finger tracing down your throat."

"Sorry, it's just that I've never done this before."

"I know," he softened his voice and drew the words out again as he spoke. "Close your eyes and imagine me kneeling over you, taking you all in. You are so beautiful, Michele. I can't believe how beautiful your smooth skin looks against the dark green of your sheets." She could hear his voice getting huskier and his breathing a little more rapid. "I'm looking down at your body as my hand is slowly moving from your throat down to the space between your breasts."

Michele's hand moved slowly following his voice, she could almost believe it was his hand, not hers doing what he said.

"Now my fingers are moving across your nipples, stroking and teasing until they stand up."

She sighed as she followed his instruction, surprised to find herself arching against the mattress to her own touches. She moaned.

"I can see them standing and the dark color puckering beneath each one," he said as his breath grew ragged. "They are so beautiful, Michele. I'm licking my lips in preparation of taking them in my mouth. I'm so hungry for you."

She continued to stroke them herself, making sure they were ready to offer to his mouth.

"As my hands knead and stroke you, my eyes are looking down the length of your body. I want to suckle at your breasts. I need to feel your nipples in my mouth."

"Yes, take them in your mouth," she whispered.

"Dip your fingers in your water glass and bathe your nipples with the water."

She did as he asked and worked her own nipples, pulling and tugging as if his mouth were on them. She moaned with pleasure as she imagined him suckling, and she could hear his breath coming faster and faster.

"I'm so close Michele," he said, breathless. "I'm stroking myself across your mound, and I want so badly to come inside."

His breath sounded so close to her ear as he spoke that she could almost feel the heat of him next to her. Unconsciously, she began moving her hips from side to side as she continued to pleasure her breasts. She wanted to help him finish; she wanted to give him what he needed.

"Yes, come inside me, David. I'm ready for you. Tell me what to do. Please. I want you."

She heard him struggling to hold himself back. "No, not yet," He drew in a large breath. "I want to watch you come, Michele. I want to hear you."

"Reluctantly, my fingers are leaving your breasts and trailing down to your navel. Both of my hands are rubbing across your stomach and up your sides. Across your breasts and down your front. I love the feel of how your entire torso responds to my touch. Oh, god. I'm so hard, Michele, just looking at you and feeling your smooth skin, the curve of your hip.

Michele's hands moved across her body as he had described, massaging her breasts, then skimming down her sides and coming back up across her belly and her waist to capture her breasts again. With each stroke she could almost feel him pressing against her, and she began tilting her pelvis up and down in anticipation of his hardness entering her.

"My fingers are working lower. My hand is massaging your mound. It is so beautiful. Your response is driving me wild. I want you so badly. I'm lifting your hips toward me. I want to prepare you. Oh God, I'm pulsing in anticipation. Can you feel me rubbing against your entrance? I need you slick and ready. Oh God. I don't know if I can wait.

"I don't want to hurt you, I want to enter you slowly, stretching you to accommodate me."

She took in a quick breath when she heard him breathing rapidly in her ear, and asking again, no demanding. "Can you feel me, Michele? Are you wet for me? Are you ready for me to enter you?"

"Yes," she responded her hips pistoning faster. "Yes, please David. I want you. I want you now."

"I need you to be really ready. I want to go deep when I thrust into you. My fingers are moving down your center and stroking you. I'm feeling your heat rise and I can smell your feminine scent. I want to feel your wetness, Michele."

She raised her hips toward the ceiling her knees opened for him as she stroked her own inner thighs.

"My finger is dipping inside your wetness. Feel my finger moving inside you."

Michele put her finger at the opening, wanting him inside her so badly. She dipped her finger in once, twice, then plunged it all the way as her hips pistoned faster. "Oh, God. Oh, God." She sucked in her breath and plunged her finger in again, and again. She added a second finger. Her breath caught and released faster and faster. "I want you," she said. "Oh God, I really want you. Now, David. Come into me now!"

She looked up, expecting to see David's eyes—expecting to see his naked torso above her. "Oh God. No!" The wail escaped and she yanked her fingers out. "Oh, God, no. It's me. It's not David. It's me. I've done it again. No. No. No." Her voice shook and she curled into a ball. "I'm sorry. I'm so, so sorry. I know I shouldn't have done that. I'm sorry. I'll never do it again. I promise. I promise I'll never do it again. I'm sorry. I'm sorry." Tears soaked the sheets below her. Her breath came in fits and starts.

"Michele?"

She couldn't answer. She felt so ashamed. Jon had told her how wrong she was to touch herself. How wrong she was to love sex so much. He'd call her a whore for needing so much pleasure. It was all true. She couldn't control herself. And now David knew it too. Oh God, David knew it too.

"Michele, are you there? What's happening? What's wrong?"

Finally, she put the phone back to her ear. "I'm so sorry, David. I thought I could do this, but I can't. I'm so sorry. I wanted it too much. I was enjoying it too much. I know it's wrong. I'm so sorry. So, so sorry."

"What's wrong?" he asked, his words releasing between pants as if he had no breath. "Nothing's wrong, Michele. What are you talking about?"

She tried to find words between the sobs. She should just hang up. Why did he insist she admit it? Wasn't knowing she acted like a whore already obvious?

"Michele, talk to me. We can work through this."

"I touched myself. My fingers, they were inside me. They…" Her stomach heaved like it wanted to empty itself and she curled back into a ball.

"It's natural, Michele." God he sounded so close. "You can do it. Pretend it's my hand, my fingers inside you."

"You don't understand. I can't control myself. I like it! Damn it, David, I like it too much." She choked out the words. "I'm nothing but a …Oh God, I'm so sorry. So sorry. I didn't mean to do it. I didn't mean to like it so much. Please forgive me. Forgive me." Now he knew everything. Anything she imagined with him was gone. Forever. She held onto the phone, unable to hang up as she cried softly.

David struggled to stop his fantasy. His hand finally dropped to his side and he let go of his own need and paid full attention to her now.

"Michele, it's okay. You don't have to do anymore." He could here her swallowing, choking back the tears. "It's okay. I don't want to make you do anything where you don't feel comfortable. I just wanted you to enjoy your body as much as I would."

"I know," she whispered. "It's my fault. I shouldn't have made the suggestion. I should have known I couldn't follow through. I just wasn't thinking. I thought, maybe with you…Oh, God, I just wasn't thinking."

He waited, listening to her cry. "Go ahead, just cry it out. I'm here."

That only made her cry harder.

He'd never heard such raw emotion pouring from anyone. He felt awful that he had caused this outpouring of pain. He assumed with the way her body had responded to him earlier, with the way she had so willingly come up with this idea, that she was free with herself—knew how to pleasure herself and enjoyed it. He wanted to learn what she liked. He wanted to be a part of that pleasure with her.

Finally he heard her breathing return to a more normal pace.

"I want to understand why, Michele. I don't ever want to hurt you. I only want to bring you pleasure."

He waited through the silence, listening as she found her voice again.

"It's all so lurid and complicated," she finally said.

"Yeah, I suspected that much. Please help me understand. Can you explain it to me?"

He heard her take a deep breath and let it out on a sigh.

"It's something to do with Jon isn't it?" He asked. "Do you still love him, Michele? Is that it?"

"Oh God, no! It's totally the opposite."

She went silent.

He waited.

Whatever it was, she obviously needed time.

"You're right, it does have to do with Jon," she finally said. "But not in the way that you think. Jon used to call me a whore when I touched myself there."

"Shit! That's just sick. What kind of a sick mind did he have? If I could get my hands on him…" His hands fisted the sheets. What kind of an idiot would say that to any woman? "The man must have had the smallest dick in the world to come up with that kind of crap."

He concentrated on keeping the violence out of his voice. The guy had really done a number on her for it to still be with her five years later. "You don't believe what he said do you?" he asked. "Pleasuring yourself is natural, Michele."

"I know. I guess. I just haven't tried to touch myself…since he left. Too many bad memories." Her voice cracked and he could hear the tears in it.

"If it's too hard, you don't have to talk—"

"No, I want to. I have to explain or there's never any hope...for me...for us." Her voice choked and he could hear her soft sobs.

"Take your time," he said. He wished he could be there holding her instead of having all this go down on the damn phone.

Michele tightened her hold on the phone. She needed to get the whole thing out. She'd never be able to move on with any man until she did, until she found someone who understood, someone who could still love her even in her wildness.

She sighed again. "I tried it once to help me come—so I wouldn't have to fake it with him anymore. He was always kind of fast."

She paused. God, was that too much? What if all guys were fast? What if...

"He was a selfish bastard," David said forcefully. "It had nothing to do with you. You deserve better than that."

She barely heard him. Would he still feel that way when he learned the whole truth?

"He caught me," she continued. "Helping myself. I knew he was ready to finish and I just wanted to be done too, instead of unsatisfied. So, I reached down... and...and my hand must have touched him. He uh stopped... mid stroke. He was so angry he pulled out and his penis was all shrunken. He yelled at me and paced. He told me that only whores do that, not people who care about each other. When I tried to explain my need, he just grew angrier. Then...then..." she took a deep breath and continued. "Then he put his fingers inside me and made me come without him. He yelled at me the whole time asking 'Is this what you want? Is this what you like?' Then he scraped his nails along the inside until I bled. He said the blood would erase my shame."

She paused, her voice choking.

"Oh, God, Michele. I'm so sorry. He was a sick, sick, bastard."

She would not cry again. She needed to get through this.

"Then he stomped out of the bedroom. I thought that would be the end of it. He stayed away for a week, and when he came back I promised never to touch myself like that again. I promised to be the woman he wanted in the bedroom."

Michele talked faster and faster, trying to outrun the pain of the story.

"Every time we had sex after that, he would force me to pleasure myself as he pumped inside me, and he called me names—some of them much worse than whore. Then, if I came before he did, after he satisfied himself he would immediately get up and put $20 on the table and walk away, saying 'That's twice as much as your worth tonight.' Once I tried not to come, but he knew it. Somehow he always knew, and that would make him even angrier. I just didn't know how to do it right. I didn't know what to do. I didn't know how to please him. I…"

Tears threatened to spill again, but she clenched her fists refusing to shed another one for Jon. She knew David would never want her after hearing all this, but she couldn't help it. She needed to purge herself. It was all over with David anyway. It was better she faced it now before her heart became involved.

"I know you're thinking I was stupid to let him do that," she continued. "But I thought I loved him. I thought we could work through it. I thought if I just did as he asked for a little while then I could go back to faking it and things would be good again. But it never happened. It only got worse.

"Toward the end of our relationship, he wouldn't even let me touch him… to help him. Night after night he would stand at the foot of the bed and stroke himself into hardness as he cussed at me. He tied up my hands so I couldn't touch him or myself. Once he got hard, he would ram into me and yell at me to come. I never could. I never could come with just him. He said that proved I was a whore because whores could never have an orgasm with a man."

Numb. She held the phone to herself, silent. It was out. It was all out now. She didn't shake. She didn't cry. She didn't feel anything anymore.

"Shit!" David whispered after several minutes. "He raped you. He fuckin' raped you."

She expected him to yell but he said it quietly over and over. Then there was silence. She couldn't even hear him breathe.

"How long?" he asked. "How long did he do this to you?"

She sighed. In the end it all blurred together. One day became the next day and the next. She didn't leave the apartment. She didn't go to work. She didn't do anything until he finally left. Even then, she didn't do anything afraid he would come back.

"Michele?"

"I'm not sure," she said. "I think it was three, maybe four months. I don't really remember. The days…they…" She sighed, and a weight settled on her chest. "By the time he finally left for good, I really did feel like a whore. Not because he told me I was, but because I allowed him to have so much control over me."

Shit! David rammed his fist into the pillow next to him as he bit off the string of swear words he wanted to yell to the sky. How could any man do that to a woman? How could any man make something so dirty out of a natural and beautiful act? He would give anything to have a woman who trusted him enough to pleasure herself and let him watch and learn how to please her.

Then he heard Michele crying softly, and repeating again and again. "I'm so sorry. I really wanted to be with you. I really did want to do this for you. In spite of everything I've just told you, I still want you. Is that sick? I don't know how to feel. You're the first man I've wanted to do anything with. I don't know what to do."

David expelled a long breath. "I don't know what to do either. I don't know how to help. God, I wish I were there!" He curled his fingers around the edge of the mattress and squeezed, imagining it was Jon's neck. The bastard didn't deserve Michele. What he deserved was a jail cell with…No! He wouldn't go there. He wouldn't lower himself to that level.

"I wish I could hold you, Michele. I wish I could hold you and show you what real love-making is all about," he said, his voice reaching to soothe her. "It's about treasuring you. It's about putting your needs first."

He could hear her breathing calm as she listened to him. After several minutes, when he could no longer hear caught breaths, only slow deep breaths, he said, "Thank you."

"For what?" Michele asked. Her voice sounded far away, like she was half asleep.

He smiled, imagining her head on his pillow next to him. Her eyes shuttered as he placed a hand on her waist and followed it to her hip. "Thank you for trusting me. Thank you for being the only woman who even tried to seduce me over the phone."

Another long pause. He waited. He wondered if she had fallen asleep. Not that he minded. He could listen to her soft breathing and fall asleep himself.

"David?" she asked, her voice tentative.

"Yes?"

"I wish you were here."

"I'm still here," he responded. "I'm not leaving. Just curl into me."

Silence.

"I can't. I can't feel you next to me anymore," she whispered. "How stupid I've been. How absolutely scared and stupid. I should have just gone to the hotel with you in Bend. I should have just gotten it over with."

"You are not stupid," he said harshly. "Don't ever call yourself that."

He softened his voice. He didn't want to cause her anymore pain. He wanted her to understand how special she really was. "You are a beautiful, generous, woman. You are intelligent and strong. You are a talented musician. You are kind and caring, and you have every right to question and think about anything in advance. You were right to be careful."

"But, what you said before…I thought…"

"I was out of control. You completely overwhelmed me, Michele. I would have done anything to be with you."

"Thank you, David."

"For what?"

"For letting me know you were out of control too…it wasn't just me then."

He chuckled "Oh, it was all you all right. You had me wrapped around your little finger. And tonight…tonight you've done some-thing with me that no woman has ever done. You completely seduced me over the phone. You took a chance. You went beyond your own comfort to please me."

"Well, I …."

"You did." His voice softened. "I wish I were there too. I wish you were spooned into me, your bottom into my belly, my hands caressing your breasts. I wish I were there to kiss away your tears of pain and to show you only joy. I wish I were there to hold you until morning, when I could make love to you again."

"Come over," she said, her voice confident. "I want you here. Physically here."

David took a big breath and then let it out. "God, Michele, I want to come over there. Really I do. I just don't think it would be right. You're just reacting emotionally after what you shared about Jon."

"I'm emotional for sure." She laughed, and he was ecstatic to hear it after so much pain. "But I'm also horny and I think…I really think I wouldn't be scared with you. Quick. Come over now before I change my mind."

David groaned again. Shit! He was really stupid for turning her down. She'd probably think better of it in the morning and that would be the end of it. His stomach clenched as he thought of not having the opportunity to get to know her better. He let out a sigh. It was the right thing to do. He was sure of it.

"Tell you what. Let's plan another date instead, and if you still want me in your bed after that, I'll gladly accommodate you."

"You're right," she finally spoke. "It wouldn't be fair to ask you to replace the memory of Jon."

"I know you want me, Michele. And God knows I want you, but…."

Michele sighed. "Let's just talk for awhile. Okay?"

"Yeah, that would be nice." David squirmed under his sheet and let the phone settle by his ear. "I'm willing to talk all night. We can even sleep together, if you want."

Michele chuckled, and it felt good. Real good.

CHAPTER 6

"Rachel, you're pushing the tempo again," Sarah said, this time with a hint of anger in her voice. "I don't know what's eating you, but we can't keep up and this isn't your solo."

"I'm not pushing it, you're all too slow," Rachel's eyes flashed in defiance. "Look, this is the tempo." She demonstrated on her fiddle with sixteen bars of the jig. "Any slower and the dancers would need wires to stay straight."

"Rachel, she's right," Kat added. "Besides, we don't have any dancers. We agreed this was going to be at the double jig tempo of 72-76. You're playing the single jig at about 120."

"No shit, Sherlock. It is a single jig tempo."

"I thought the pacing was okay," Michele added. "I actually liked it being a little faster."

"See!" Rachel said. "Even the newbie knows a good tempo when she hears it."

Sarah turned her back on the rest of the band. Her shoulders slumped. It appeared she was going to cry.

"Let's take a break," Theresa said. "I think we can all use a little space right now. Anyone for lemonade?"

A round of "Nah" went up from everyone except Kat who rushed from the room following her mother.

This rehearsal hadn't been going well from the start. Rachel was in a snit and no one knew why. Kat had been thirty minutes late, having come from a matinee show at Sandy High School where she played accompaniment for a theater production, and the usually calm and collected Sarah was on edge. This was the first time since Michele had joined the band that it seemed no one was getting along.

"You okay, Sarah?" Michele asked, quietly noticing Sarah's turned back.

"She's just being anal," Rachel said. "She's worried about the bookings."

Sarah placed her guitar on the stand and turned to Rachel, no sign of tears just the grim clenching of teeth. "Well, someone has to worry. You obviously don't care if we starve on the road or not."

"That's Theresa's job," Rachel said. "You've got to trust her to have it together by the time we leave. Besides, she has a Midwest booker now that will handle most of the tour back there.

"But that still leaves a lot for us to do and you're too busy chasing men every night to help."

"And you're too busy guarding your virginity to even notice new guys!" Rachel stomped from the room, shoving the glass door closed with a resounding ping. It was a miracle the glass didn't break.

"That was a bit harsh," Michele said. "It's not like you to be mean."

Sarah took a deep breath. "You're right. We know how to push each other's buttons. I just don't understand her choices."

"Are you really worried about Rachel or is it the tour? Or something else?"

"Oh, I don't know. I guess it's everything." Sarah paused. "I was so excited about the band going on a tour when we first planned it, and I know this is the way for us to grow our fan base...but...I just don't want to end up in Timbuktu, broke and with nothing to show for it."

"I can see that, but what have you got to show for yourself now?"

"At least I have a job and I know I'm making enough money to make my rent and put food on the table. I'm just not like Rachel, able to throw caution to the wind and not worry about it."

"Yeah, I know what you mean. I've been wondering what to do about my apartment. On the one hand, I should let it go because it's silly to pay rent for four and a half months and not even live there—particularly if I'll need that rent money on the road. On the other hand, if I let it go, the chances of finding something that reasonable when we get back is really slim. Students will be back for fall term and my apartment would be one of the first to be rented."

"Exactly." Sarah paced in front of the sliding door. "What if we don't make it? What if some of the bookings fall through or we don't get enough? What if, God forbid, something happens like an accident or the motor home breaks down?"

"It's easy to get caught up in the what-ifs," Michele said. "I guess it's just something we each have to deal with in our own way."

"Yeah, you're right." Sarah paused. "So, what are you going to do about your apartment?"

Michele sighed. "I guess I'm going to give it up. I just don't think I have the money to pay the rent and be on the road without a regular monthly income. And, if worse comes to worse, I'll beg Theresa and Kat to let me bunk here for a couple weeks until I get back on my feet.

"At least there is that option," Sarah said. "Though by the end of the tour you may be so sick of us, you'd rather live under a bridge than spend one more day in the same house with any of us."

Michele chuckled. "I don't think that will happen."

"Maybe not, but we can be pretty awful sometimes."

"You especially," Michele teased.

Sarah smiled and gave her a hug. "Let's get some of that lemonade before it's all gone."

Michele followed her through the sliding door, tamping down her own fears. The thought of giving up her apartment of six years was something she'd only recently contemplated. But this was her chance to prove to herself she was committed and she could make it. After all, it was just a couple weeks ago she'd decided to give up the dream of being a full-time musician. Then Theresa approached her at Meinig Park and her life changed.

Sometimes you have to give up everything to make your dream come true. She just hoped it was worth it.

MICHELE LOOKED through the peephole to make sure it was really David at the door. It had been a whole week since the Allison Krauss concert—plenty of time for second and even third guesses. He'd called her every night after rehearsals and they'd talked about philosophy, books, politics, and yes even sex. She figured she knew more about him from all their telephone conversations than she had known about Jon after their entire two-year relationship. So why was she so nervous now? Oh yeah, the big decision—she was probably—make that definitely—going to bed with him tonight. Maybe. Darn! Her confidence was still on edge.

"Just a minute," she said, then peeked through the peephole again.

David's pose was a combination of arrogance and vulnerability. His thick, dark hair was mussed as if he rode over with the windows down. That clean shaven chin drew even more attention to those mesmerizing blue-green eyes. One hand checked his belt and then disappeared into the jean pocket.

She opened the door slowly. He immediately looked her up and down and smiled as he stepped inside and closed the door behind him. She moved to close the distance between them, but he put out a hand to stop her.

"Don't move," his voice caressed the air between them.

She melted like a spent candle..

He took a long, frank look at her from head to toe. "I like the dress," he said softly, nodding at the yellow bit of chiffon she wore.

She knew it skimmed her figure and showed it to advantage. That's why she'd chosen to wear it tonight. Not to mention, it was pretty easy to get out of.

"Definitely inviting, the way your white shoulders barely hold up those little straps." He looked at her chest and she could feel her nipples pucker in excitement. "Mmmm hmmmm. I didn't think you could get a bra under there. Trying to tempt me, Michele? If so, it's working." He stepped forward and placed his palm against her cheek.

She blushed and backed herself against the door. Already, she could feel the heat as he traced a finger over her shoulder, dislodging one of the straps.

"Oh, I…I…" Michele stammered. "Uh, I think we should get going. Don't you?"

Everything inside her went still as he closed the space between them. The warmth of his body soothed her while the deep fragrance of musk spoke of unfettered sexuality.

Michele trembled at the contrast.

David's lips followed the same curve of her shoulder as his hands, but this time he worked back from the tip of her shoulder toward her neck then to her lips. He brushed her lips softly, then worked on her mouth in a tender massage with his, but not taking the kiss any deeper.

After what seemed like minutes, she heard his intake of breath and he took two steps away from her. "Now we can go." His husky voice speared her with promise.

She could barely move. He'd done it again. This time it wasn't the quick passion that she had felt in Bend. Instead it was this soft, sensuous, caring. God, he was good. She wasn't sure how she was going to make it through dinner and a movie before getting back here tonight.

In a daze, she gathered her purse and offered him her key as she wrapped her arms in a shawl. He ushered her out the door and locked it behind them, neither one speaking as they headed down the stairs to his car.

MICHELE MARVELED AT THE VIEW. They were on the thirtieth floor of the big pink building—the tallest building in Portland, known as the US

Bank Tower. David had made reservations at the Portland City Grill. They'd passed through the noisy bar, where happy hour was in full swing, and were seated in a quiet corner with windows to the north and east. They were seated cate-corner, so they both could enjoy the view of Mt. Hood on the eastern horizon as the sun set. A golden glow highlighted the scarred, timbered ceiling beams, giving the room a cozy, lodge-like feel even though she knew they sat in a modern high-rise 300 feet in the air.

The menu had a variety of choices from sushi to fine steaks and seafood. Having never been to the grill before, Michele asked for David's recommendation. He'd ordered a bottle of Pinot Noir, then started them with a light sushi plate followed by a blackened tuna appetizer. Michele enjoyed the sushi and the wine, perhaps drinking just a little too much as she began to feel a slight buzz.

"Hmm…" she murmured. "I hope the dinner comes soon or you may have to carry me back to the car." She smiled with a twinkle in her eye.

"As appealing as that sounds, I think I'd rather not carry you out of the restaurant if at all possible. People may think I'm taking advantage."

"Little would they know I'd be the one taking advantage of you." Michele pointed a finger back at David, and couldn't help the broad smile that followed.

He offered her the blackened tuna appetizer. "Try some of this. It's a little more substantial than the sushi."

Michele looked at the plate. Raw ginger wrapped around baby watercress and bright yellow swirls on the plate. She loved watercress and immediately took a bite, then she forked a small piece of tuna and swirled it liberally in the yellow sauce."

"Uh, I don't think you want quite that much…" David winced as she popped the piece into her mouth.

"Yow!" she let out a yelp as she realized the pretty yellow was hot mustard. She downed a glass of water with several quick gulps and then reached for his glass as she could still feel the burn on her tongue.

David tore open two packets of sugar. "Here, pour this on your tongue and swallow."

Michele looked at him in disbelief.

"Trust me, it works."

She opened her mouth and poured both packets directly on her tongue. Immediately, the hotness began to dissipate. She swallowed.

"That's amazing." She opened another packet and poured it into her mouth as well, then sighed with relief.

"A little trick I learned from a client in Mexico after ingesting jalapenos I thought were bell pepper pieces."

"Ouch!"

"Yeah. Water actually makes it worse, because it sends it all around your mouth. Believe me, it took a lot more than two teaspoons of sugar."

Michele loved the way the skin near his temple crinkled when he laughed, and his eyes twinkled with the memory. She looked up and caught her breath, squeezing his hand in hers.

He turned to follow her gaze and they watched for a moment as the sky gradually darkened and the lights of downtown Portland illuminated its city neighborhoods. "Beautiful isn't it?"

Michele nodded. "I'd heard about the view from here, but I'd never bothered to come see it. Can you imagine having a view like this every night? I could just stand and watch it for hours."

"Yes, I..." David stopped himself.

He had been about to tell her he had this same view from his loft and that he would love to share it with her tonight and again in the morning. Whoa! He'd never slipped like that before. He reeled himself in. No women in my bedroom, he reminded himself sternly. He'd never even had second thoughts about having a woman over before—Michele was really starting to get to him.

He smiled. "I'm sure the view would be exquisite," he said in his best Cary Grant voice. "As exquisite as a view of New York from the Empire State Building."

Michele tilted her head slightly to the right and her brows creased together.

"What do you want to know?" he asked softly.

"Your family," Michele blurted. He blinked in surprise. "You've never talked about your family."

"Not much to tell—good that is."

"Oh." She paused and looked down at the table. "I'm sorry. I don't mean to bring up bad memories."

David sighed. She deserved to know. "Well, I'm not being entirely fair," he said. "It's not like I had an awful childhood. In fact, quite the opposite. I had all the material things and love any child could wish for. It was just …uh…prescribed."

"What do you mean by that?"

"My parents are both very successful. Dad's a CEO of a computer consulting firm just inside the D.C. beltway. Lots of government contracts. Mom sells over-priced McMansions in McLean, Virginia."

"Brothers and sisters?"

"No. I'm an only child." He paused, deciding how much to tell. "My parents were great to me. I really did have a loving home and lots of attention. My father's expectations couldn't always be met, but then when does any son truly measure up? I tried to meet his expectations. Worked at the firm every summer from age fourteen on—that's where I got my computer skills."

Michele nodded. "But you went to Oregon State. How did you decide to travel 3,000 miles to come to college here? You probably could have gone anywhere."

"Yeah, well, Dad and Mom had it all planned. Four years at Yale in Electrical Engineering, followed by an MBA at Harvard, then return and take over the firm so Dad could retire after he'd trained me in the way I should run things. But when it was time to go to college, all I wanted to do was get away—as far away as possible. My best friend's family had been transferred to Oregon when I was in High School. When we both started looking at colleges, he told me he was going to Oregon State because he loved living there with all the outdoor activities. He made it sound like heaven. Actually, I chose it just because it was far away from the east coast, and it happened to have a decent computer science program."

"I can understand wanting to get away. I kind of felt that way about Digby, Montana too, though it wasn't to get away from my parents. It was just the small town living and the expectation of marrying a farmer or rancher and having babies right away that I was running from."

David looked at her with renewed interest. She had talked about her family in one of their many conversations. How much she loved them. How supportive they had been of her musical career, and especially of her decision to play the bass.

"So, your parents must be dying that you are so far away now."

"Well, not exactly. They don't much pay attention to anything I do these days."

Michele didn't speak, but the way she leaned forward and covered his hand with hers told him all he needed to know.

"My parents were divorced after 26 years of marriage, and since then...well...they're pretty caught up in their own lives. Dad is in Maryland now, and Mom is still in Virginia."

"Oh. I'm so sorry."

"Yeah, well" he shrugged, withdrawing his hand as he took another sip of his wine. "They've been divorced more than three years now."

"Did they remarry?"

"I wish they had. At least that would be more normal."

Michele didn't say anything. She simply waited for him. Her eyes wide, inviting confidences.

"What about your parents? Divorced? Together? Happy?"

"My parents have been married for thirty years and it seems they have never been happier. I've always thought that is how it was for everyone. That is until after I left Digby. Not that I didn't know about divorce—it just wasn't part of my daily life. I know for sure that I won't get married until I find a person who can last that long with me."

"So, divorce is not your childhood aspiration?" he mugged as George Clooney. "But with the Massey Pre-Nup, you can get divorced as often as you like."

"It really hurt didn't it?" Michele asked, her hand reaching to cover his again. "I can't imagine what I'd do if my parents suddenly let me know they were splitting."

David shrugged. "Well, now that they're both divorced it seems nothing is permanent with either one of them. The last thing I knew, Dad had shacked up with someone about your age and Mom was reliving her glory days with someone only five years older than me. About once every six months they both look for someone else— usually someone younger than before. At this rate, by the time I'm forty, they'll be dating minors."

Michele didn't know what to say. He sounded angry and vulnerable at the same time. His eyes flashed with derision, but his posture had bent slightly as he spoke. She couldn't begin to imagine how it would feel if her parents were dating people nearly half their age.

"Are you ready for marriage, Michele?" His eyes held hers with that same anger, mixed with questioning. "Do you think you could maintain a relationship for twenty years? Thirty? How about fifty?"

"I…uh…don't know." She wasn't sure what he was looking to hear. Surely, he wasn't thinking about them, together, marriage and all that. It was more of a question about himself. "I think…if I found the right person… I could be ready. But no one has even come close. What about you?"

"Nope," he said with finality. "Not looking for commitment. Definitely never going to marry. Just havin' fun."

Well, that was a pretty clear message. David would never fall in love, no matter what. Good thing she knew that. Not that she planned to fall in love with him. Their relationship would last all of two more weeks, then she'd be touring with the band, and that would be the end of it.

Great sex, as Rachel would say. Take some of her own and enjoy it, her best friend had told her; and that is exactly what she was going to do. Then why was it she felt so hollow all of a sudden?

"I guess that sounded a little harsh," David said softly. "That doesn't mean I'd never care for a woman. But it's only fair you know it won't ever lead to marriage." He paused. "I hope we're still okay."

She forced her lips to lift at the corners, but she couldn't quite make the smile full. "Oh sure," she said a little too brightly. She waved her hand at him to shrug it off. "That's just the way I want it too."

David looked up and leaned back to watch the waiter set their tray on a folding stand. "Ah, our dinner."

The waiter first served Michele the Opakapaka. It looked beautiful, with the colorful Asian-style vegetables and saffron rice. She'd said she loved seafood and she'd allowed David to order for both of them. She waited as the waiter placed David's swordfish meal in front of him. Then he refilled both of their glasses and left.

Michele cut a piece of her moonfish and put it on her tongue. "Mmmmmm. Coconut." She smiled. "Great choice. Thanks." Her eyes held his for a moment, then he looked away and took in his own plate.

He cut a piece of his swordfish and sampled. "Yes, nicely done. Taste?"

Michele nodded and opened her mouth. He carefully placed a piece on her tongue and she savored it slowly before swallowing. "Oh my, what is that flavor? Cilantro and…?"

"A reduction of shitakes," he answered. "It's a specialty with the swordfish."

"Mmmm. I think I've died and gone to heaven."

"Not quite yet," David teased. "But you are definitely on the way. More wine?" She nodded and he filled her glass half way.

Michele giggled softly. "Don't get too cocky, Mr. Blackstone. You don't know what I have planned for after dinner."

He leaned back in his chair and sipped his wine slowly. "No, I don't. But I'm dying to find out."

The rest of the conversation was light and easy, mixed with tales of David's travels and some funny things that happened with clients.

She told him what she hoped to do, describing her music in a way she had shared with no one but family. She spoke of her excitement and apprehension at touring for four months, at letting go of her apartment, and how she was finally making headway in writing another original song.

Over dessert, under soft lights and the slight haze of good wine, she felt herself fall over the edge. It seemed so natural she barely even blinked at the realization. She forgot the vow she'd made that she would never, ever love anyone so much again that she'd be vulnerable to him. That she would never hook her heart to a man and give him the power to break it, and her.

~

DAVID OFFERED his hand to help Michele from his car. She faced the stairs to her apartment and swayed slightly. She looked at the stairs with a little hesitation.

"Hmmm…not sure if my foot will slip through those open treads."

David laughed as he easily swept her up in his arms and carried her, taking two treads at a time. "No need to walk," he said and then carefully deposited her at the front door. He fished her keys out of his pocket and opened the door, steadying her as she leaned against it and almost fell inside.

She giggled as she kicked off her shoes and led him past the kitchen to her living room. She pointed to a large bookcase and cabinet. "Bed," she said, then giggled again.

David quickly remembered that she said she had a Murphy bed. He ran his hand along the top, looking for a release. Finding it, he easily pulled it down from the wall, releasing the legs and making sure it was secure on the floor.

Michele jumped into the center of it. Lying on her back she crooked her finger at him. "All right, computer man. Show me your routines." She giggled at her joke as she gazed up at him.

David couldn't believe how gorgeous she looked against the bed. The bright yellow dress hugged her frame, the hem on one side most of the way up her thigh. He had never seen her so relaxed, or so inviting.

He groaned. "Michele. Are you drunk?"

She giggled. "Yup."

"I don't want to take advantage, if you're drunk."

"I'm not that drunk," she said. "I know what I'm doing, and I'm the one taking advantage."

She sat up in one fluid motion, reached behind her and unzipped her dress, letting it fall to her waist. Her breasts spilled out easily and he took in a breath of appreciation.

Then she leaned back again and lifted her hips as she slid the dress off her legs. He groaned again. She had on only a thong. She flicked the dress toward him and it landed on his head. He slowly removed it, taking in the scent of her perfume. By the time he looked at her again, the thong had been removed and she laid before him, her long hair fanned on the pillow, her lips pouting, and one leg raised slightly and crossed to cover her mound.

"If you don't come here soon," she said, "I'll think you don't like what you see."

David swallowed hard, unmoving. "Please. Just give me a minute to appreciate you—all of you. You are so much better than my fantasy."

She smiled broadly, then levered herself onto her elbows and opened her eyes wide with invitation. He took his time looking and she began to blush.

His gaze moved from her eyes to her chin, following the curve of her shoulder to the defined arms he had admired earlier. But now he could look beyond her collarbone and follow the pulse at the base of her throat down to the swell of her breasts. He licked his lips as he saw her body soften and respond to the intense awareness sizzling between them. Her nipples stood erect, and her diaphragm worked overtime as her lungs filled and expelled lifting her breasts up and down, up and down with each deep breath.

His eyes traveled down to her navel and he noticed the tiny waist, and how the curve continued out to her hips.

"Damn," he muttered. Then he shucked his clothes as quickly as possible and slid onto the bed next to her. His eyes met hers and he let her see all his passion there, and promises of more to come.

She grinned broadly, pushed him back against the bed and strad-dled him, her loose curls obscuring her breasts. She wiggled her hips against him, then leaned over and rubbed her breasts against his chest as she moved her mound up and down his length, working him to hardness. He stiffened quickly and she sat up with triumph in her eyes.

"If I remember correctly, you had pretty quick hands in Bend," she smiled. "Care to show me again?"

"I can be slow when the situation warrants. Just tell me what you want."

"I definitely don't want slow," she said, her hips continuing to work him up, as her eyes twinkled with mischief.

"We'll, you don't always get what you want." He took possession of her breasts, teasing her nipples—alternately caressing and pulling until he heard her moan for more. "But I'll make sure you get all you need."

She bent forward and brushed her breasts across his mouth, offering them. He quickly obliged, taking a nipple into his mouth while continue to work on the other. She keened with pleasure. Then he released the one and took the other in his mouth until her breathing quickened. He wanted to go slow. He wanted to meet her every need. He wanted her to beg for release.

Before she could recover from his mouth on her breasts he pushed her up and pulled her to his lips, to take her mouth in a carnal kiss. At the same time his hand worked down her waist and across her butt. He massaged and kneaded, his long arms working up and down her sides while his mouth continued to ravish her.

She moaned and moved to the side. "I want you inside me," she whispered. "All of you."

"Not yet. I haven't even begun to pleasure you."

"We'll see about that."

He gasped when she took his cock in her hand. Her fingers worked up and down his shaft with feather-light touches that made him shudder. The pressure of her fingernail drawn down the length of him made him catch his breath. The tight clutch of her fist around him, the firm stroke up, down, up, down, made him groan.

When she dipped her head and took him in her mouth, he thought he might go blind.

For the next ten minutes—or maybe ten hours, David wasn't sure

—Michele taught him the real meaning of slow. She teased him, tantalized him. Tortured him. Then she straddled him, poised to sheath his cock with her wetness.

"Michele, no," he rasped. "A condom. I need a condom."

"It's okay, I'm on the pill."

"No. It doesn't matter…I'm always safe."

"I believe you. That's why I'm trusting you. I want you to feel me, all of me."

She slid herself onto him, first a little then withdrew, then a little more, getting used to his size. He moaned with each withdrawal. Finally, she settled on him completely and started moving, up and down, clenching, massaging, enveloping.

"Oh, God," he whispered as he grabbed her hips and held her to him unmoving. "Slow down, I want you to enjoy first …" then he whimpered as she moved again, this time faster.

"I am enjoying," she panted.

She rode him with freedom and abandonment, and he didn't have the strength to fight it. As he built toward climax, he saw her hair flashing around her as a crown fit for a warrior queen who knew her own power—the power to make him respond as quickly or slowly as she desired. When she brought him to climax, she cried out in confident victory—not a scintilla of guilt or shame.

She collapsed on top of him, kissing his neck, his throat, his forehead, his eyes. Finally, he had enough breath to bring her to his lips. "Michele, oh God, Michele," he whispered between kisses. Then in one roll, he was on top of her, trapping her beneath him this time.

She laughed and stretched like a cat beneath him. Her fingers traced his shoulders and she purred.

"Nice muscles." Her finger continued down to his stomach. "Great abs." Her eyes traveled down between his legs. "I won."

She started to roll away, to get off the bed.

"No you don't." His hands grabbed both of hers and held them above her head. He pulled them together and trapped both wrists in one hand alone, his other moving to her cheek and down her throat.

His strong thighs still trapped her legs between them. "Now it's my turn."

His gaze met hers, burned into hers. She swallowed hard. Her breasts seemed to strain toward him, begging him to take them in his mouth again. Greedily his mouth opened wide to take in as much breast as he could. She arched her back, offering more. He backed off and captured her nipple, and sucked hard, then gentled his attentions, lapping her lazily with his tongue, massaging her other breast with his free hand. Then he repeated the process all over again until she whimpered aloud. He released her, only to devote his mouth to her other breast, offering the same, sweet torment.

Michele thrashed beneath him, keening sounds of need escaping from her throat. "Let me touch you," she cried out.

"Oh no. Not yet," he answered. "You had your way. Now I'll have mine."

David had made a promise to himself on the way over. He was going to show her the kind of pleasure she deserved. He was going to worship and treasure every curve and crevice, and then do it all over again. She'd surprised him a few minutes ago, but now he was in control and he was going to keep that promise.

She lifted her hips and rotated against him, he shifted and evaded and counter-moved. His hand moved down to the slight, tight flesh between her thighs. He used his palm to massage her mound, and when he thought she was ready he moved his finger toward the opening. Her thighs immediately snapped together to stop him. He retracted his finger and fanned his palm against her. He didn't move backward or forward. He released her wrists then and put his other hand behind her neck and raised her head, looking directly into her eyes.

"I want to love you with my fingers," he told her. "I want to pleasure you, Michele. I want to see you come and learn what you like. Can you trust me?"

He watched her eyes and saw them change from fear to agreement. Slowly she released the tightness in her thighs and her knees inched open. His hand still didn't move as he held her eyes. He wanted her to know, the decision was completely hers. He wanted to be the one to untangle the knots Jon had tied in her self-confidence. He wanted to show her the beauty and sensuality he saw in her. He wanted to return the exquisite splendor that she had shared so freely with him earlier.

"Yes," she finally said, and he realized she had allowed him into a place he would never want to leave.

He held her in the palm of his hand, pressing the heel against her mound and slowly kneading the tender spot on her backside. "You are so beautiful. I want to watch you take pleasure from me."

"David," she said on a sigh.

He lowered slowly to her mouth, first languidly brushing her lips with his tongue as he continued to massage her with his whole palm. Then his kisses grew more impassioned. When she finally began returning them with abandon again, her fingers tangled in his hair and her hips pressed into his palm. He slowly allowed first one then two fingers to enter her wetness. She groaned against his lips.

He stroked her, worked her. He made love to her with his hand, his mouth. As his tongue probed her lips and her throat, his fingers searched deep within her, driving her wild and he hardened again. He watched as her need became a clawing, raging beast within her and finally she cried out as the orgasm overtook her.

He waited a moment and then began kissing her again, his mouth moving down her throat, again to her breasts, his fingers working her again. She moaned and arched toward him, calling his name.

"David, please…please."

He thrust inside her, burying himself to the hilt. Holding still, forcing himself to wait for her body to tighten around him, he indulged in a deep, urgent, infinitely carnal kiss.

Michele's hands clutched his shoulders as he nipped the side of her neck and moved within her and against her. After a few more strokes, he found a rhythm that pleased them both. He changed the angle to give her the most pleasure. Soon his breath panted, his muscles quivered as he strained to make it last. He wanted her to come one more time before he released. He slowed and moved her legs to his shoulders. Stroking deeper her nails dug into him and her eyes went dark with bliss. He picked up the pace.

"I don't know if I can take any more," she panted as he felt her go up again.

"Just one more time, Michele. I want to see you in exquisite pleasure one more time." Sensing he couldn't hang on much longer, he slipped a hand between them and thumbed her nerve center.

Her inner muscles gripped him harder, and she gasped. He thumbed her again and increased his pace faster...faster...until Michele pressed upward, grinding herself against him, and let out a long, throaty groan. When the rhythmic waves of her climax stroked his erection, he finally gave himself to the animal within. He pumped into her once, twice, three more times, then called out her name in reverence as he erupted in a hot explosion of pleasure.

"God," she breathed as he collapsed atop her. "Kill me now because it will never be this good again."

Heart racing, fighting to catch his breath, David somehow found the strength to lift his head and tease, "Is that a dare? Again?"

She laughed and rotated slowly beneath him.

He groaned as the sensitiveness after orgasm reminded him of all that had gone before. He rolled to his side, his arm still wrapped around her, holding her close so he wouldn't slip out. She nuzzled her head against his chest.

He closed his eyes and drifted in the pleasure of the moment—a warm, satisfied, naked woman in his arms, the sated heaviness of his limbs, the musky scent of sex in the air, and he realized how hard it would be to one day let her go.

CHAPTER 7

"That was the best rehearsal we've had yet." Theresa said as she stirred the homemade lemonade. "We worked out a lot of little details." Then she washed fresh raspberries and added them to the pitcher.

Michele sat at the counter, Earl the cat in her lap, and Sarah and Rachel on either side of her. It was going to be a long evening. They still had all the band business to finish before anyone could head back home. She stroked Earl's fur until he purred. Hearing that little motor going helped Michele relax.

The icemaker churned as it spit out cubes into each glass Kat shoved under the spout. Belle cat waited, ready to pounce on any stray cubes.

"I really screwed up on that last round," Kat said. "I completely lost my place." She handed the glasses to her mother who filled each one and passed them out.

"Did you?" Michele asked. "I didn't notice."

"You weren't noticing much," Rachel muttered, loudly enough for everyone to hear her clearly.

Sarah held the cold glass to her forehead and sighed. "I know this tastes great, Theresa, but right now I just need to cool my skin." She leaned back in her chair, her legs extended straight out.

"You lean any farther and you'll be drenched in it," Rachel commented sourly.

"Come on, Rache, please don't bitch today," Kat said then ducked her head when Theresa gave her a stern look.

"I'm not bitching, I'm just noticing." She pushed back from the counter and paced, scaring Earl from Michele's lap.

"So, Michele, I want to hear what happened with you. Wasn't last night your big date with Mr. I-can't-keep-my-hands-off-him-even-though-I-just-met-him guy?" Sarah turned her full attention to Michele, a smirk playing across her lips.

Michele lifted an eyebrow and smiled. "Me?"

"Oh yeah, I almost forgot. Spill it," Kat commanded, leaning forward as if a state secret were about to be told. "You know you want to."

"Well…the date was great."

"Uh huh…" Sarah invited more.

"It was exciting."

"Better…" Theresa leaned across the island, refilling Michele's glass with a broad, knowing smile.

"He was amazingly romantic." Michele's gaze flicked over to Kat, wondering how much she should say.

"Don't worry about me," Kat caught her look. "Believe me, I've heard it all with this bunch. Once, this guy named Chet came to a rehearsal with Rachel, and he said that she was the best piece of—"

"We don't need that story," Rachel speared her with an angry look.

"Oh, yeah, right." Kat returned her attention to Michele. "Go on."

"Well, I was scared. And excited. And confused."

"Shit, I knew it. Hot, excited, and sweaty, right? Ah hell." Rachel kicked her foot against the wall as she backed toward it.

Michele furrowed her brow and looked up at Rachel.

"Go on," Kat invited. "Was the sex great?"

"Kat!" Theresa raised her voice. "Don't be cheeky." Then she smiled as she turned back to Michele. "Well?"

"And yes…it was great. And that's all I'm going to say." Michele blushed again. She couldn't believe she just admitted to all of them that she slept with the guy on her second date.

"So, our goody-two-shoes has finally had a one-night stand," Rachel said. "You've joined the ranks of the wicked."

"It's not like that," Michele defended. "David wants a relationship too. I can't explain it. I know it sounds ridiculous, but somehow we just knew. We just knew we were right for each other and we wanted it to be longer, to be a commitment, to be exclusive."

"Oh sure, that's what they all say, at least for the first week or two. Then they get tired of you and off they trot to the next one. Believe me, I've been through it several times."

"Rachel, just because you keep choosing the wrong guy, doesn't mean Michele will too." Sarah said.

Theresa patted Michele's hand across the island, offering her reassurance. "I'm sure he's everything you've said, Michele."

"Me too," Sarah said quietly. "I'm really happy for you. Not every man is a jerk, as Rachel would have you believe. I know. I have three wonderful brothers. I admit they're definitely demanding, and their good looks get them plenty of offers, but not one of them would enter into a one-night stand—or a one-week stand for that matter. Not one would be intimate with a woman without a complete understanding of what the relationship was about. You have an understanding don't you, Michele?"

Michele paused before answering. Come to think of it, she wasn't sure what their understanding really was. The beginning of the evening seemed one way, but the end was another. Well, she wouldn't worry about that right now.

"Well, yes. At least I think so." Out of the corner of her eye she saw Rachel roll her eyes, but Sarah stayed steady looking at her. "Yes. I know so," she added with growing confidence. "We talked about it. In fact, I wasn't going to let him…uh…do anything." She flicked her eyes toward Kat again. "I was thinking clearly when I made my decision. In fact, I initiated it. And I don't regret it."

"Good for you!" Theresa said, patting her on the back. Then she turned away and started clearing the glasses. "Let's head down stairs to the office and get the routing settled and do the planning for at least the first ten or eleven gigs on the tour."

The group reassembled around a large rectangular table in Theresa's office. Above the table hung a four by six foot map of the United States. For each confirmed booking, Kat had put a red pushpin at the town location and the date. Yellow pins represented bookings that were still being negotiated. So far the combined pins included Oregon, Idaho, Montana and Wyoming on the way out. That took care of June through mid-August. Then difficult choices needed to be made between the mountain states of Utah and Colorado in late August or heading up to Canada for potential bookings in British Columbia and Manitoba. The group split on which ones to pursue.

The fall dates in September and October were skewed toward the Midwest in Kansas, Missouri, Indiana and finishing up with a slight dip to the south to hit Tennessee. The contracted agent in the Midwest had primarily booked those. At the end of October they had a choice to make between the Desert Bluegrass Festival in Tucson, Arizona or returning to Dornan's in Wyoming, the first bluegrass festival the band had played two years ago.

"You've done a good job with the schedule," Michele commented as she checked the route with Sarah. "The only big hole we have on the leg out is that dead eight days between the Montana gig and the three confirmed in Wyoming."

"Yeah, going out is pretty good. I'm concerned about the coming back," Rachel said. "We only have half the dates booked in September and October. I don't want to get caught in some small town in Tennessee for two weeks with no possible gigs. This is the only income I've got."

"We're all in the same boat," Sarah said quietly. "Theresa's doing the best she can, given the circumstances. This is the first time we've tried a big tour."

"I'm not questioning Theresa's planning skills, I'm just worried about the money. We need a professional booking agent. We don't know where we're going next half the time."

"You know we aren't big enough to get a decent agent yet. We're not doing that many shows—we need to do at least 150 a year before anyone will look at us."

"Yeah, well that's another problem. All because of Kat here who can't miss too much school."

"She already misses the fall term," Theresa said. "I can't afford a tutor for more than that."

"Well, the truth is we don't need an accordion in the band," Rachel looked away from Kat. "No other Americana band has one."

"Fine! Just go without me! I don't want to be in your stupid band anyway. I'd rather be home with my friends." Kat ran to the sliding door, slamming it open and closed as she barreled through it.

"What is with you lately, Rachel?" Theresa asked. "First you were picking on everything someone played in rehearsal, then you were trying to make Michele feel bad about her date, and now you're taking your frustrations out on Kat."

"Well it's true, we don't need an accordion and her age means we can't even do bar gigs to fill in, unless we leave her in the motor home. Did you ever think maybe she'd be better off not going with us?"

"You know I can't go without her. She's always been part of the deal. Or are you suggesting I shouldn't be in the band either?."

Rachel didn't say anything and didn't apologize.

"I see. Well, maybe you better just find yourself another band then. I think you're the one out of line here." Theresa turned her back and made her way through the slider to comfort Kat.

Michele could hear Theresa knocking on Kat's door, her voice coaxing Kat to open the door and let her in. Then she heard a tear-filled voice invite Theresa inside. Michele softly closed the sliding door separating the room from the rest of the house. She had something to say to Rachel and she didn't want to have Theresa or Kat add that to their problems.

"You're just full of problems today, aren't you?" Michele fisted her hands at her sides, wanting to land a punch.

"And who asked you," Rachel stared her down. "You've barely been with us a few weeks and you think you know what's going on? You think you have a right to a say here?"

Michele stood tall and stepped toward Rachel, her temper flaring. She pinned Rachel with a glare. "Look, I don't know what crawled up your ass all of a sudden, but no one should have to take this shit from you. I may not have been here as long as you, but I've been working my ass off to make this tour work and I haven't complained a bit. We've all been putting in some long hours and you just need to back off before someone gets really mad. Or hurt."

Rachel's lifted her chin. "Back off."

Michele didn't move.

Rachel raised a hand and pushed Michele back a step. "Back off, Michele."

"Don't try to push me around, Rachel, I won't take it anymore."

"Anymore? When did you suddenly grow a spine?"

"Just because I don't pick on people like you do doesn't mean I don't stand up for myself."

"Not that I could tell. Your talent's always been good but you've sure let people roll over you a lot here."

"I don't remember anyone taking advantage of me in this group."

"Oh yeah? Whose ass has been putting in long hours to take publicity shots? Whose ass has been finagling friends at PSU to let you use the darkroom? Who's been using her own personal savings to create bookmarks with our name on it to hand out at gigs? Who's recorded and cut sample songs for our website with MP3 downloads? We've taken plenty of advantage of your cute little ass."

Michele wasn't ready to relax yet. She wasn't sure if Rachel was actually giving her a compliment or just reserving her strength for another hit.

"Screw it." Rachel shrugged and turned away. She slouched into an easy chair, crossing one leg beneath her.

Michele stood in place, her mouth slightly open. She couldn't believe how Rachel's mood suddenly changed.

"Hmmm. There sure were a lot of asses in that speech," Sarah said.

"And, Michele, I've never heard you use a swear word before, outside of damn."

Michele relaxed a little. "Well, I was a bit miffed."

"Really?" Sarah drew out the word.

Michele returned to her seat at the table. "I apologize." She looked at Rachel. "To both of you. I don't like to swear." She began rearranging the play list on a sheet of paper. Another job she'd taken on was to make the initial list and then work toward consensus with everyone else. "My parents always said that people who swear show their ignorance, because they don't know enough words to express themselves. I only do it when I'm really mad."

"Speaking of your cute little ass," Rachel chimed in, resting her chin in her hand nonchalantly. "That was really what set me off today."

"What? You don't like it?"

"No. The fact that you got some last night."

"But you didn't know that until after the rehearsal."

"Wrong, Sherlock. When you showed up this afternoon, you were just too damned pleased with yourself. I could tell by the way you walked, by the way you sang those love songs we do, that you were on cloud nine."

"What does my love life have to do with your moods?"

Rachel slouched into a chair at the table. "Just envious that's all."

"Not again?" Sarah asked.

"Same old story. It was nice, you're beautiful babe. Blah, blah, blah. Gotta run."

"Ouch." Sarah agreed.

"Yeah. Well, at this rate, I might as well just start charging and make some money. That's about as long as my relationships last."

"Oh Rachel. It's not that bad, is it?" Michele asked.

"Almost. Since Kavan left me two years ago, there have been twenty-two first dates with no follow-ups. And I didn't even sleep with those guys. Then there were the twelve that lasted a week—each with a bedroom preview of course. So far, only three that have lasted a month."

"Not that you're counting or anything," Michele said.

"Yeah, a bit anal of me, do you think? Maybe you could put it on one of your lists or something and keep track for me."

"Sarah's the one who is good with spreadsheets, not me," Michele said.

"Wrong, I'm the one who's good at spreading sheets," Rachel said.

Sarah and Michele laughed uneasily.

"It's not that I'm interested in anything really long term. Kavan made sure to ruin any illusions I had about marriage. But I thought maybe Bill and I really had something going. You know, maybe I could even expect to come back to him after the tour. Instead last night, while you were getting all cozy and feeling secure, Bill was doing the let's-just-be-friends-I-want-to date-other-people routine. Or, as I've come to know it, the wham-bam-thank-you-ma'am-and-don't-let-the-door-hit-your-butt-on-the-way-out routine."

"I'm really sorry, Rachel." Michele gave her a quick hug. "Really. I didn't know things were like that for you. You've never talked about it to me before."

Michele thought back to last night and everything that happened with David. Everything seemed right, and she did believe him and trust that he wanted some type of relationship—though he was clear on the no marriage part. Was it that way with Rachel's dates too in the beginning? Maybe Michele was foolish to believe everything David said. After all, men will say almost anything when they want sex, right?

"You know, Rachel," Sarah spoke quietly. "I've watched you over the past two years, since your divorce, and I've often wondered why you jump in the sack so easily. Not that I'm judging you. It's just that... well... it seems to me...emotions get tied up with sex. Then it hurts so much more when the guy leaves."

"Really? Ya think?" Rachel asked, sarcastic. "I'm not always looking for commitment ya know. It's just sex, Sarah. It's not as if I'm jumping in the sack with any guy who tilts his head at me."

"I wasn't suggesting that."

"Yeah? Well, who are you to talk? When's the last time you had any?"

Sarah was silent.

"Thought so. I bet you can't even remember it's been so long ago. Or are you still a virgin?"

"I can remember," Sarah said angrily. "It was on my twenty-first birthday and it was very special and with a guy I had been seeing for six months."

"Uh huh, and now you're what? 28?"

"Twenty-nine, but...."

"No, buts. We just don't have the same needs. You don't mind practically reclaiming your virginity. Jeez. Seven years. I think I'd die first if I had to go that long."

Michele smiled. Before David, she had visions of herself being more like Sarah—waiting for Mr. Perfect. Entering the dating pool, but never going too deep. But now—now that she had experienced how her body really could respond—she had a little more understanding of Rachel. Though she still couldn't imagine having so many relationships over a two-year period. As it was, David was only her second.

Rachel opened the sliding door and looked down the hall. "Crap. I really blew it this time didn't I?" She took a deep breath. "I guess I should go apologize to Kat."

"You better leave that to Theresa," Sarah offered. "When Kat's ready to come out she will. Then you can apologize."

"Yeah, you're right. It's not like this is the first time I've stepped into it with her."

"Do you really think the band shouldn't have an accordion?" Michele asked.

"Sometimes. But then I also realize it's something that makes us unique. And she mostly plays chords which do help to fill in the sound." Rachel paused. "I guess I'm just really nervous about the tour, and I'm grasping at straws. Not that I want to play bars at $200 a gig, but it's better than nothing."

"I don't want to be playing bars at all," Sarah added. "Those kind of gigs require us to play a lot of cover songs, some we don't even like; and the requests can really be difficult when they insist on us trying to play something we don't even know. And the drunks are horrible. There are a lot more drunks in bars than at festivals. Also, we haven't really been rehearsing those covers we used to do years ago. Can you even remember half the requests we used to get?"

"Nah. I just want to be prepared. Nothing else seems to be going right in my life. I just can't have this go bad too. Having a teenager does kind of cramp our style. And, to be honest, I can't imagine spending the next four months in that motor home with her talking all the time."

"Now there's a point." Michele squeezed her lips with her thumb and forefinger indicating silence, as she heard Kat's door open. The three of them scrambled back to the table as if they hadn't left the map and tour discussion.

Theresa came in first and Kat followed. Kat went directly to the computer in the corner, not saying anything. She also made a point not to look at anyone else. She sat down and began typing in the gig schedule.

Rachel sighed as she stood and walked over to Kat. She placed a hand on her shoulder. "I'm sorry, Kat. I was being a real jerk."

"Yeah, you were. Big time."

"It's not your fault. Things just kind of fell apart with Bill and I'm nervous about the tour, and you were the closest thing for me to hurt."

"Do you really want me out of the band?"

"Nah. If you left who would I have to pick on?"

Kat looked over at Michele and grinned. "Well, how about Michele, she's the newest one."

"Hey, thanks a lot. It's not like Rachel doesn't already rag on me."

"Good idea, Kat. Maybe we can work on that together." Rachel winked at Michele then turned back to Kat. "Forgiven?"

Kat paused. "Not yet. What you said really hurt. You can't always go around picking on people just because your life is crap."

"You're right, I don't know why I do that."

"You do it because you want everyone to feel as miserable as you do. But, you have to stop. And I'm going to think of something you have to do during the tour to pay me back, something really hard. Something that will make you want to be nice to me everyday."

"Oh nooooooooo—not spend more time with you," Rachel teased. "You're killing me here."

Kat grinned and her eyes twinkled as she thought of the appropriate punishment. "I've got it." She paused for effect. "You can teach me to fiddle. Then, next time you make a comment about my accordion, I'll say you can leave the band because I can take your place with the fiddle."

Rachel laughed long and hard. Then she shook Kat's hand. "You've got a deal, kiddo."

CHAPTER 8

Michele bent her head upside down and brushed out her long hair. It was still a little damp from her shower, but it should be dry in time for her date with David. She peered in the mirror and took stock.

No bruises, in spite of the table practically falling on her when she tried to load it into the truck. The move with the U-Haul had gone well. She'd bought pizza for her friends and they all left with plenty of hugs and well wishes for her new adventure.

Her eyes were bright in anticipation of this evening and her cheeks a healthy pink after the heat of the shower. She was fortunate her skin was smooth, as she'd never liked to wear makeup. It was just too much trouble and she always felt as if she were clogging her pores. She was so nervous tonight that she figured she needed every part of her to breathe as much as possible.

She imagined her heart beating like a cartoon character with it popping out of her chest. She checked the mirror again and chuckled at herself. No bulges or beats visible.

She walked back toward her bed and looked around her empty apartment. It was harder than she thought to leave. Six years and a lot of memories. Now the unknown loomed before her. "Well, it's time to make new memories," she said aloud.

She glanced at the clock above the kitchen counter. 6:30. She still had half an hour to get ready. And, if she played it right, she would have some lasting memories tonight in this very bed to take with her.

Her clothes for tonight were laid out on the bed. Everything else was packed in two suitcases she'd take on tour. The outfit she'd chosen for her date tonight wasn't fancy, but it was silk and she liked the way it felt against her skin. She'd found it at a local thrift store last week for only $10 and it just felt so decadent, she had to have it.

She stepped into the ankle-length silk skirt and zipped up the back. She had chosen it for the print, an intricate mosaic pattern in varying shades of blue and aqua. She skimmed her hands down each side of her hips. The movement of the pattern reminded her of the ocean and walking along the water in a cool spring breeze. She liked the way the length made her look taller.

She slipped the solid aqua top over her head. It had thin double straps that added a little sophistication to the simple top. The scoop neckline was lower than she usually felt comfortable wearing—especially without a bra—but the silky feel against her bare skin was sensual and she knew David would love it. She added a pair of strappy sandals, then quickly ran a brush through her hair one more time.

Just as she finished brushing she heard the knock on her door.

She looked through the peephole and saw David leaning lazily against the opposite wall. He wore tight black jeans and a short sleeved button-down shirt that emphasized his broad shoulders. A roguish grin curved his lips. She opened the door slowly and beckoned him in. Her eyes twinkled with invitation.

He moved into the apartment with two quick steps and quietly closed the door behind him. He stood for a long moment and looked her up and down thoroughly. "You look amazing, Michele."

The hunger in his eyes tied her in knots. She swallowed and licked her lips in anticipation.

David groaned and caught her to him then turned and backed her against the wall, taking her mouth in a hard demanding kiss. She wrapped her arms around his neck and pulled him closer, giving him back as much as he could take. As he ravished her mouth one hand moved over her breasts. Her nipples jumped to attention as he made them pucker through the clingy silk.

She reached toward his shirt, her fingers moving fast to unbutton it, to feel her skin against his. But he backed away, grabbing both her wrists in one hand. She let out a little yelp of surprise as he lifted them above her head trapping her hands against the wall.

Then his mouth followed the same path as his hand had before. First he kissed the pulse in her neck, then sliding his lips along the top of her shirt, his other hand dived underneath to push first one breast then the other up toward his mouth. He kissed along the tops of them, all the while continuing to tease her nipples with his limber fingers.

"Oh David, please!" she begged, as warmth poured down her belly and into her legs. She didn't think she could stand it much longer.

He obliged her by placing his hand beneath her legs and carrying her to her bed, where he lowered her beneath him. Finally, pushing the silk blouse up to her neck he grabbed both breasts and placed his face between them, laving the insides with kisses. Then he cradled one breast in both hands massaging and suckling, nipping and pulling as if he was starving for her. Michele arched toward his mouth and pulled his head full into her breast, her fingers tangling in his hair. When he had his fill of one he switched his attention to the other. Michele groaned in pleasure, lifting her hips toward him, signaling her willingness to be taken.

After another minute of suckling, David returned to her mouth, finishing with a wet, probing kiss. "Oh, how I've missed you." Then he rolled to his back, carrying her with him to rest on top. He wrapped his arms tight around her, holding her head to his chest and breathing hard.

"Me too. Me too." Michele could now feel the hardness of him. Her own need throbbing within her, she rubbed against him in a blatant invitation to finish what he started.

He groaned but pushed her to one side. Lying side by side he looked directly into her eyes and she saw the need flaring there. "I could easily take you now. God knows I want to. But I want tonight to be special. We have to wait."

With a low growl of barely contained lust, he pushed himself off the bed and offered his hand to help her up.

She looked up wide-eyed, questioning, taking his hand in silence as she stood and rearranged her blouse back to its original shape. Was this the beginning of the end? Every other night he'd come over, they weren't able to stop in their rush to her bed. He said he wanted it to be special, but what could be more special than what they were just engaged in?

David glanced around the apartment. "It's a little bare in here. How are you feeling about leaving it?"

"I…I'm a bit sad and excited at the same time."

He pulled her to him again, letting her bury her head in his chest. "You are one of the bravest people I know. You are taking a chance most people would never take, a chance to live your dream."

Michele couldn't speak. He really did understand and that meant more to her than anything he could have said. She wrapped her arms around him tighter. How could she ever leave him? How could she ever say good-bye?

"I thought we'd go for a ride and dinner."

"Alright," she said, adding a tremulous smile to her agreement as she looked up at him. "Where are we going?"

"Some place with a lot of room and a lot of privacy."

Her eyes widened with unspoken questions.

"Do you trust me?" He put his hand beneath her chin and looked directly into her eyes.

She nodded, and his mouth dipped to hers to brush her lips in a sweet, slow kiss.

"Good. No questions until we get there, then you can ask whatever you want."

He released her and grabbed both her suitcases. "Let's get going. You can drop your keys at the office. I'll get these and you get your bass. I want to spend every last moment with you before you leave. I want to drive you to Theresa's and hold you until the last minute when the motor home drives off. I don't want to waste any time coming back here."

"But—I .."

"I have special plans. No questions. Please, Michele."

Puzzled, she hefted the bass over her shoulder, took her house keys off the counter and held them out to him. She took one final look around and then closed her eyes in surrender. "Take me where you will."

"Oh, I will, babe. I will." He took the keys from her, and brushed her lips once more with his. "I'm hoping you'll love it." He guided her through the door, locking it securely behind him.

Michele had learned to expect the unexpected when it came to David, which was part of what made him so breathtakingly appealing. But this time she was a little scared. She'd been building her anticipation of his return over the last two days and she'd had the weekend all worked out in her mind. It included sex when they saw each other. Well, she'd almost managed that. Then she'd planned to order take-out and have a picnic in the bare apartment, followed by more sex. A kind of saying goodbye to him in her apartment, even though all the furnishings were gone.

She'd relished the idea that their last weekend together would be the same as the other days they'd had. Comfortable, sensual, and full of memories in her apartment—memories for her to treasure over the next four months as she slowly let go of him. She wanted one last picture of him here, not in a hotel as he probably had planned.

Resigned, she dropped the keys at the office and met him at the car. Once settled into the passenger seat, she closed her eyes and leaned back, determined not to think too much and just go with the flow. At least they were together. That was what was most important.

Michele looked up when she heard the car slowing. She recognized some of the buildings in the Pearl district; then he made a sharp turn into a private garage. A brick façade faced the street with seven stories above, each one having four medium windows looking over the river.

"Where are we?" she asked as he lifted the door and took her hand to help her out of the car.

"Which suitcase is the one you'll need to get ready for tomorrow?"

She pointed at the smaller of the two, and he retrieved it from the car.

"Where are we?" she asked again.

Instead of answering, he entered a code at the keypad by the elevator and then kissed her passionately until it arrived. When the doors opened he backed her into it, all the way to the back wall, his attention to her mouth relentless. When he released her lips she could see the hunger in his eyes. At least part of her plan for the evening was still sure to take place.

A moment later the elevator opened at the top floor onto a small dark hallway, with a slender table against the wall and a single lamp on top of it. A black, painted concrete wall stood in front of her and blocked off anything to the left. To the right down the hall was a glass door that allowed some daylight into the hall.

David held her hand, stopping her from exploring further. He took a key from his pocket and turned it in a cylindrical shaped hole near the elevator. She heard a click and a red light engage above it. She assumed it was some type of locking mechanism, but she wasn't sure, as she'd never seen anything like it before. David emptied his pockets into a basket on the table and set her suitcase down next to it.

"Close your eyes," he said.

"But..."

He stopped her with another passionate kiss. "Please. Close your eyes."

On a sigh, she lowered her lashes. He put one hand at her back to guide her and then the other on her arm to steady her and moved her toward the glass door. She could hear it click open and then close again after they stepped through. Then she felt him let go and step away.

"Welcome to my home," he said quietly.

Michele opened her eyes and sucked in a deep breath as she took in the view. The room was filled with light. The all glass wall in front of her and to her left framed a 180-degree view encompassing down-town Portland, Mt. Hood, and the Columbia Gorge. And because it was a clear blue sky, she could even see Mt. St. Helens and Mt. Jefferson.

Tearing her eyes from the view, Michele finally noticed the room itself. The two-story loft had no walls separating the rooms, yet each area was clearly defined with carpets and furnishings. The generously sized furniture still looked small within this room of high ceilings. The two walls without windows were painted a sky blue to reflect the outdoors.

In the living room, two large love seats, in a deep hunter green, were placed perpendicular to each other and set on angle to take in the best of the view to the east. A carpet, patterned with autumn leaves on a rich, golden brown background, defined the space, suggesting a feeling of woodlands in counterpoint to the plush comfort of deep throw cushions dotting the other side of a wide square table.

An open kitchen commanded the center of the room, defined by two crescents of cabinets. One side opened to the living room and the other side to a space divided by a large piece of oak.

Turnings and decorative woodwork made the deep, cherry cabinets appear to be antique. White granite countertops finished the surface, striking a perfect balance between warm and cool. Michele could barely make out the appliances, as most of them were faced in the same wood as the cabinets. Suspended from the ceiling, on long thin wires, small spotlights provided task lighting to various parts of the counter. She ran her hand along the curve of the sensuous wood, her heart tapping a single jig rhythm so fast she could barely catch her breath.

David watched as she took in the details. She was as awestruck by the view as he had been when he bought the place. Though he'd lived here for four years now, he never tired of it. As much as he appreci-ated the views on a clear day like today, he also loved seeing the storms come up the Columbia and gather over the mountains, some-times blotting them out completely. He treasured waking to the sunrise and watching the city lights wink out, followed by a pink glow slowly rolling across the buildings like a carpet being taken up to start the day. And tonight he was looking forward to sharing a sunset over his bed, with Michele lying in his arms as the reds and pinks caressed her body bringing shadows into the room.

She looked right standing in his home. He swallowed hard, knowing that after tonight it would be four more months before he'd see her standing here again. That strengthened his resolve to make sure she wanted to be here far into the future.

He walked up behind her and wrapped his arms around her shoulders, pulling her close as she looked back out to the view. Michele shuddered as she leaned into him and he rained kisses along her neck. Having her in his home felt so right, so good.

She tilted her head back and looked up at him. He could read the questions in her eyes.

"I've never brought any woman to my home, Michele. It's a rule I have to keep my heart safe. But you've already captured my heart and I wanted to see you here. Feel you here. Make love to you here."

He turned her toward him and lowered his lips to hers, barely grazing them. Then he drew her closer and gave her the sweetest softest kiss he could muster. He wanted to let loose his raging hormones, but tonight was as much for her as for him. He wanted her to know how much he treasured her. He wanted her to agree to spend the rest of her life with him.

Michele gasped as he teased her bottom lip and then her top one. When she opened her mouth to receive him, he continued his slow exploration. His tongue caressed every part of her mouth in a slow and inviting ballad with a story so filled with promise and longing that when he withdrew she thought she would cry. She'd never known for sure his feelings. She'd never allowed herself to believe there'd be anything left to come back to. But now…

"I'd planned an entire salmon dinner, along with champagne to toast your upcoming tour with Sweetwater Canyon, and even dessert." David gestured toward the kitchen. "But I have to admit I'm thinking of skipping all of it right now, and taking you to bed instead."

Michele gulped, but said nothing. She'd be fine with skipping dinner.

"But we need sustenance for the night and the day and the night and..." he took her in his arms again, this time the kiss was passionate and fast. He so thoroughly ravished her lips that she could barely breathe when he finally withdrew.

He turned toward the kitchen refrigerator. "I don't want you to leave without knowing what a great cook I am."

Michele still held his hand in hers, not wanting to let go. "Then, let me help."

She tore the red leaf lettuce into a salad bowl, reveling in the texture of the leaves. She used a special knife and peeler to shape the carrots into slivered rosettes.

"Tomatoes?" she asked as she held up a small cherry one between her thumb and forefinger.

"Definitely." He turned and opened his mouth. She placed one on his tongue and smiled when he held her finger in his mouth, refusing to let go.

He pointed her toward the pantry to select other condiments. She chose sunflower seeds to finish the light salad.

He ground herbs together before mixing them in melted butter, then basted the salmon and set it on the open grill on his stove. Her mouth watered as the scent of the salmon wafted her direction.

He poured a glass of wine for each of them as they worked together in a sensual dance of smells and touch. There was no need for words as the motions of preparing a good meal took over.

When he reached around her for a spice, his lips grazed her neck. As she reached for the whisk to add the spices to the rice, she paused to trace the strength of his jaw and lift her lips briefly to his. Throughout the preparation, they were unable to stop their constant touching, looking, memorizing of each other.

It felt right. It felt natural to be here in his kitchen. The dinner had been amazing. Every nerve ending ached for him so much it hurt. But she had to know first if this was a memory for the scrapbook in her mind or if it was the start of something more.

"Champagne?" David asked.

"Maybe just a little," she said.

David drew out two champagne flutes. He put the bottle on the counter and Michele giggled nervously when she heard the cork pop. He poured first her glass, then his. As he handed her a glass he drew her closer and raised his glass for a toast.

"To the most beautiful woman ever to enter my life. May your career be long and prosperous. May all your songs be filled with joy, and may you fall into my arms with a happy heart."

"Thank you." She lowered her eyes and blushed, as he clicked his glass against hers. *Oh, God, please give me strength to accept whatever he's offering.*

She sipped slowly, then set her glass on the counter and looked up at him. She took a deep breath and gathered her courage. "David, I have to ask you something."

"Not yet, Michele. Please." He handed her glass back to her. "Please, no thinking tonight. Just feel. Just indulge me a little longer."

Silently, he took her hand and led her past the kitchen to the one area she hadn't yet explored.

A massive, solid oak divider faced the kitchen. As they walked around to the other side she entered his bedroom. He took her glass from her and laid both of them on a side table next to the bed.

The large, king sized bed centered on the oak divide as a headboard. A small lip at the top housed a track light that shined down to the pillows. The large painting above the bed, in the style of the old masters, depicted two nude lovers in a passionate embrace beneath the shade of a tree. In the distance a village perched on the side of a hill, and in the foreground soft grass provided the bed where the lovers lay together. How she wished her life could be as simple and free as that picture.

David turned her away from the bed. "I have something for you."

A white sheet draped something large in the corner of the room, like a sculpture awaiting the grand opening in a museum. Her eyes opened wide. "A present?"

"Uh huh." He put his hands lightly on her shoulders and urged her forward. "I wanted to buy you something special—something I knew you would enjoy for years to come."

Her fingers hovered at a fold in the drape. It looked huge and she couldn't imagine what it might be. She looked back at David, her eyes asking if she could remove the drape. He smiled and nodded.

"Oh…" Michele dropped the drape at her feet as she took in the full size carousel horse. "It's beautiful." She wiped away a stray tear as she realized how much he understood her, how much he remembered. She ran her fingers along the dark, wavy chocolate mane.

"It reminded me of your hair," he whispered as he stepped to her side, holding her close to him. Her hands trembled as she followed the curve of the neck and the back. As she traced the shape of the saddle, she realized that the color was the same as the aqua in the silk shirt she now wore.

Her hands continued down to the sculpted tail giving a sense of freedom as the horse ran through the wind.

"I don't know what to say," Michele whispered. "It's so perfect. It's so…" She turned and her arms went immediately around his neck. She kissed him slowly and softly, then moved deeper. She felt the love pouring from him and for the first time she realized he loved her too.

"I know you've just put everything in storage, but I hoped you would let me keep it here while you're gone." He held her in his arms, stroking her hair. "I know that every time I look at it I'll think of you."

Michele blinked back tears, then giving up she buried her face in his chest and sobbed quietly. "Oh, David…I just didn't know. I wondered if …" She couldn't continue. After all the tension of packing, putting things in storage, wondering how she would let him go, she couldn't believe her dreams were coming true.

She heard his intake of breath and he squeezed her even tighter against him. "I thought you knew. I love you, Michele. I love you."

She sobbed even more as it overwhelmed her.

"I didn't want to fall in love, but I did from the first moment I met you. I love the way your chin juts out when you're angry. I love the way your eyes twinkle when you discover something new or rediscover something you've forgotten. I love the way you accept me so easily without question. I love the way you put your trust in me from the beginning, sharing your deepest secrets and allowed me to fill your needs. While I was traveling I realized I didn't want to say goodbye. I don't want to let you go on tour without knowing. Michele, I want you in my life everyday…forever."

She looked up again, the tears glistening on her cheeks. Unable to speak now that he had finally said the words she longed to hear, she took his hand and walked back to his bed.

CHAPTER 9

*D*avid followed willingly. How could he have been so stupid to not guess she didn't know how strong his feelings were? He thought his heart had been on his sleeve for her to throw away at will. He marveled that she had been so giving all this time while wondering if he was going to walk out the door, or if he would be here when she returned.

As the sun set behind him it cast a pale pink glow against the golden silk sheets and coverlet on the bed.

Michele unzipped her skirt in the back and stepped out of it, revealing what David had already surmised earlier in the evening. No underwear. Then she slowly lifted her top over her head and also let that drop to the floor. Without a hint of shyness she laid back against the bed, her long hair draping across her breasts and down her sides. Her eyes bored holes into his as they clearly invited him to join her.

David sucked in a deep breath and stared in appreciation. The bright orange and red sunset slashed a passionate pattern across the floor and windows, making his fantasy for this evening complete. He quickly shucked his clothes and moved to lie beside her, tracing her curves.

He let his fingers take their own sweet time as he feasted on her response. He began along her jaw then brushed across her lips as her mouth opened to his touch. He expanded his tracing to his full palm as he moved down her throat and across each breast, mapping each delicate nipple as it swelled and arched toward him. His hand continued down her stomach and she raised her hips in invitation as he neared her center. But he ignored her thrusting invitation, instead tracing down the inside of her thigh and down toward her toes. Then back up the other leg as Michele moaned at the gentle torture he inflicted. He enjoyed keeping her waiting and watching her passion build.

His fingers finally worked back up to her mouth. He tilted her chin toward him and then slowly kissed her, teasing her lips alternating between slow, languid movements and deep passionate strokes with his tongue.

He raised his head to look deep into her eyes. "Your beauty leaves me breathless."

Her lips lifted in a shy smile. "Thank you. Again. That's the third time you've told me."

"It's the twentieth time I've thought it." His hands moved back to massaging her breasts, then he laved each nipple and blew cool air across them, causing them to pucker instantly. She arched toward him again.

"I've been thinking of this moment for the past week," he said between suckling one breast and the other. "I've wanted you in my bed, with your entire body before me. I've wanted to watch you come, again and again as the sun set through my windows. I want to memorize every part of you. I want my fingers, my mouth, my body to remember you and be able to bring you to me at will while you are away."

Michele reached out, and the muscles in his stomach flexed and rippled as her strong fingers caressed his heated skin and moved down from his belly. Knowing he'd never last as long as he intended with her hands over him, he stayed her hand.

"Do you trust me, Michele?"

She nodded, her hips rotating begging for action. "I need time to pleasure you. I promise not to hurt you, only to love every part of your body."

She nodded again. "Yes, yes I trust you." Her words begged for release.

At that he reached for his shirt, and lifted her arms above her head, making sure her elbows were relaxed. Before she realized what was happening he had tied her wrists together with the arms from his shirt. She tugged on the bindings, her expression reflecting concern.

"Are you okay? I won't hurt you," he repeated. "I just want this to be slow, and I can't do that with your hands stroking me." He waited for her response. He did not want to scare her. He did not want to remind her of Jon.

"Yes," she finally said. "But...if I ask, you will release me."

"Just say the word."

She nodded and lifted her face toward him. He caressed her cheek with his palm and lowered his mouth to hers. He calmed her jitters with a lush, deep kiss, and tamed her passion with the slow, lazy stroke of his tongue against hers.

Then he slowly skimmed his hands down her body, between her thighs and lifted her hips as he knelt before them. She looked deliciously sensual with her breasts swelling, nipples stiff and dark, and her long curly hair teasing her pale skin.

As his hands moved back around her thighs he noticed their gentle curve—the kind that could cradle a man's hips in infinite softness. His cock pulsed, already hard and aching for her.

Drawing his eyes away from the vee between her legs, he slowly worked his hands back up to her breasts, straddling her and alternating his slow strokes with kisses. First her navel, then working up her sides. He made a point not to take her nipples into his mouth this time. Instead dancing all around them, blowing cool air across them, and finally back up to her luscious mouth, which he took with abandon.

Noticing the champagne still on the nightstand he dipped his fingers in the champagne and flicked the liquid across her skin. Her nipples automatically puckered and darkened to a deep raspberry hue, and her deep brown eyes widened in astonishment.

Dismissing her moans, he did it again, misting her throat and breasts with the droplets of champagne, then did the same to her belly and thighs. He watched as her entire body trembled, and her breathing deepened as he stared at her, fascinated at the way the dewy moisture sat as if on an opening flower after a soft, drizzling rain. God, he'd never seen anything so sexy, so mouthwateringly tempting as the feast she presented. She was the only woman to allow him complete trust with her body and so much control over her pleasure.

Aching to taste all that slick, glistening flesh he put his mouth to work lapping up every last drop of champagne. Beginning with her forehead, and moving over to her ears and across her cheeks. "You slay me with your response," he whispered. "Why did I take so long to tell you how much I love you?" He took a long time again at her mouth, sucking on her lips and her tongue until finally moving to her chin and down her neck. He stopped at the pulse at the base of her neck. "I love everything about you."

She moaned and begged him to hurry, but he refused.

Michele had never even dreamed of such sensual attention to every part of her body. Her hands ached to be touching him, to be returning the favor. She felt so selfish as he treasured her every crevice with his tongue.

She arched when he moved from her shoulders to her breasts, continuing to suck every last drop of champagne he had sprinkled on her. She moaned loudly when his teeth grazed her erect nipples.

"Ah, you like that," he said then sprinkled more champagne on them as if he needed an excuse to spend more time there.

As his mouth moved down across her belly, his hands trailed above him, working over every place his mouth had left, giving no respite to the sensuous torture he lovingly exacted. She gave herself over to David's hot breath and roving lips as he brought her feminine nerve endings to vibrant life and aroused her to the point of dizzying torment. As he suckled the inside of her thighs and teased at her center, she went over the top again.

Michele panted in short staccato breaths. "Please, David. I'm going to die. I can't take it anymore. Please let me touch you."

"Not yet, love. Not yet."

He smiled and slowly worked his mouth back up her body, until his hands finally came to rest on the headboard behind, surrounding her with the full male scent of him. She could see his hardness and she whimpered to feel it inside her.

The sun had set and a full moon now beckoned over David's shoulder. He closed the distance between them, rolling his hips, letting her feel the full effect of his cock against her stomach and she reacted with a low purring sound.

"You want me?" he asked on a whisper.

She set her feet apart, her knees widened and arched toward him, seeking more. "Yes. Please," she begged, frustrated at his slow seduction and her inability to use her hands to take what she wanted.

"I'm almost ready," he answered. "Just one more thing I need to do."

He lowered his head and brushed his mouth across hers. When she opened her mouth, he deepened the kiss, voracious and hungry, and she answered by sliding her body sensually against his trying to capture him between her legs as she wrapped them around him.

He chuckled as he finished the kiss, easily slipping back down and through her legs, his arm spreading them so he could stare down at the dark patch that protected her center. Lifting a hand, he glided one long finger through that thatch and working in a butterfly stroke, teased her toward climax.

She felt swollen, slick with desire. She rolled her head from side to side, willing to beg. "Oh God….Oh God…please, David."

He rested an arm above her head, bringing her face to face with him, and held her eyes as he continued his stroking. She could see the arousal blazing bright in his blue-green eyes as he pushed a finger deep inside her and watched her enter the fog of his loving again. Before she could recover, his teeth began to gently tug at her nipple and he added a second finger, stretching her to accommodate him, making her whimper at the dual sensations he'd inflicted upon her.

She bucked against his hand, her inner muscles beginning to contract. He looked directly into her eyes as he delved the pad of his thumb against the hood of her sex. The steady pressure of his stroking with a knowing touch brought her to the brink, and he watched in delight as her eyes widened in passion, her insides clenching deep in a wrenching throb of pleasure as she went over the edge with a scream of release and drew her knees together to stop the sensations.

But he wasn't through yet. His biceps flexed as he splayed his hands and slowly pushed on her quivering thighs, opening them wide again. His palms slid upward, and he used his thumbs to expose the tender nub of flesh hidden within her. He leaned in close, inhaling deeply and groaned as his breath gusted over her. Then he tasted her with a long, slow lick.

The air in her lungs felt trapped, and when he used his tongue to push inside her, all she could manage was a whimper of sound. He leisurely slipped in and out of her feminine folds, leaving burning trails in the wake of his intimate kiss. He found her center and his tongue circled it with flicks and slow swirls, accelerating her heart rate beyond what she thought she could stand. Then his lips closed over her, and he took her eagerly, hotly, greedily, as a second orgasm slammed into her.

Spent, her entire body quivering with spent passion, she cried out to him. "Oh, God, no more. Please no more."

He laughed huskily and leaned forward.

"I love you, Michele. You have given me the greatest gift – your trust. No woman has ever given me so much freedom." He paused as his breath faltered, and she felt him struggling to hold back as he finally released the bonds on her wrist. "Now," he said, barely able to talk. "Now!"

Eagerly, she fingered her hands through his hair, ran them along his shoulders and down his sides and back. She wanted to give back to him now. She wanted him to be inside her to have the joining she'd been craving all day and night.

"David." She whispered his name like a prayer.

He gathered his long body and knelt between her legs. She reached for his manhood and found it engorged and ready. He groaned as she circled her finger around the head.

Hooking his fingers beneath her knees, he dragged her toward him until her thighs were draped across his chest. Her knees over his shoulders, her pelvis tipped up in offering. He eased over her, using his weight to effectively trap her beneath him. His forearms came to rest next to her face, and he shifted his hips, lodging the thick head of his shaft against her very core.

"David," she splayed her hands against his stomach. "I love you."

He captured her mouth in a possessive kiss. "You're the only one I've ever loved," he said. "You will always be the only one."

He pushed into her an inch, letting her feel him, teasing them both with the promise of more. She groaned in anticipation.

"I want to feel every part of you, Michele, and I want you to feel me."

Then he pushed in another inch. She ran her fingers across his shoulders and pulled his face to hers for a wet and passionate kiss. She tasted herself in his mouth and it renewed the feeling of the orgasm he had given her only moments before. Rotating her hips, she worked him in further, as deep as he could go.

He lowered his chest to hers, covering her breasts with its broad expanse. "Do you feel my heart, Michele?"

Her eyes widened. She could feel the beats of their two hearts, beating together in double time, interweaving a riotous fugue.

David kissed her passionately as he stroked slowly and deeply. He kissed her again as the pace increased to a frenzy. This time the pounding of their two hearts threatened to drown her in its forcefulness.

"I love you, Michele. I want you to be mine. Not just tonight. But every night. Forever."

She couldn't find her voice as her inner muscles clamped tight around him and his eyes flared wide in response, giving her a chance to see his passion rise. He held still and she could see something else there too. Love. His eyes devoured her, made promises to her. Then his body followed through with more promises. In answer she wrapped herself in the interplay of the complex melody their two bodies shared.

Tremors radiated from her. Her heart pounded the strong bass undertone. His hands, his tongue stroked her strings. All the music of her emotion and her body fused with his heat. She felt thoroughly possessed by him, body and soul, in a way that was deeper and more passionate than ever before. A low, on-the-edge moan escaped from her throat as she climbed the peak again. He crushed his mouth to hers, kissing her with a deep, fierce passion that caught her off guard. She abandoned herself to him and went over the cliff, her nails digging into him.

David tossed his head back and screamed out her name. His hips driving hard, stroking long and deep until his body convulsed with the force of his release. When the shudders subsided, he released her legs from his shoulder and pulled her tight as he rolled to the side.

Michele buried her face against his throat, her ragged breathing hot and moist against his skin, her heart racing just as unsteady as his. When he caught his breath, he shifted to keep himself buried inside her as they slowly fell into a sated, languorous sleep.

DAVID SAT at the kitchen counter and poured himself a second cup of coffee as he worked the New York Times crossword in the morning paper. His fingers gripped the pencil hard and it broke in two. His thoughts were on other things…like the woman he'd made love with at least three times last night and how she had taken over as the sun rose behind her in the shower.

Michele was the only woman he'd ever had in his home. In his bed. Having her there all night had felt so amazingly right. His sleep this morning had been fitful. Afraid she'd already gone, he woke several times only to find she'd just rolled slightly away. Then he'd gathered her close again and she'd sighed in her sleep as she fit her hips back into his stomach.

He felt Michele's hands go around his waist and she pressed herself against him, nuzzling the back of his neck.

"Is that fresh coffee, I smell?" Michele's deep-husky voice asked, still filled with sleep.

David smiled and turned in her arms. He swallowed hard when he saw she wore his dress shirt from last night. It reached to her knees. Though it was buttoned, everything was easily accessible. She'd left the top buttons open just enough that the rise and fall of her breasts teased him with every breath she took. He slipped his fingers into the vee of the shirt and unbuttoned it the rest of the way, then pushed aside one panel to reveal a breast. He dipped and nipped at it then sucked with a groan. Not wanting to play favorites, he reluctantly let it go and did the same to the other one. Then he forced himself to withdraw his mouth and lazily watched as she caught her breath and her eyes filled with passion. He continued to caress the nipples and she closed her eyes, arching into his hand.

Oh, yeah, he could get used to having her at his place on a permanent basis, waking up to her in the morning and having her every day. The shirt burst open as her arms went around his neck and he pulled her closer. He cupped her bottom and lifted her up to the stool with him. Her legs straddled his waist and she automatically locked her ankles behind. Her broad smile indicated she knew the power she had over him as she wiggled in his lap and he immediately hardened. On a groan he dipped his mouth to hers.

Michele sucked on his lips then opened wide, inviting a quick exchange of tongues. Then she closed her lips over his tongue and sucked until he whimpered.

"Coffee?" She said, fluttering her lashes once.

Reluctantly, he slid her from his lap back to stand on the floor. "Yes. Fresh." He adjusted his pants and stood. "Would you like some?"

"Mmm. Hmm." She stepped to the other side of the counter and retrieved a mug from the stand near the coffee pot.

David lifted the pot and filled her mug with steaming liquid. He stirred in half a packet of equal and a little cream, noting how she stood with ease watching his every move. He'd memorized how she liked her morning coffee after their first night together, and every morning he'd made a point to pour for her and fix it to her specifications.

"Thank you," Michele said. She leaned against the counter as she raised the mug to her lips and sipped.

His shirt closed to a slit as she closed both her hands around the coffee mug and lifted it to her lips again and again. His eyes focused on the small trail of beautiful skin from her neck to her knees. His gaze stopped at the vee between her legs. He swallowed hard, forcing his tongue to stay in his mouth instead of following that trail once more.

After several more sips, Michele sighed. Setting the cup on the counter, she crooked her finger and he moved to her. Her arms wrapped around his torso and she laid her cheek against his bare chest, her warm breasts flattening against his stomach as he pulled her tight.

He needed to know. He needed a commitment. But he couldn't bring himself to ask her. If the answer was no, he'd be devastated.

She tightened her grip around his waist. His heart pounded hard and fast as he waited for her to speak. When she finally looked up at him again, he could see the question glimmering in her eyes. He felt her take a deep breath as she gathered her resolve.

"You know I'm going on tour," she said, her voice breathy, unsure. "The thing is my heart aches every minute I'm not with you, and I'm not sure I can stand this ache for four months."

He gulped and closed his eyes as he leaned his chin on her head and held tight. She'd spoken his fear, a fear that she couldn't wait—wouldn't wait. It had only been three weeks, what did he expect?

"I fell for you on our first date," she continued, her breath soft against his chest as she spoke. "I've been wrapping the memories into a special place in my heart for every day we've had together, holding them tightly in my core so I could live on them as we toured." She paused, and her hand pushed against him, making a space for air to pass between. "But…"

"But what?" He whispered his question, realizing how much her answer would hurt him, how much he didn't want to hear anything but her profession of love.

"But…how can I be sure whatever we have together will survive the separation?" She'd whooshed it out in one quick breath. "Since our first date, the longest we've been apart is only two days. What happens when it's a whole month, or worse two or three months? Once I'm not around for great sex, or just to remind you everyday that I'm here, that we are growing together, what then?"

She pushed further away from him and her jaw clenched as she looked to one side. She closed her eyes. When he tried to draw her back in, she backed up several more steps and looked at him, her brows furrowed, her lips pursed.

"And what about when other women in your life come around, you know…offering themselves? I'm not naïve enough to believe there are no other women." She spoke faster and faster with barely a breath, and paced back and forth in front of him. "Just three weeks ago you had someone in mind to take to the concert. What if she comes looking for you? I know I have no right to ask you to pass that up—especially with me gone for so long. You've never said anything about being exclusive."

"Michele, no—"

She held up her hand, palm facing him. "Let me finish. I have to get this out. We've only been together three weeks. But the problem is, I just can't stand the thought of you being with anyone else; and if that's the way it's going to be then I have to be able to go on tour knowing that's where I stand. I have to deal it with now, not later. I can't be worrying about it every night before I go on stage. I have to be up. I have to be positive. I have to be ready to perform."

She stopped her pacing and looked over at him, her mouth half open, her eyes wide.

A muscle in his cheek pulsed as he fought to tamp down his feelings. He struggled to restrain his desire to shout at her. "Do you think I'm so shallow that I can't go without sex for a few months?" he asked.

"That wasn't what I meant. What I meant was—"

He paused, concentrating on breathing deeply. Getting angry

would not help anything. "Did you hear what I said to you last night and this morning? What I said with my body? With my heart? Were you listening when I made love to you?"

"Yes," she said quietly. "It's just that —"

"No!" he almost shouted the word.

She backed up a step as if she were afraid of him.

He took long strides toward her and framed her face with his hands, holding her head strongly, forcing her to look into his eyes. When he saw fear in her eyes, he dropped his hands and pulled her to him, speaking softly and urgently. "I. Love. You. Only you, Michele. No one else. I've never been in-love with another woman. You are the first and you are the last. That is the way it is with me. I always knew there would only be one chance. You want to be in control? You want to understand what your power really is? It's my heart, Michele. My heart has been yours every day of the past three weeks and it will remain yours for the rest of my life, even if you throw it away."

He held her head to his chest, afraid to look into her eyes again, afraid to get a glimpse of her true thoughts. He'd bared his soul, and he wasn't sure he would survive if she trampled on it right now. But he had to make her understand, he had to get this straight before she left.

"I will wait for you," he continued after several moments. "That's what love does—it waits when it has no other choice."

He felt a wetness against his chest. His gut clenched at her soft sobs.

"I didn't know," she choked out the words. "I mean you said it, but I didn't believe. I thought it was to get me to bed. Then you said it in the throes of passion. I hoped. But I couldn't let myself believe. I had to be strong."

When she calmed and her breathing slowed, he released his hold on her and tipped her chin toward him. Seeing the love there, he smiled. "And you damn well better believe I expect the same from you."

Then he kissed her, a long, deep, soulful joining that expressed all his feelings for her. When he lifted his head they were both breathing hard, and he couldn't wait to be inside her again—to be part of her.

Michele sighed and arched into his touch. "You're everything I want, David."

"Then you'll come back to me? You'll live your life with me."

"I can't promise forever…yet."

His heart clenched. He closed his eyes to shutter the hurt before she saw it.

"But I can tell you that I love you more than I ever thought possible. And every day on tour I will think of you. There will be no other men." She paused. Her voice shook as she spoke against his chest. "I do want to be with you…forever. It's been in my dreams since we met. But I just can't let go of my fear—my feeling that it is just too good to last."

He would have to accept that she needed more time. At least he didn't have to worry about her seeing other men, meeting someone on the road who would turn her head.

David lifted her chin again and looked deep into her eyes. "I'm very greedy, Michele. I want it all. I want you physically and emotionally. I want to have children with you. I want to grow old with you."

He waited a long time for her response, but she didn't offer him any words of assurance. Instead, she took his hand and placed it on her heart, and looked into his eyes with invitation.

He gathered her to him, accepting what she could offer right now. He carried her back to bed. At least he knew her body could express without thinking what her mind couldn't yet accept. That would have to be enough for now.

CHAPTER 10

*D*avid sat at his computer, staring at his day planner once more. It had only been a week since he'd driven Michele up the mountain to join the rest of the Sweetwater Canyon band. As he'd waved goodbye to her and the lumbering RV, named Annabelle, he'd vowed to find a way to meet her on the road for a night or two as soon as possible. He looked again at the Sweetwater Canyon website for the tour schedule. She'd be leaving Washington and heading to the Telluride Bluegrass Festival. They'd be playing there for four days before heading to Arizona.

If he worked 15-hour days Monday through Thursday this week, he could finish up his current project and meet them in Telluride for the weekend. He smiled. Surely she wouldn't mind spending a few nights in a hotel instead of the RV. He tapped a few keys and booked his flight and the hotel, then got back to work on his project.

"Okay," Michele said, seating David at the end of the CD table. "The fans will line up here first. Once they pay for the CD, you then direct them to one of us to autograph it. Don't forget to get their email addresses so we can add them to our mailing list."

David sat in the chair and checked the inventory. The band had two CDs they'd produced in a small studio in Portland. Michele had told him that small bands often made as much, if not more, money selling CDs than doing gigs. The gigs were all about getting known and selling product.

He smiled, sold the CDs, made change, directed traffic, and whenever possible kept his eyes on Michele who was only a foot or two away. She was good with people. She laughed at their jokes even when they weren't funny, and listened to mothers and children who wanted to know why such a petite woman would play such a big instrument. Some of the men in line flirted with her but so far he didn't feel the need to deck anyone. That didn't mean he liked it, but he knew it was part of the job she undertook as a performer.

After about an hour he saw a man, maybe in his 40's approach the table on a zigzag course. He'd obviously had too much to drink. The man zeroed in on Michele. First, David watched the guy mentally undress her and lick his lips. Then he asked her to sign the promo photo, and purposely pulled it to the edge of the table so he could peer down her top. David stood and edged closer.

Michele stood and handed the autographed photo to him with a smile. "I hope you enjoyed the concert."

"Sure did," the man said, drawing out the first word. Then he laughed and pulled her hand toward him until her face was only inches from his. He purposefully stared down her blouse and licked his lips. "I bet you're the best fuck any man could want."

David stood, ready to strong arm the man out of the area.

"No!" Michele whispered, as she yanked back her hand.

His jaw locked tight and his heart pounding, he settled for putting a protective arm around her. "No one talks to Michele that way," he said between gritted teeth. "Now I suggest you take your photo and back off or I'll make you sorry you ever came."

The man gave Michele another leer and then laughed heartily, both palms up in a sign of surrender. "Lucky bastard. I see she's fucking you already."

David lunged across the table toward the guy, and he danced away, laughing all the more. "She must be real good. Yeah, real good. Let me know when you're tired of her. I don't mind sloppy seconds."

David rounded the table and Michele forcefully pulled him back. "Stop it! What do you think you're doing?"

Theresa, Rachel, and Kat came running over. "What's wrong? What's wrong?"

Now twenty feet from them, the man laughed, lewdly grounded his hips, then licked his lips and winked. David struggled with a need to pound the hell out of him.

"What a jerk," Kat said and gave the stranger the finger. The man laughed and finally moved one. "We always get one or two of them at every show." She looked at David and then looked at Michele. "Ohhhh. You were doing the protector thing. How sweet."

"Kat, David and I need some privacy," Michele said, her back ramrod straight.

Theresa hooked her arm in Kat's. "Come on, let's start packing everything up and getting it to the van." They walked toward the back of the stage.

"Take it easy on him," Rachel said to Michele. "I'd hate to see any bruises on that fine body." Then she smiled at David before turning to join the others.

Michele marched away from the tables toward the back side of the tent. David followed, still seething.

When she stopped and turned toward him, he said, "That man had no right to talk to you that way."

"Wrong!" she corrected him angrily. "You had no right to threaten him. Do you think I can't take care of myself? Do you think I don't know how to handle jerks like that? This is part of the territory, part of my job. You can't come riding in on your shiny white horse guns a blazing and save the little cowgirl."

"He was practically slobbering over you. I could see what he was thinking. I could see what he wanted."

"So! If he'd tried anything do you think that Theresa or Sarah or Rachel wouldn't have been there to help me?"

"Well, yes, but…"

"Did you see how everyone stopped coming to the table after your little possessive display? We must have lost a good ten or twelve names for our list because you had to make sure that everyone there knew I belonged to you."

"I'm sorry, Michele, it's just that…"

"Sorry doesn't cut it, David. If you can't handle other guys flirting with me at gigs, you just can't come to them anymore. Being nice to people after we play is part of the job."

"You can't mean you wanted to flirt with that jerk."

"I don't want to flirt with anyone. Sometimes, I'm so tired after we play I don't want to be nice to anyone at all—men or women—but I do it anyway. It's part of being a musician. It's part of building your fan base. It's part of promotions."

They stood only feet apart. David worked on unclenching his fist. He didn't come here to fight with Michele. He came to be with her, to keep their relationship alive.

He took a deep breath and concentrated on calming his voice. "I obviously have a hard time with someone like that…that…"

"Asshole," she supplied.

He laughed and it felt better. "That's a much cleaner description than I was thinking, but it works."

Michele stepped forward to within a foot of him. She didn't touch him; she just looked up into his eyes. "I appreciate that you care enough to protect me, but it wasn't helpful, and it didn't solve anything."

"Yeah," he admitted. He reached for his wallet and pulled out four $50 bills. "Look, I'll make up for what you lost in sales."

She folded the money back over his hand and closed his fingers with her own. "Put it back, we'll make it up another day. Just promise me something."

He put the money back in his wallet. "Not to help with the CDs anymore?"

"Can you do it without jumping to my rescue?"

David shook his head. He knew he couldn't stand and watch one guy after another flirt with her and trust himself. He knew if another drunk acted even remotely like this last guy, he couldn't stop himself from wanting to pound the hell out of him.

"I think after your concerts, I'll uh…take a walk and go listen to another band. Okay?"

She smiled and raised her lips to his as she pulled his head down. He lowered his mouth and tenderly returned her kiss. He wanted to show her he didn't have to be violent. She deepened the kiss and he groaned in relief as he pulled her closer. Forgiveness. Sweet, sweet forgiveness.

"There you are!" Kat shouted, interrupting their long kiss.

"Mom sent me to look for you. We're heading back to the campground. You two coming or are you going back to that swanky hotel to have wild, orgasmic sex."

"Kaaaaaat," Michele chuckled. "You know your Mom would kill me for letting you get away with that."

"Yeah, well she thinks I don't know anything about sex—even though I think about it all the time. Just haven't found a likely candidate yet."

"No need to rush anything," David said. "You still have plenty of time before entering into any kind of relationship."

"Yeah, easy for you to say, boyo. You've got Michele any old time, and I don't have squat. Anywho, what's the verdict? You in love again? Or are you spending the night with us in Annabelle?"

"In love," David answered for both of them and squeezed Michele around the waist.

Michele laughed. "Yeah."

"Thought so," Kat nodded back in the direction of the van. "More room for me then. See you at 10 tonight for the next set." Then she ran back toward the tents and the rest of the band.

"What would you like to do for the next seven hours?" David asked, squeezing Michele back against him.

"You have to ask?" She wrapped her arms around him and looked up with a twinkle in her eye.

"I didn't want to assume," he said. "After all, we did have all of last night together."

"And this morning," Michele added.

"So…."

She brushed her lips against him. "So, we only have two more nights and I have a lot more memories to fill of you and me together to get me through the next weeks after you leave." Then she turned and took off running. "First one to the room gets to call all the shots for the evening."

David laughed and ran after her. He'd keep a good pace but he wouldn't even try to pass her. He was very interested in learning exactly what Michele found exciting when she was in control.

FOUR WEEKS LATER, Sweetwater Canyon picked David up at the Salt Lake City airport. He'd arranged another long weekend to ride with them. This time to Digby, Montana and meet Michele's family. While motoring up Interstate 15, David added his baritone to the rest of the band as Rachel led them in a traditional Scottish pub tune. "Just got in from the Isle of Skye / I'm not very big and I'm awfully shy / The lassies shout as I go by…"

Kat pointed a finger at him and sang alone. "Donald where's your troosers?"

He laughed along with everyone else. This was what he imagined family was like. The band had certainly gelled since they'd started this tour. He could feel the easy camaraderie among the women. For a moment, he wished he could give up his consulting and join them for the rest of the trip.

David had been surprised to learn that following the Telluride festival Michele had become the chief driver for the RV. Being the shortest and most petite of the five women, it amused him that she would be the one driving this thirty-nine foot behemoth they had dubbed Annabelle. Evidently adept at maneuvering it into close quarters at gigs, so far she was the only person who hadn't hit anything even once.

He placed his hand on her thigh and squeezed as he joined them in the last line of the funny song. "So I hiked up my kilt and I gave it a blow / now you can't do that with troosers."

The women laughed uproariously and Kat slapped him on the back. "I bet you can't blow your nose on your trousers, David."

"Aye now," he answered in his best Scottish brogue. "I'll have to pull out me kilt in that case."

Michele flicked her gaze toward him for just a minute and smiled. She was so happy he was here, and so happy the band accepted him. Soon, the other women were talking among themselves leaving Michele and David to converse alone.

"So, I'm going to get to meet your family?"

"Yup. Are you nervous?"

"A little, but more excited than nervous. I want to see where you grew up, and meet the people you love. I want to know everything about you. I want to smell the air, feel the pastures beneath my feet, watch the sheep graze, see the mountains where you played hide and seek."

Michele could feel her heart fill with the love she had for him. In all the time they'd spent together, Jon had never wanted to meet her family. In fact, he never wanted her to tell his friends that she'd come from a small town like Digby or that she grew up on a sheep ranch. Every hour longer she spent with David she realized how wrong her entire relationship with Jon had been.

"My parents are kind of quiet. But they'll love you the minute you walk through the door. I've told them all about you, from the beginning."

"Yeah, you told me. I'm still not certain how I feel about them knowing we've been sleeping together."

She laughed as he turned red. She'd never seen David blush before. "It's not like they think I'm a virgin."

"It's just that if some guy my daughter had only known for three weeks had taken her to his bed, I would probably want to kill him."

"Would you, really?" She cocked her head and winked at him. "Even if your daughter told you how much in love she was with him? Even if your daughter told you how kind he was and how he made her realize what a fool she'd been with her previous boyfriend. If your daughter told you that she didn't know love could feel so wonderful, would you still want to shoot him?"

David smiled so broad she thought his cheeks might crack. "Well, now that you put it that way, I guess not. You told them all that?"

"Yup, and you know what my Mom said?"

"What?"

"It's about time!" Michele laughed giddily.

She laughed again as she remembered her brother's aside when she'd told him about David. "My brother said he wanted to buy you a beer and shake your hand because I sounded so happy."

"Well, I'll take him up on that."

Michele wanted him to know all about Digby and her childhood. She eagerly talked about her parents and her brother's family, sharing funny details about growing up on a sheep farm. By the time they pulled onto the ranch, she felt she had taken another step closer to the permanent commitment he wanted from her.

Michele deftly parked the motor home between the large trunk of the old oak tree and the side of the barn. She opened the door and immediately heard the music issuing from inside—Big Rock Candy Mountain, from the soundtrack of Oh Brother, Where Art Thou. Her steps unconsciously timed to the beat. When the soundtrack from that movie was released, her father bought it the first day he could get to Butte. She'd never known him to be so anxious to by a CD.

David stepped off behind her and the rest of the band followed close behind, each person taking a moment to stretch out the kinks of riding so long in the motor home. Michele took David's hand and pulled him toward the barn. She wanted to formally introduce him to her parents before they had to set up.

As she rounded the corner, she heard squeals and what could only be described as enthusiastic laughter. The dog came first, a rocket of brown and white fur racing around the corner and then coming to a dead stop in front of her. Barking with enthusiasm he nudged his nose into her crotch and wagged his tail enthusiastically.

David laughed heartily. "I know boy, I like it there too."

Michele pushed at the dog as she laughed. "Zeke, come on now. You know that's not polite."

After getting the smell of her he reared on his back legs and put his paws on her shoulder then lapped at her face as she laughed and stroked his thick fur. "I've missed you too," she said.

Moments later, a child's voice shouted, "You better run. 'Cause if I catch you on my property again, you'll wish you'd never laid eyes on me." A boy streaked past her in quick retreat as his brother chased with a play bow and arrow. Looking over his shoulder at who was following, the first boy ran right into David.

"Whoa, there," David said lifting the boy right off the ground. As the second boy came to a dead stop in front of him, he snatched him into the air as well. He immediately inverted both of them and the second boy dropped his weapon as they both giggled with glee.

"Well, well, I see you've caught yourself a couple of live ones," a gruff voice addressed David.

"Daddy!" Michele pushed Zeke off her and ran into her father's warm embrace.

David turned the boys upright and lowered them to the ground. They immediately scampered off, with the dog following them, shouting something about getting grandma.

David put out his hand. "Pleased to meet you, sir."

"We've heard a bit about you, son." Michele's father gripped David's hand firmly and looked him in the eye.

"All good I hope, Mr. Scott."

"Please, call me Matt. Should it be all good, David?" David swallowed hard and Matt laughed. "Just teasin' ya. It's nice to hear Michele smiling and talking again when she calls on the phone."

David was amazed at the easy acceptance of her father and the obvious love he had for his daughter. Not that he hadn't been loved growing up, but his parents were... reserved. At least they used to be. They didn't hold much for physical displays of affection; and his father certainly would not have invited anyone to call him by his first name.

Mr. Scott gave Michele another squeeze. "Ready to see the set up we've got for you and the gals?"

Michele nodded, her arms around his waist as her father walked her into the barn with David following close behind.

Three men were putting the finishing touches on a makeshift stage. Hay bales had been lined up in neat rows for seating, and a spattering of promo pictures were clipped to fishing line strung above the stage. Teenagers of various sizes and shapes set up tables with large pitchers of drinks—it looked like maybe lemonade and some kind of punch. One of the teenage boys emptied bags of ice into a lined trashcan, while the girl beside him dropped in cans of pop and beer.

On the other side a group of women bustled in and out, bringing in casseroles and vegetable trays, cookies and cakes. The table quickly filled and David couldn't imagine there was enough space for what appeared to be a long line of deliveries still to be deposited. At the end of the table were paper plates of all different colors and patterns, as if everyone brought whatever they had left over since the last picnic. Next to them were plastic knives and forks, also sporting many different colors.

Michele took David by the hand and introduced him to her mother, Carol, who gave him a big hug and whispered in his ear, "Thanks for loving Michele properly." He blushed, wondering exactly what details Michele had told her.

Then she introduced him to her brother, Rob, and his friends Justin and Morgan. They all agreed to get together for beers and talk after the band played.

As David helped the band unload and set up, he watched all the preparations of Michele's family and neighbors in amazement. A large mayonnaise jar had been set up at the end of the buffet table and already he saw it was bulging with small bills. David discreetly stepped over and stuffed five one hundred dollar bills into the center where they wouldn't show. He knew the band ran on a shoestring, but Michele refused to let him give or loan them money. She wanted complete financial independence from him. So, the least he could do was support her hometown fundraiser.

As the start time drew near, he saw more of the men coming in and lending a hand. Several of them looked like they had just washed up after a hard days work. Some of them carried food and had children trailing behind them, others stopped to add some bit of decoration to the barn at the behest of what appeared to be a decorating supervisor. And each person who entered added some bit of money to the mayonnaise jar.

Michele's mother and father were in the middle of all of it. In their own quiet way, delegating, guiding, keeping everything organized and on time, while listening to all the stories and catching up with the gossip. The whole lot of neighbors and friends were loud and laughing, as if they were one big family. Once the stage was set and the tables were brimming with food, Michele's mother took the microphone.

"May I have your attention…may I have your attention, please?"

The group silenced as mothers grabbed their children to them, and fathers stood close.

"Michele, would you come up here please?"

Michele made her way to the stage and joined her mother at the microphone.

"We are all so proud and happy to have our Michele here," her mother continued. Everyone clapped and whistled in agreement.

"When she decided to go off to Oregon… to college, most of you know we were scared for her…and for us. It seemed so far away. But we knew we had raised her right. And we knew she had the intelligence and the heart to become anything she wanted."

Eyes filled with love looked at Michele, and she blushed at the compliment. "Ah, Mom. I love you." She kissed her mother on the cheek and put her arm around her waist.

"Of course, little did we know she would join a band, especially a band that plays our kind of music." The audience laughed and her mother beamed. "So, tonight, we are having a bit of a homecoming and raising some money for the music program that helped put my little girl through college. I appreciate everyone who brought potluck. So let's pray and let's eat. Then we'll have some music." Again everyone clapped as Michele and her mother hugged. "Michele, will you start the prayer?"

Michele and her mother stepped down from the stage, hands joined. Michele gestured at David to join her, as they began a blessing circle. She took his hand in hers, Michele's father took David's other hand, and then everyone else filled in hand-to-hand, making a large circle around the edge of the barn. When there was no more room, a new circle began just inside it. Then Michele began to sing, and everyone else joined to sing the blessing.

A blessing upon your home
A blessing upon your hearth
A blessing upon your dwelling
And upon your warming fire
A blessing upon your animals
and upon your land
A blessing upon your kith and kin
A blessing upon you in dark or light
Each day and night of your living.

The song ended and there was a moment of silence. David's eyes misted and he squeezed her hand. Such love. Such faith. Such simple acceptance. Exactly what he wanted when he and Michele had a family together.

Michele pulled David toward the food tables and they took their place at the end of the line, which David soon learned put them right in the path of those who wished to give a hearty congratulations and a hug to Michele. As each person stopped, Michele attempted to introduce him. The women tended to hug David with one arm, and the men usually gave him a slap on the back to welcome him. Then a story of some type would follow about Michele's childhood. He knew he'd never remember most of the names, but he would remember the feelings he'd had as he met each one. David had never received so many hugs and slaps on the back in his life.

Neighbors easily shared their stories and personal lives as they regaled the troubles or triumphs a child or sibling had experienced. David heard about someone's brother jailed for hitting his wife, and another whose daughter had gotten pregnant and wasn't married. He also heard the proud story of a son who had joined USAID to help refugees in Sudan, and a daughter who had graduated from medical school and was doing her internship at a big city hospital. Occasionally he heard a bawdy story, always followed by a laugh and a wink as Michele blushed.

As the dinner hour passed, David realized he had heard more stories and learned more about the lives of this group of strangers than he knew about his own extended family or the friends he grew up with. It was nothing like the social events his parents would have sponsored in their suburban Virginia backyard. His parents would have hired a string quartet to play in the background throughout the evening. The conversations would have been calm and ordered. Any kisses would have been air kisses, followed by some type of congratulations for a job well done. If there had been a scandal to discuss, it would have been in furtive whispers, not openly shared with everyone else at the gathering.

Many years later, when his parents divorced, he'd learned his father didn't have so many business engagements—instead he'd had a string of mistresses throughout their marriage. When he called to console his mother, he was flabbergasted to learn she hadn't been faithful either. When David asked his father about all the other women, his father just laughed and said when you have enough money and enough power women were one of the perks. No one could expect a man to be happy with only one woman. Why, the sex would be utterly boring within a few months.

Before meeting Michele, David could almost understand his parent's lifestyle and constantly changing partners. He personally had never found sex boring, as his father claimed, but he had to admit that in the past he had found it a little more exciting whenever he began a new sexual relationship. But that was all before Michele. Now he couldn't imagine being with another woman ever again.

The benefit concert picked up again with another dance tune, and more than once David found himself pulled into a traditional dance as someone tried to teach him the steps. He usually failed miserably, but his partner, most often a young lady of the age of ten or twelve appreciated the fact that he'd tried.

On one of the ballads, David caught a glimpse of Michele's parents watching from the background. Her father stood behind her mother, arms wrapped about her waist as they both looked on with love and pride. The intimacy was palpable to David, even from across the room. He knew that was the kind of love he wanted to have for Michele in the long term. How long did she say her parents had been married? Thirty years or so? He'd bet neither of her parents had ever strayed.

The band finished with a rousing jig, led by the fiddle and then the ballad These Are My Mountains. Several people in the audience joined in the chorus as they began packing up their things. No land's ever claimed me tho' far I did roam / For these are my mountains and I'm going home.

David helped carry two coolers out to a truck for an older woman and her husband who were the last to leave. Tired, but happy, he returned to the barn for a last check to see if anyone else needed help.

"How 'bout that beer and a walk?" Rob had a glass of dark beer in each hand. He held one out to him.

"Sure." David reached for the glass and lifted it to his lips, taking a big taste. "Not bad. A stout?"

"Yep. Oatmeal. Dad's own recipe. He taught each of us to brew at the age of ten."

"Ah, that explains how Michele knows so much about beer." He followed Rob outside as they headed away from the house and the barn. "Does your Dad brew his own all the time?"

"No. Only a couple times a year—usually for special occasions. Truth is it's usually cheaper to buy it than make it. But nothin' tastes better than a good home made stout. Hard to find good stout anywhere nearby."

David took another long drink.

They walked without talking for a while. Then Rob stopped by a creek that ran through the property. Even though it was nearing 9:00 at night, it was still half an hour until dusk. David stood and looked over the fields of sheep grazing on the other side of the creek.

"So," Rob said. "It seems that my sister is pretty stuck on you."

"Yep. Seems so."

"She's made it pretty clear to all of us how she feels about you," Rob paused. "What I want to know is how you feel."

"Ah. Trying to protect her, huh?"

"That's right, and proud to do so. I don't know how much you know about Jon, but I can tell you he wasn't any good for her. The family never met him, but I saw the results of that relationship. I watched her go from being this optimistic, happy go lucky, confident young woman to someone with black circles under eyes, and losing too much weight. And whenever she came home to visit she never had much to say. Mom asked her if Jon was beating her and she denied it. I never saw any bruises or anything, so I guess she was telling the truth. But he was doing something, and whatever it was it was really bad."

David knew all about Jon, but he wasn't going to divulge anything Michele had chosen not to tell them.

Rob looked past him and didn't speak for a while. Then he turned back and smiled tentatively. "I can see you're not making her sad. In fact, I've never known her to be so happy since she left home." Then his expression became stern. "But…if you don't love her. If you're just being nice till you're done with her, I want to know now."

"And you'll take me out behind the barn and beat the crap out of me, right?"

David saw Rob evaluate the possibility of that, and it looked like he was actually considering it, even though David had a good six inches and probably at least a thirty-pound advantage. David didn't say anything and Rob didn't push as they both eyed each other for a few minutes. He appreciated that Michele's brother wanted to protect her. If he'd had a sister, he was sure he would do the same.

"I love her," David said simply, looking Rob in the eye. "I want to marry her. I want to raise a family with her."

Rob let out a breath and David laughed.

"Would you have really tried to beat the crap out of me?"

"Oh, yeah. Me and about ten of my friends." Rob's eyes twinkled as he chuckled. "I don't think you realize who you've fallen in love with. Any guy for about fifty miles around would give his right arm for Michele."

"That's not too surprising." David said.

"Outside of Justin, the guy she dated all through her junior and senior year of high school, she was just never all that interested in other guys. In fact, when she went off to college, I thought maybe she was still carrying a torch for him, as it seemed she wasn't seeing anyone. She never talked about dating and she never seemed in too much of a hurry about it. Until that jerk-off she met in her senior year."

"Jon?"

"Yeah."

"So, it's been only Justin and Jon."

"Anyway, if you ever did hurt her, Justin would be one of the ones to come after you. We've been friends a long time. My kids play with his kids. He cares as much about Michele as I do."

"I guess I better never hurt her then."

They both stood in companionable silence as the sun began to set.

"Better head back before we can't see," Rob suggested.

"We straight now?"

"Yeah. I can see that you love her." Rob looked down and toed his boot into the hard packed dirt. "So, when you getting' married?"

"When she says yes."

"She hasn't said yes yet? The way she talks about you, I would have guessed it was next month."

David's heart filled with gladness. "Seems she has to think about it. Seems to be unsure I'll stick around."

"Wow, sorry, man. I know how hard that is. Dana pulled the same shit on me."

"Yeah? What did you do to get her to make a decision?"

"Nothing you can do. No man really understands how a woman thinks."

David laughed. He used to think he knew all he needed to know about women. But now that he really cared. Now that he was in love with someone, he realized he knew very little.

CHAPTER 11

"*I* was in pain. I was in sorrow," Michele sang as she strummed chords on Sarah's guitar. "I couldn't see into tomorrow. Then you came..." She stopped and rubbed her temples, then swung her legs off the small sofa into the small aisle. "God, that's awful."

Sarah came out of the bathroom and walked sideways until she reached the sink. She washed her hands and dried them on the tea towel hanging from the cupboard door. She looked toward the cab of the motor home and gestured. "Rachel's still driving?"

"Yeah. It seems that she and Theresa were involved in a discussion about the sound guy at last night's gig, so she didn't want me to take over yet."

"Oh no, not again."

"Yeah, again," Michele shrugged her shoulders. "Rachel thought he was hot. Didn't you notice her smiling at him and flirting when we did our patter between songs?"

"I noticed something was going on, but I didn't know if she was aiming it at someone in particular or if she was just feeling good."

"She was feeling good alright. I think they shared a couple beers as we were packing up, then I started seeing that libido dance she does

151

with a new guy, and sure enough they walked away together with his hand on her butt and she was giggling."

"But she made it back on time for us to leave this morning?"

"Oh yeah, only one problem."

"Problem?"

"He's beside us in the red car."

Sarah barely pulled the curtain at the sink aside to peek through the window, then groaned. "I wonder how long this one will last."

"Who knows?" Michele crossed her legs under her then stretched forward, her torso flat against her legs and her fingers touching the floor.

Sarah flinched. "How can you do that? I'd be hearing my hips springing apart if I tried that."

Michele laughed. "No you wouldn't. It feels good…works out all the kinks from sitting cooped up all day. You should try it. Keeps you limber."

"No way! I didn't have all those years of ballet like you. And I'm a lot taller than you, so I have more tendons to pop."

"Well, I have to do something to keep my body from tensing up. I never realized how much time bands spend just getting from one place to another. It can be pretty boring."

"I hear you. You know, I always laugh when my friends try to tell me how lucky I am to be living the bohemian life of a musician, traveling from town to town, getting all the adulation of our fans. I think they get that from watching too many road movies. You know, the ones where the band is in a big, luxury bus with their own manager and driver, and the musicians sit around jamming all the time and being really artistic."

Michele rolled her eyes, understanding completely. "Oh yeah. They're not stuck in a thirty-nine foot motor home, sharing living quarters with five people, one toilet, and a shower that breaks down as often as it works."

"Can you imagine having our own driver? That would be heaven."

Michele gestured toward the window. "I'm sure we could leave it up to Rachel to always find us someone."

Sarah giggled. "You're bad, Michele."

"You're right, I shouldn't pick on her. She just sets herself up so well." Michele smiled and looked toward the front of the motor home to make sure Rachel and Theresa were still deep in conversation.

"I'm sure that once these guys realize we spend more time sitting in the motor home and driving to the next city than actually playing gigs, and how tired we are after driving 300 miles and then playing until midnight somewhere because our 9:00 slot was being used by the band before who was an hour late—that even Rachel wouldn't feel like having a romp between the sheets."

"Or have to help with all the business stuff we have to do before we go on tour," Michele added.

"We don't make it sound too glamorous do we?" Sarah leaned back against the chair and stretched her long legs in front of her. "To listen to us, you'd have to wonder why we do it."

Michele smiled. "Yeah, but we're still really lucky. There is a lot of work and a lot of boring road miles, but we are living our dream."

"Yeah, there is that," Sarah agreed.

"It's hard to find a woman our age who hasn't dreamed about being a singer or a musician," Michele continued. "At least we're all doing something we love and making enough money to pay our rent and buy food. Even with the miles, the spats, and the boredom in between, it's worth it every time I step out on stage."

Michele closed her eyes as she brought the memory forward. "And Rachel starts the intro, and you or Theresa pick up on the guitar. Then I start to feel the music. When I begin plucking the strings and the beat rocks my body it starts to seep into my every fiber." She sighed and slowly opened her eyes. "And then I hear the audience responding, and I know...I know I'm making a connection...well, there's just nothing like it."

Sarah quieted for a moment and nodded her head in understanding. "You've got a good point. God only knows this is a hell of a lot better than waiting tables. I left my teaching job to join the band, thinking the money would start rolling in within a few months. I was so naive. When it didn't, I picked up waitressing on the side."

"I was filling out bankruptcy and divorce papers, sometimes both for the same person, for the umpteenth time," Michele said, remembering the brief three-month temp office stint she did at a law firm before she joined Sweetwater Canyon.

Sarah stood and took two steps to the sink. She opened the mini-fridge and pulled out an orange. "Want one."

"No thanks, I already had breakfast two hours ago."

"OK." Sarah peeled the skin from the orange into the sink before gathering them into the trash bag. Then she carefully arranged the orange wedges on a small plate.

Michele tried the song again, this time changing the key and the words slightly. "I was in pain. I was in sorrow. I let all my fears, keep me from my tomorrows." She paused. "Hmmm. Better."

Sarah brought her orange slices back to the chair and sat. She popped a wedge into her mouth and chewed. "What's that you're working out?"

"Just a song I've been working on in my head. I have the melody, but I can't get the words to fit with it."

"Sing it to me."

Michele sang the melody using the words da, da, da, then launched into the chorus.

"Pretty. What's it about?"

"Oh, a girl who had lost all confidence in herself and then found it again with the help of a good man. Then he asks her to marry him, but she can't make a commitment because she's afraid it won't last."

"Another one about David, huh?"

"Yeah," Michele dipped her head.

"You've got it bad, don't you?"

"Oh, yeah. These long drives from one gig to the next doesn't exactly take my mind off him."

"Ever tried reading?"

"I did bring a couple of romance novels."

Sarah laughed. "Like that would help you."

"True. They just make me yearn for him all the more." She plucked out the melody for the next line. "This song is special."

"Yeah? Why?"

"Because it ends with the woman accepting his proposal," she said softly.

"You have? You are? Oh that's so great!" Sarah launched herself toward Michele and gave her a big bear hug, dropping the plate of orange slices in the process. "Darn it!" She bent to pick them up off the floor and then proceeded back to the sink to rinse them off.

Theresa turned from the cab. "What's going on back there? Is everyone OK?"

"Michele's getting married!" Sarah shouted.

Theresa immediately left her seat and gave Michele a big hug too. "It's about time," she said softly. "I was beginning to think if you didn't do something soon I was going to throw my hat in the ring. That is one hunk of a man, and he's really good to you."

"Yeah, congrats, Michele," Rachel said sourly, without turning around.

"Thanks guys." Michele smiled as everyone returned to their seats.

Then she heard Rachel's side comment to Theresa. "Big fuckin' deal. It's not like it was going to be a surprise or anything. She's been mooning over him ever since we left Oregon."

"Rachel, keep it to yourself," Theresa hissed. "Let her be happy. She deserves it. We all do." Theresa pulled the road map out of the glove compartment and began looking at it. Then she said loudly, "Let's see the next turn will be..."

Sarah turned back to Michele as Theresa and Rachel picked up their previous conversation again. "So, what made you change your mind?"

"He's been so patient, and I know how hard it's been for him. You know, we haven't seen each other since Billings. He's been really busy and hasn't been able to find a time to get away and meet us again."

"Yeah, two months is a long time to go. But it's not like you never talk. You call him every night before you go to bed."

Michele blushed, wondering how much anyone heard her conversations. She usually tried to talk to David outside of the RV but, if it was raining or they were parked side by side with ten other rigs, it was frequently a choice between a stranger overhearing her conversation or the women in here who she at least trusted.

Sarah took another slice of orange and put it in her mouth. "So, I see Rachel is at least talking to you a little."

"Not exactly. Since Sunrise Mountain we've been at least civil to each other, but she's still being disagreeable."

"You know, you shouldn't have told her about that guy. What was his name?"

"Bill."

"Yeah, Bill, when we were in Edmonton."

"Look, if I'd just woke up with David in the morning and planned to see him again that night, then one of you saw him go into a hotel with a blonde in the afternoon, I'd want to know about it."

"Well, that's different. You and David have a commitment. Rachel and these guys she hooks up with, there are no promises."

"Maybe not a promise like we have, but there's certainly an expectation that the guy doesn't hop from one bed to the next in just a couple of hours—even for Rachel."

"I 'spose. But, she doesn't want to hear it. So she's bound to shoot the messenger."

"I know, but it's not going to stop me from trying to protect her," Michele's tone was fierce.

"Protect who?" Kat asked, peeking her head out the door of the back bedroom. "And what's this I hear about marriage?" She opened the mini-fridge and poked around for a minute. "No more yogurt? But, I'm starving." She drew out the last word with exaggeration.

"About time you showed your face around here." Michele giggled, noticing that Kat had her nightshirt on inside out. "Rough night, huh?"

"What?" Kat followed Michele's eyes. "Oh, geez. What an idiot I am. Can't even put on a t-shirt right." She whipped it over her head, turned it right side in and then put it back on again.

"There's cereal in the cupboard, milk in the fridge. Or if you want something warm, there's instant oatmeal that you can stick in the microwave," Sarah said.

Kat opened the cupboard above the stove. "Nope. Nope. Definitely not." Then she closed the door and opened the mini-fridge again. Finally, she stood up with a bowl of leftover spaghetti and a slice of garlic bread. "This will have to do."

Sarah and Michele looked at each other and started laughing.

"What? What?"

"We're not saying anything about your choice of breakfast," Michele said, holding back a smirk.

"Good, because you just don't know what a good breakfast is. This has all the nutrition I need right here. Meatballs for protein, pasta for carbs, tomato for vegetable."

"Tomato is a fruit not a vegetable," Sarah corrected.

"And the garlic bread is?" Michele asked.

"More carbs, but I'm young I can take it. Garlic is good for you. I read it in some magazine."

Kat stuck the pasta in the microwave and punched in a number. "Now, who's getting married and who are you trying to protect?"

Michele and Sarah looked at each other again, and silently agreed not to say anything about Rachel.

"I'm getting married," Michele said, smiling broadly. It was starting to sound right. Natural. She tried it again, this time a little more giddy. "I'm getting married!"

"Whoopee!" Kat clapped. "Can I be a bridesmaid? When is it? Right after we get back? What kind of a dress are you going to wear? We can pick up a brides mag at our next stop. What about flowers? Oh my God, yellow roses. It's got to be yellow roses."

"Hold on, hold on," Michele waved her hands like a person drowning. "Slow down."

Kat clamped her mouth shut, but she couldn't help her smile and she kept dancing around the motor home humming Here Comes the Bride.

"Good question," Sarah said, giggling at Kat's antics. "Have you thought about a date?"

"Well, as I haven't even told David yet, I can't really say."

"Come on, Michele. You know he'd be on a plane tonight and at the justice of the peace tomorrow if you just said the word."

Michele smiled. "Yeah, I guess he would."

"So?"

"I was kind of thinking mid-December, maybe at Timberline Lodge. We get back from the tour the first of November. That would still give me about six weeks to get everything ready. I love how the lodge is decorated for Christmas, and it is close to Theresa's place."

Kat danced back and forth, like a child who had to go to the bathroom. Michele looked up at her and Kat stared back, pointing to her mouth, indicating how it was closed on Michele's command.

"Okay. What is it? You don't have to keep your mouth shut, just one question at a time."

Kat let out an embellished breath. "Christmas! That's perfect! Timberline will be all decorated for Christmas. You won't even have to buy a lot of flowers. White dress. Your long dark hair. You'll look just like Buttercup in the Princess Bride. Hey, instead of a crown you can wear a wreath in your hair. You know, with evergreens and berries and all that stuff."

Michele's eyes misted, as she got caught up in Kat's fantasy. "That would be beautiful wouldn't it?"

Sarah took her hand. "You would be beautiful, Michele. You're glowing already."

"I'm going to start planning right now," Kat announced. "I can picture it already." Dreamily she walked back to the bedroom.

Michele giggled. "How long do you think it will take her to remember she still hasn't eaten?"

"Oh, maybe two minutes," Sarah said. "So, how are you going to tell David?"

"Well, that's what this song is about. It's my acceptance song."

Sarah's eyes misted now. "Oh, Michele, that's so romantic."

"I wanted to start practicing it now, so the next time David can get to see me I'll have it down cold and I won't get nervous."

"Oh, you'll still get nervous," Sarah said. "But it will be the good kind of nervous."

Kat sprang out of the bedroom like a Jack-in-the-box. "Hey, where's my breakfast?"

Michele looked at the watch on her wrist. "Ninety seconds." Sarah giggled.

Kat retrieved her pasta from the microwave then took the second chair across from Michele. She tucked one leg under her bottom and her other one rested on the ball of her foot. She used her free foot to twirl the chair slowly from one side to the other. Kat dug into the pasta and took a couple of big mouthfuls before speaking again. "So, who are we trying to protect?"

Sarah and Michele sighed and didn't say anything.

"Come on you guys." Kat looked from one to the other. "All right, let me guess. Michele? Michele's being followed by rabid fans who want to steal her soul and send it to aliens?"

Michele raised an eyebrow as she laughed, knowing that Kat often used humor to wrangle secrets.

"Mom?"

Sarah giggled.

"Mom forgot one of the bookings, and we will be met by a phalanx of cops when we reach Muskogee."

"Phalanx?" Sarah asked. "I think you're not using the word correctly."

"Whatever. I read it in my history book and it sounded good. It's my word for the day."

"Good word," Michele said.

"Now I know! It's Rachel. Right? We have to protect Rachel."

No reaction.

"That's it isn't it? I can tell because you did absolutely nothing. Your face suddenly went blank." She paused and looked again for a reaction. "Oh, God, not another one?"

Michele was immediately reminded how five women living in a motor home couldn't keep anything private. Kat probably knew more about Rachel's comings and goings than anyone. Still, she forced herself to keep her face impassive.

"I knew it. I knew it! Do we have someone following us again?"

Sarah gestured toward the window. Kat turned around and threw the drapes open behind her. Then she stuck her tongue out at the driver and pulled the drapes closed again.

"Gross! He's not even cute. At least the guy who followed us from Edmonton for a few days was hot." Kat made her way to the cab and leaned over the seat. "Hey, Rache, are you going to dump this guy or what?"

"I tried to, but he wouldn't take no for an answer." Rachel replied between her teeth.

"So, call the cops. They'll make a courtesy stop and distract him while we get away. They've done it before, you know."

"I'm going to try talking to him one more time before we get to our next gig. If that doesn't work then I'll call for help."

Kat made her way back to the chair and slouched into it. "Man. I wish she wouldn't do this. Every time we go somewhere for more than a few days, something like this happens."

"I think the worst is yet to come," Sarah said softly. "Branson always brings them out."

There were still a couple of days before they hit Branson. They had one more gig in Oklahoma, at Muskogee. Then they dropped down to Little Rock for two nights before coming across the Missouri border to Branson where they were scheduled for three shows. Branson was their biggest gig of the tour. They would be opening for Laurie Lewis.

"Oh, yeah," Kat agreed loudly. "Remember, last year when she hitched up with the sound guy? The one she dumped and then he followed us around for, what was it? Three or four months. What was his name?"

"Drake." Rachel threw the name out over her shoulder. "His name was Drake, and I don't appreciate you talking about me behind my back."

"Well, we can hardly talk to your front 'cause you're driving." Kat quipped.

Rachel let out a string of swear words. "I don't appreciate you talking about me at all. It's my life, and I'm free to screw it up as much as I like."

"And you're doing a great job with it too," Kat flung it back.

"It's my life and stay out of it."

"Fine with me," Kat replied and she stood with a dramatic sweep of her arms. "I have a wedding to plan." Then she flounced back to the bedroom and closed the door with a resounding thump.

"That went well, I think," Sarah said and Michele curled into the sofa with the giggles.

CHAPTER 12

The large arrangement of flowers stood just to stage right of Michele's bass. The aroma of the beautiful pink and yellow roses mixed with the chrysanthemums and day lilies wafted on to the stage throughout the performance. She couldn't believe David had arranged for them to be delivered to the stage in Branson just before they opened. They were absolutely gorgeous! And the arrangement along with the stand was huge. Big enough to make a definite statement without upstaging her bass.

"Those things are absolutely garish," Rachel commented as she packed up her fiddle and the stagehands began moving equipment in for the next band. "What does he have to prove? You already have him by the short hairs."

Rachel had been in a bad mood all day, and Michele just wasn't willing to let it spoil her happiness.

"I think they're beautiful," Kat offered, snapping the strap across her accordion. "You are so lucky. What are you going to do with them?"

"Don't even think about bringing it back to the motor home," Rachel said. "I won't be able to sleep with that smell trapped in there."

"I checked with the theater's director," Michele said. "She told me about a nursing home just down the road that would love them. She even volunteered to take them down for me so we wouldn't have to move the motor home."

"Thank God," Rachel said.

"I'm beat," Theresa spoke for the first time since their set ended. "I have a headache and I need to lie down. Kat, let's get going." The two of them headed out the back door.

"I'm heading over to that Mexican place. I have a craving for a good burrito. Anyone hungry?" Sarah asked.

"I need to make a phone call first, but I'll join you in awhile."

"Yeah, she has to call Mr. Google Eyes and talk dirty," Rachel said. "Well, I'm starving so I'll go with you now."

Sarah rolled her eyes, gave Michele a hug and whispered. "See ya later. Enjoy your call." Then she headed out the door with Rachel.

Michele moved her bass to just outside the door and leaned it against the back wall as she hit her autodial for David.

"Yeah. Dammit! Ouch."

Michele giggled. More often than not he seemed to answer the phone swearing. "Now, that's not a very nice greeting to someone you claim to love."

"Sorry. I just got out of the shower and tripped over a chair trying to grab for the phone. I guess I'm falling at your feet."

"Poor Baby. You want me to come kiss it and make it better."

"Yes, can you leave right now? It's an emergency. I think my toe will fall off if you don't get here soon."

She laughed. "I wish I could."

She held the phone closer to her ear and reveled in just hearing him breathe on the other end. He seemed content not to talk either.

"David, they are so beautiful. But you shouldn't have. All I could do was smile through the whole concert—even on the sad songs."

She heard his sigh, then a rustling, as he must have found a way to sit back and relax for a minute.

"I'm glad you liked them. Miss me?"

"Not particularly."

"I don't believe it."

She sighed, making it as loud as possible so he'd be sure to hear. "Why should I miss you? You call me almost every night and talk more than anyone else I know."

"And you don't talk enough. Talk to me now."

"I don't know what to say, except Thank You. You do too much. I don't think I'll be able to ever repay you."

"You can repay me the rest of my life by marrying me."

"I've been thinking about that."

"And…"

"And you have to come see me to hear my answer."

"Well, I'll definitely come then." He paused. "I had a dream about you last night, all soft, watery colors and slow motion."

"Again?" Michele loved to hear about his dreams. She had dreams too, but she couldn't ever tell him about them. "Tell me."

"We made love on the bank of the river in back of Theresa's house, and the wild grass was cool and damp with flowers. I woke up with the taste of you in my mouth."

There was a moment of silence, a quiet catch of breath. "That's very interesting."

"Is someone standing right there listening to you?"

"Uh huh." She turned her back to the people moving things onto the stage, trying to block the background noise of other people talking.

"That riverbank is a very public place, you know."

He laughed so hard she thought he might bust a gut.

"I'm seriously crazy about you, Michele. Just two more weeks and I'll be with you."

"Really?" She could hardly believe he'd arranged something so soon. "Where?"

"I'll meet you in Asheville at the folk festival. Think you can get us a private room in town? I don't want to embarrass the rest of the band by taking you three times a night in the RV."

Michele practically purred. "Well, with a promise like that I'll definitely come up with something."

After twenty more minutes of quiet fantasies, Michele hung up and meandered back inside to pluck a single yellow rose from the bouquet before it was taken away. She took a deep breath and inhaled the sweet smell. She was getting closer every day—closer to singing her song—closer to admitting to the world that she was indeed in love with David Blackstone and willing to give up her fears and commit to a life with him…forever.

~

RACHEL CHECKED the keycard Flint had given her as she road the elevator to the tenth floor. She was so depressed. All she wanted to do was make the pain go away. And she knew only one way to do that. Sex.

It just wasn't fair. She'd done everything right with Kavan. She'd followed him to America. She'd supported him as he grew his business, and then he'd dumped her for his secretary. She'd tried looking for the right guy after that, but they just never seemed to show up. Then Michele, who was six years younger, met the perfect guy in only three weeks, fell in love, and now they were getting married. Not that she hated Michele. She actually loved her like a sister. But, it just wasn't fair.

The elevator doors opened and she peered at the sign in front of her. Rooms 1001-1049 to the left. 1050-1099 to the right. She turned right, added a swing to her hips and held her chin high. She knew how to take away the pain, she'd done it before. Fast and dirty, hard grinding sex would make her feel great—at least for a while.

Flint had that hard edge to him and she could tell he was the kind who took control immediately. She needed that tonight. She needed someone who wouldn't let her think. Reaching the end of the hall, she took a deep breath, unbuttoned a few more buttons on her blouse to make sure her cleavage showed just right, then knocked on the door.

"Well, Rachel, come right on in." Flint looked her up and down greedily as he opened the door wide and gestured her inside. "Join me for a drink?"

Rachel studied Flint's leer, something wasn't quite right. She scanned the smooth surface of the bar just inside the door where two glasses of beer rested. She looked beyond that to the bed in the middle of the room. She didn't see anything wrong. Must be her imagination. Michele just had her too upset. She stepped inside and smiled, draping her finger at the vee in her shirt to draw attention to her cleavage.

Flint licked his lips, handed her a beer, and motioned her toward the bed. She sat down on the edge and crossed her legs. He took a big gulp of his own beer and his eyes darted toward the bathroom.

"Something wrong, Flint?" she asked taking a sip of her beer.

"Just gettin' hard for you, babe," he said his voice low. Then he drank the rest of his beer in one large gulp. "Drink up. I can't wait too long."

Rachel took three large swallows as he approached.

He sat on the bed and his hands immediately dipped inside her shirt. She gasped as he forcefully ripped it open, scattering buttons all over the floor and beer sloshed from the mug she held. Then he jammed his fingers down her bra, feeling for a nipple and pinched hard. She gritted her teeth.

"Careful there, big boy. You have to give me a little chance to get worked up."

"Oh, I'll work you up honey. No need to worry about that. Come on, finish that beer so we can get started."

Well, this was what she wanted wasn't it? This was what she needed to forget Michele and David and all that sickly sweet happiness swirling around her all the time. She chugged the rest of the beer and handed the mug to him, smiling.

"Give it your best shot," she invited.

He pushed her into the bed and then ripped her bra in half, immediately going for her breasts with his mouth. Before she could even react he tugged hard at her jeans, ripping the zipper and pulling them down her legs. He didn't even stop to take her boots off. He just pulled the pants down far enough to get to what he wanted.

She moved to raise her hand toward him to ask him to slow down, but realized she couldn't move her arm. She tried the other one. They weren't bound, but she didn't seem to have any control over them. Oh, God, no! There must have been some kind of drug in the beer.

"What did you do to me? What did you give me."

Flint laughed and pulled her boots off, then stripped the rest of her jeans away.

She tried to raise her leg to kick at him, but like her arm, she had no control of them either.

Next he pulled a large knife from a sheath in his pocket and waved it toward her. "Now we're getting' somewhere." He slid it beneath her panties and sliced the fabric in two. His hands almost reverently moved aside the last bit covering her. "Oh yeah, he wasn't kiddin' when he told me you were sweet."

"Who?" she asked. "Who have you been talking too?"

"You'll find out soon enough."

She bit down on the inside of her cheek. She knew this would hurt. There had been no kisses, no attempt at all to help her prepare for him.

She heard him unzip himself, then he straddled her, his cock in her face.

"Suck bitch," he said.

"Look, you don't want to do this," she said, trying to sound confident even though she couldn't move.

He slapped her. "I said suck."

Tears in her eyes, she did what he asked. It took only a minute for him to get an erection and he moved his cock away from her mouth.

She couldn't see what he was doing, but she knew he wasn't done with her yet.

"Fucking condom!" She heard a snap and figured he'd managed to put it on. At least she was safe. She groaned at the irony. Safe and drugged.

He grunted at her tightness as he entered her and she winced at the pain.

"God you're tight. Just how I like it." He grunted and pumped and then finally fell on top of her sweating.

Thank God he was quick, she thought. Now if he'll just go to sleep, the drug might wear off and she might be able to leave before he woke.

He caught his breath and rolled off her, then removed the condom and threw it to the floor. "Damn things. Can't feel enough with it on." She saw him pull on his pants and head toward the door.

"Okay, she's warmed up. She's all yours." Flint laughed raucously and she heard the door slam as he left the room.

Then she saw another man standing at the foot of the bed.

"Drake?"

"Hi Rachel," he said, unzipping his pants. "Flint get you worked up good and wet?"

"Drake. I can't…I can't move."

"You got that right. I'm not takin' any chances with you gettin' away. It keeps you awake and knowing everything I'm doing to you, but you can't do nothin' to stop me."

Rachel moaned. They'd been together maybe three months over a year ago. She'd dropped him because he was into some frightening stuff.

He knelt between her legs and as his eyes looked at her, the grin was so evil she knew she'd be dead in the morning. Then he pulled a gun out of his waistband.

"I've been watching you, Rachel. I've been watching you flirt and fuck since you left me. Now I'm going to do what I've wanted all along. Every time I saw you go off with some other guy, I promised I'd make you pay."

Rachel closed her eyes. God, how many men had she been with? She wasn't even sure. Had he been following her for the past year? How did she not know?

He slapped her. "Look at me, bitch."

She looked at him, knowing it may be the last thing she ever saw. She couldn't help her tears.

"I'm going to make you pay for leaving me. For every guy you fucked, you are going to pay me tenfold. And you are going to pay all night long." He held the gun to her forehead and leaned his hard shaft toward her mouth. "Make me feel good, baby, and maybe I won't pull the trigger."

RACHEL OPENED her eyes and moaned. She was on the bed, stomach down, and every part of her hurt. Slowly she rolled to her side and drew her knees to her abdomen. She could smell beer and whisky, and the bed felt wet liked it was soaked in it. She had a vague memory of Drake pouring the bottle over her, before using his gun on her several times. She remembered passing out twice, only to have him slap her awake so she would be certain to feel whatever his next indignity was.

Cautiously, she looked around the room. No sign of Drake anywhere. She tried to sit up, but couldn't. Then she noticed her arms had deep bruises all over them. She didn't even want to look at her legs. Tears came to her eyes and she curled tighter, rocking back and forth on the bed.

Michele woke early and looked to the sofa. Still no Rachel.

Rachel had been pretty good the first two nights they'd spent in Branson. In fact, she'd even made up with Michele and helped her to finish her acceptance song for David. Michele had thought maybe Rachel had turned a corner, but Michele saw all the signs last night just before the show. It began with Rachel bitching about Michele's bass being in the wrong place on stage. Then between sets she accused her of speeding up the tempo and ruining the fiddle's solo. That was the way it always started when Rachel was ready to spend the night with a new guy. She alienated everyone close to her.

This time it was another musician. Some guy supposedly from a country-western band. After Rachel took off, Michele did some asking around. She couldn't find the band on the schedule anywhere, and no one she talked with had heard of this guy. What was his name? Flint? Something like that.

She rolled off the makeshift bed and stood, stretching her arms overhead trying to touch the ceiling. Then she bent over and touched her toes with ease. Holding her head to her knees, she stretched her back and then slowly rolled back up making sure each vertebra aligned correctly.

She folded the sheet and blanket and stowed them in a cupboard above her head, then separated the two chairs that had been pushed together to make her bed. She stretched again, this time from side to side, working out the last few kinks she had from sleeping. Finally, she tiptoed to the bathroom, making sure not to wake anyone. She could still hear Sarah's soft breathing in the bunk over the cab and she assumed Theresa and Kat were still in the back room, behind the closed door.

After finishing in the bathroom, Michele retrieved a glass from a cupboard above the sink and took it, along with her toilet kit and her cell phone. She eased open the door of the motor home and stepped outside.

She took a deep breath and looked around the parking lot as she got her bearings. It was a little past dawn, but she could already feel the muggy air closing around her. Michele would be glad when they got back into mountain country. This humidity, and the temperature that barely changed five degrees from day to night, was oppressive. She longed for the dry summer heat and the cool nights of the Pacific Northwest.

Feeling a little more awake, she slipped on sandals and made her way to the campground showers. She picked up a beer can and a McDonald's bag along the way and deposited them in the trash. It made her angry when people couldn't take the time to walk a couple more steps to throw things out.

Michele turned off the shower and sighed as she toweled dry and stepped into a clean pair of underwear, shorts, and a top. It felt so good to have great water pressure and plenty of hot water. It was nice to have the convenience of the motor home shower, but it was a pain to use. She heard a ringing and realized it was her cell phone. It wouldn't be like David to call her early in the morning she thought. She fished it out of her toilet kit.

"Hello?"

"Please, come. I need help."

She could barely hear the whispered plea between the sobs.

"Rachel? Is that you?"

"God, I don't know if he'll come back. I can't move. I can't walk. Michele, please."

Michele's heart pounded against her ribs and her chest tightened. She could hear the desperation clearly in Rachel's voice now. She started running toward the motor home. "I'm coming, Rachel. Where are you? Hold on. I'm coming."

"1099. Tenth floor."

"Got it. Tenth floor. Now which hotel are you in?"

Rachel started crying again. This time really loudly.

Michele threw open the door to the motor home and yelled. "Rachel's in trouble, get up. Get up." She shook Sarah awake, then bounded into the back bedroom and kicked at the queen bed that Theresa and Kat shared.

"I know you're hurting, Rachel." Michele pointed to her phone as each of the other women gathered around her sleepily. "You have to think now. Which hotel are you in?"

"I don't remember. It's the one with the big western hat on top. I don't remember the name."

"OK. That's good. That will help." Michele worked to keep the panic from her voice. "Now you stay on the line. Don't hang up. Do you hear me? Don't hang up. I'm going to bring the cavalry."

She could hear Rachel's sobbing get quieter.

"What's wrong, what's wrong?" Each of the women were asking in a dissonance of sounds as they bumped into each other and hunted for clothes.

"I don't know, exactly." Michele answered, her hand over the mike in the phone. "Rachel's in real trouble. She sounds hurt. She sounds scared."

Then Michele took control. "Theresa, call the police and tell them to meet us at the hotel with the big country-western hat. I don't know the name. Room 1099. Tell them to make sure the hotel manager has a key to the room."

"Sarah, call a cab and have them meet us at the park entrance. We can get there faster in a cab than we can maneuver Annabelle out of this spot and get on the road."

"Oh my God. Oh my God. Rachel. Poor Rachel." Kat was showing signs of hysteria.

Michele grabbed her by the shoulders. "Kat. She's going to be all right. You have to pull yourself together."

Kat nodded, her eyes wide and tears falling. Sarah used her own cell phone to call the cab company

"Hold on, Rachel," Michele said as she gathered everyone at the gate. "Don't let go. I see the cab now. Keep talking to me, okay?"

Michele kept talking in a calm voice as she listened to Rachel sob, then talking about stupid mistakes, then sob again. The cab finally arrived and they all piled in. Theresa gave a description of the hotel. The cabbie knew exactly which one it was. Michele talked to Rachel as they drove through town, and she talked to her as they rode the elevator to the tenth floor and walked down the hall.

She found the police at the door to the room, along with a hotel manager. She signaled them to knock. "Do you hear us at the door Rachel? We're here. We're finally here."

"I hear you." She heard the relief in Rachel's voice, then it rose in panic again. "Don't let them see me like this."

"Like what?"

"I don't have any clothes, I can't move. Oh, God, Oh God." Rachel started sobbing again.

Michele waited impatiently while the hotel manager opened the door with his master cardkey. She asked the police to please wait outside until she could at least get Rachel covered.

Reluctantly, the officers agreed but told her not to move anything, as it would disturb any evidence at the crime scene. The police stepped back from the door as Michele stepped inside with the rest of the band members edging through the door.

The smell hit her first. It smelled like a combination of whiskey, urine, and vomit. Michele's hand went immediately to her mouth, and she bit down on her knuckles so she wouldn't scream. She swallowed hard, determined not to lose her stomach. Tears streamed down her face.

Kat and Sarah gasped. Theresa grabbed Kat to her, turning her away from the sight. Sarah froze, her eyes wide.

Rachel was curled in a fetal position on a bed soaked in urine and alcohol. She rocked back and forth, crying softly. Scorched blankets and pillows lay in a heap in the corner. It looked like someone had tried to take a match to them. Black and blue splotches bloomed on Rachel's legs and arms, and what looked like razor cuts made a criss-cross grid on her thighs. Her hair had been shorn completely. Some sections were almost completely bald, while others were irregular patches of short matted white. Dried blood crusted on the bed behind her and broken glass was scattered on the floor.

Michele turned and looked at the women behind her. "Kat, I want you to go with your mother and tell the police we need an ambulance."

Kat nodded into her mother's chest. Theresa mouthed a thank you. Red-rimmed eyes turned away from the scene as she guided Kat from the room.

Sarah didn't speak. She covered Rachel with the blanket she'd brought, then sat on the edge of the bed holding Rachel's hand.

Michele sat at the head of the bed, her fingers caressing Rachel's shorn head in her lap. "It's all over now, Rachel," she said. "We're going to take care of you."

When the police entered, Rachel shivered and a keening cry rose from her throat as she curled tighter. Michele held up her hand to stop the police moving forward. Sarah shifted and leaned into Rachel blocking her view of the police.

The lead trooper nodded and silently pointed the others to check around the room. As officers moved to bag evidence, Michele's shoulders sagged and she closed her eyes. But the horror continued to build. It continued to choke her with every intake of air.

She wanted to scream until she couldn't breathe. She wanted to cry until she was blind. She wanted to run until her heart stopped. No one deserved this. No one!

Instead, all she could do was to wait, to listen for the ambulance, to pray the doctors could end the pain—for everyone. All she could do was to keep Rachel warm, to say words of comfort she knew would never be enough.

Rachel's cry was barely a whisper now.

"I'm here," Michele said again. "I'm here."

CHAPTER 14

The following three weeks were the hardest the band had ever faced. They cancelled the next thirteen bookings while they worked together to bring Rachel back to health. She'd only been in the hospital four days to take care of her physical problems, but it was the emotional trauma that really worried Michele.

The doctor said that Rachel was so torn up inside that it was doubtful she'd ever be able to conceive a child in the future. The gun had breached her cervix and gone into the uterus. She would be fighting the infection for a while, and he just didn't know if the repairs they had done were enough.

The worst part was that Rachel seemed to take the damage as her due. She kept saying she deserved it after all her running around, and no one in the band could convince her otherwise.

"It's not your fault, Rachel," Michele had said time and again. "No matter how much running around you did, you didn't deserve this. No one deserves this. It was rape. It was premeditated assault and he almost killed you."

But Rachel wouldn't listen. Michele knew, from her work with the crisis line in Portland, that for some women it took years to get past this kind of brutality and the self-blame. She knew she couldn't force Rachel to believe differently, but she wasn't going to agree to just let it go.

Rachel didn't cower from pressing charges though. She took her anger out by making sure the police knew it was Drake who had done this to her, and she described Flint to them as well. Unfortunately, no one had heard of a Flint and there was no country-western band named The Bandits. As for Drake, the police knew him well. With a long list of felony assaults they immediately put out an APB. But it seemed he'd left town in a hurry and the chance of finding him again soon was pretty slim.

Michele looked down the road and saw the sign for the intersection of Interstate 40. She looked over at Rachel, who was the navigator today, and smiled at the platinum blonde wig she was wearing. It framed her face nicely, and the color was a good match to Rachel's natural hair color.

"Which direction am I going?" she asked.

"East," Rachel chuckled. "You know girl, you are the worst with directions."

"Yup, but I'm the best with driving."

It was good to hear Rachel laugh again. The band hadn't been sure they should continue the tour. They'd all agreed they would be happy to take Rachel home and just take it easy for a few months. But Rachel had insisted she wanted to—she needed to finish the tour. She said she wasn't going to let Drake take her dream away from her and, besides, playing the fiddle was the only thing that could heal her now. She said if the band didn't want her to play she would join another band.

Michele looked in the side view mirror. Sure enough, the black minivan was still behind them. She grimaced.

"Are you and David OK?" Rachel asked, following Michele's eyes to the mirror.

"Yeah, we made up last night."

"I'm sorry to cause you so much trouble."

"Oh, Rachel, it wasn't you. It was me. I'm just so stubbornly independent that I can't see straight some times."

Rachel looked into the side mirror and nodded. "Well, I'm glad they're with us. Knowing Drake is still out there somewhere, having security makes me feel more secure."

Michele nodded. For once she was thankful that David was more stubborn than her. "Me too."

"You two really have something special, you know. I can see it whenever you're together. He worships you, Michele. That's a rare thing in a man."

Michele smiled. "I know. I have to admit, though, sometimes it's a little scary. I mean, I love him with all my heart; but I'm still amazed that he loves me."

"I'd give anything to have a man look at me the way he looks at you."

Michele reached over and placed a hand over Rachel's. "It will happen to you someday too. You're an amazing woman. You're strong. You're talented. You're passionate."

"Well, I don't know about passionate anymore." Rachel frowned. "I'm not sure I'll ever have sex again and enjoy it."

Michele's eyes misted. She'd heard similar things from other rape victims. "Just don't rush yourself. Take your time and only do what feels right to you. When the right man comes along, you'll know it. You'll be able to trust him and it will happen as it's supposed to."

"Like David did for you?" Rachel whispered, her voice filled with hope.

"Yeah, like David did for me."

DAVID HUNG up the phone after the seventh phone call. He had now successfully cancelled the entire next week of his appointments. He was going to Asheville as he and Michele had planned, but he was staying longer than the weekend they'd discussed. He just couldn't stand the thought of being away from her right now. In fact, if he thought he could swing it, he'd take the rest of the tour off work and spend it all with her.

He threw clothes into a suitcase, not even stopping to fold them. He wanted out of here and on that plane now. Every moment he couldn't see personally that Michele was safe burned in his gut. After their last disagreement, he wasn't taking any chances that she would tell him not to come.

When Michele had called David in tears after checking Rachel into the hospital, she'd told him everything that had happened. He'd been so afraid for her he was ready to cancel all his appointments and fly out immediately to protect her. They'd had a shouting match over the phone with Michele declaring they could take care of themselves, and him saying that was highly unlikely, and her hanging up on him. He called her back trying to get her to listen to reason and, when she stubbornly refused, he ended up getting angry and hanging up on her.

The next morning he was on the way to the airport when Michele called back to apologize. After a slightly less emotional argument, she agreed he could pay for 24 hour security—for Rachel's sake—and he agreed to stop taking over and making decisions for the band, even if his intentions were good.

David opened the drawer by the bed and drew out a small velvet box. He checked the contents to make sure it was still there. His grandmother's engagement and wedding rings, and his grandfather's ring as well. They were simple bands and the diamond on the engagement ring could hardly be seen, but the love they had held after more than sixty years of marriage was represented in these rings.

Just before his grandmother had died last year, she had given them to him. He had told her many times before that he was never getting married after seeing what it was like between his parents. But she wouldn't listen to him. She told him not all marriages were that way. His parents were just two selfish, self-absorbed people who never should have married in the first place—though if they hadn't she wouldn't have had the chance to know David.

David had to agree with her—especially at the end, given that his father had only visited once even when his own mother was on her deathbed. And his mother said there was no need for her to visit at all as they weren't married any more, completely ignoring the fact that Grandma had been an integral part of their lives for twenty-six years.

In the last two days, as he sat alone by her side in the hospital, his grandmother had shared what her own marriage was like. She had shared not only the romance but the passion she'd had with her husband—the man David remembered as Grandpa Hal—who had died two years earlier. He knew him as a man of quiet confidence, a man who was probably more of a father to him than his own dad. Thinking back, he could remember how they'd been together. Grandpa's hand was always on his Grandma somehow, on her shoulder, on her waist, on her hand. And her eyes, every time she looked at him held a love David didn't understand then. He did now—now that he had Michele in his life.

Grandma wasn't even afraid of dying, she'd said, because she knew her Hal was waiting for her and would guide her to wherever it was that souls really went. Then she'd asked him to hand her the little velvet box.

She'd put it in his hand and curled his fingers around it, and made him promise that when he found the right girl she would wear these rings. She knew they could bring him as much happiness as she and grandpa had.

At the time, David made his promise only because he loved her and he didn't want her to die knowing he could never find that kind of love—that his experience told him that kind of love didn't exist anymore. And after the funeral, he had stored it in a safety deposit box and practically forgotten about it. Until now.

He snapped the box closed and tucked it safely into his front pocket. It was far too valuable to check with luggage. Finally packed, he closed the suitcase and walked to the elevator. He secured the alarm for his home and stepped inside as the elevator doors opened.

Besides making sure Michele was safe and secure, he was going to get her to marry him on this trip. He wasn't willing to wait any longer while she tried to figure this out. He'd proven himself to her and she obviously loved him. He refused to take no for an answer. If she couldn't make up her mind when he got there, he'd just follow her from town to town until she did.

CHAPTER 15

"Could you turn the monitor down a little?" Michele asked into the mike. "And we need to move this speaker." She pointed behind her. "It's too close. All I'm getting is the vibration from my bass."

Rachel played a few bars on her fiddle, then sang a chorus into the voice mike. "The middle tones on the fiddle don't sound right," she said. "Voice is OK."

Michele listened out of one ear as they each went through the sound check with the engineer. They weren't playing until 8:00 tonight but, as there was a band before them, they had to get all the sound worked out this afternoon. There wouldn't be a lot of time for fine-tuning once they did the switch.

She plucked a few more notes on the bass and then took out her bow. She rarely bowed, as most of the songs just required her to set the tempo, plucking the undertones in the background. But tonight they were doing two pieces where she actually led the rest of the band in with a bass melody line. She listened to the monitor again and then stepped up to the mike. "That's good for me. Thanks."

"Is that Michele Scott?" she heard a familiar voice below the stage and looked down.

"Justin!" She laid her bass on its side and hurried down the stairs, throwing herself into a big hug. Then she stepped back and took a long look at him. "Justin, what are you doing in Asheville? How's Mary and the kids? What is it now, two or three babies?"

"There's three now. They're great," he answered, smiling wide. "Little Carrie is just two months old. Mike is in first grade now and he absolutely loves it. His favorite subject is reading. Can you imagine? Every night he wants to read to us. And Elizabeth is three. We are beginning to wonder if we should have given her a different name though. She's such a tomboy. She's out catching frogs, running bare-foot, and she has pretty much refused to wear a shirt all summer."

"You look really happy, Justin. I'm so glad. You and Mary are a perfect match."

His eyes twinkled and he smiled again. "Yeah. So, how about you, Michele? We wanted to make the shindig at your parent's place, but that was right about the time Mary was ready to pop and she didn't want to deliver in the middle of your party. We heard it was great though."

"It was a blast," Michele agreed. "Mom and Dad and all the neigh-bors went out of their way to welcome us, and can you believe we made over seven hundred dollars for the music program?"

"Yeah, I heard. Everyone was really surprised at the amount. I think the most they've ever raised before was about two hundred. I guess you really know how to pull in the money."

"I'm just so glad we were able to stop there. Maybe you'll catch us another time."

"Well, Mary's at the hotel getting gussied up. The kids are home staying with grandma and we're kind of having a little break just for ourselves. We were heading out tonight, but I saw the poster with the name Sweetwater Canyon on it and knew we had to come hear you play. Mary agreed we should stay. In fact, she said I better record the whole thing or everyone back home would shoot me when they found out."

He held up his cell phone. "I use this for meetings so I don't have to take notes. It's probably not equal to the sound you gals will be putting out, but at least everyone back home will hear it. Do you mind?"

"Of course not!" She gave him another hug. "I'm so glad you're here. Hey, I've got a couple hours before we have to get ready to go on. Why don't you go get Mary, then come back to the motor home, meet the rest of the gang and have a little supper?"

"That would be great, just show me where it is."

He offered her his arm and she took it as they picked up Mary and caught up on old times all the way back to the motor home.

DAVID CHECKED the hotel suite over one more time. Michele had done a nice job of finding something for the two of them. Nestled between the peaks of the Appalachian Mountains, Asheville was known for its summer music festivals and its romantic getaways. Now, he wanted to be sure everything would be romantic and soft tonight. It had been ten weeks since he'd seen Michele. Between his business, everything that had happened with Rachel, and his agreement that he wouldn't come flying to her rescue and take over her career, it had taken every bit of patience he had to wait until Asheville to see her.

Now that he was here, David was determined to never let her go. He was proposing tonight—and he wanted to make sure there was no way she could say no. When he'd arrived at the hotel he immediately upgraded to a suite. The room had floor to ceiling windows on two sides, both overlooking Asheville's skyline and the Blue Ridge Mountains. The bathroom was large and sported a deep, two-person Jacuzzi he intended for them to use to good advantage.

David called room service and ordered a setup of wine glasses, along with a bottle of Willamette Vineyard's pinot noir. He had been pleasantly surprised to find an Oregon wine on the list. He wanted to remind her of home. In their most recent phone conversations she had been sounding tired and a little homesick for Oregon scenery. He asked for the wine to be delivered at 9:00pm so it would be ready when they returned to the room. He expected they should be here no later than 10:00. He double-checked the mini-bar to confirm that the Brie was still there, just in case she was hungry when they arrived.

His gaze swept around the room one final time. He was finally satisfied. David patted his pocket to make sure the rings were still there. His heart pounding and his mouth dry, he wasn't sure how he was going to make it through the entire evening before popping the question.

SWEETWATER CANYON WATCHED from the wings, tapping their feet as the band ahead of them finished their set. Michele surreptitiously checked her watch. On time. Thank God, she thought. Tonight they might actually get to bed at a decent hour.

The MC thanked the band and announced a break, with a promise that the next band was going to be something really special. Then the chaos of one band packing up instruments while the other one gets on stage ensued.

They each smiled and chatted briefly with the other band as they unpacked their own instruments and began instructing the stage hands where to move mikes and chairs, and how to position the monitors. Though there was a half hour between bands, it never seemed like quite enough time.

Theresa reviewed the play list with everyone, double-checking that they all knew the order for tonight. "Any changes or additions?" Everyone shook their head.

"Hey is one of you named Michele?" a young man asked, standing at the backstage stairs.

"Yes, that's me." Michele walked toward him. "What's the problem?"

"No problem," he said and handed her a piece of paper. "Guy out front said to give this to you."

Michele took it. Her brow rose, puzzled. As she unfolded the paper she could hear the back door close behind the young man.

"What is it?" Rachel asked, a slight shakiness in her voice.

"Ohhhhhhhh." Michele hugged it to her. "David's here." Then she shouted it as if no one heard her. "David's here! He's out front!"

They all gathered around. "What did he say, what did he say?"

She clutched the paper to her. "It's personal, but let's just say he has a night of passion planned." She blushed.

They each gave her a hug, sharing in her happiness.

"This is it then," Rachel finally spoke. "You've been waiting for the right time to sing your song to him. This is it."

All eyes focused on Michele.

She looked from one to the other. Was she ready? Was she really ready? She'd been talking about it the past month. She and the girls had been making plans for a December wedding. But now that it was really time to let him know, was she ready?

She could feel them holding their breaths, waiting for her to confirm it. Finally she nodded. "Yes, this is the night."

"Whoopee!" Kat yelled. "We're having a wedding, we're having a wedding."

"We've got to change the order then," Theresa unfolded the play list again. "You were singing your song in the middle, but that was just for practice. You've got to do it at the end. It has to be the last thing he hears."

Michele was shaking with anticipation, her eyes misting as she realized it was really going to happen. "Yes," she said softly. "It should be the last one. Is that okay with everyone?"

"Of course," Rachel gave her a big hug. Then Sarah joined in too. Theresa and Kat filled out the circle.

"On in five minutes," the stage manager announced.

"Oh my God," Kat said. "This is it. Come on. Let's hit it." And they all scrambled to their places, big smiles and knowing glances exchanged as the curtain opened.

DAVID HAD SECURED a spot in the front row after paying a premium to get the seat. As the curtain opened, the band immediately started into a quick reel that got everyone tapping their feet. He tapped along with them, his body humming, but his eyes were fastened only on Michele. God, she looked good.

The band slowed the tempo to a ballad. Though they were singing in harmony he could always pick out her voice. The sounds coming from her throat were pure honey, and she moved with graceful confidence. She stood beside the bass and stroked it when she wasn't plucking, then placed her fingers expertly on the neck and joined the foundation at the right times.

No longer even aware of where he was, he sank into the chair and listened, mesmerized. Between numbers, each woman had a story to tell. When it was Michele's turn, he smiled. She laughed and chatted with the audience like they were old friends. She shared her story about growing up in Digby and how she thought she'd run away from old-time music only to find herself traipsing across the country in a motor home named Annabelle, losing directions, and then suddenly finding themselves in Asheville. The audience laughed appreciatively and the band launched into their next tune.

Every time she moved, every time she sang, David felt his heart reaching out, as if he could wrap a cocoon around this moment and hold it forever. As they worked through the list, he could feel his anticipation growing.

Finally, Rachel stepped to the mike and said. "We've had a great time here in Asheville. Your hospitality has been wonderful and I hope you'll ask us back." The audience clapped raucously with shouts of "We will."

Then Michele stepped to the mike and the lights dimmed, casting a golden glow with her in the center. Rachel started the melody on the fiddle, a slow ballad, and Theresa came in on the guitar with Sarah plucking her own guitar in counterpoint. "I have a special song to sing tonight," Michele began. Then she smiled flirtatiously. "It's for a special man in my life who was able to offer me the kind of love I never knew existed. This song is meant to answer a question he posed. A question I didn't think I could answer. But now I hope he'll understand."

The sudden silence in the audience was electrical, and David tensed as he leaned forward and could hear his own heart beating so loud he thought certain everyone around him could hear it too. Then she began with almost a wail—but not the kind of wail that hurts your ears. It was the kind of wail that wrests your heart from you, the kind that makes you feel broken along with the story. Her eyes were closed as she began to sing.

"I was in pain," her voice pulled the emotion forward. "I was in sorrow. I couldn't see my tomorrows."

No one in the audience moved. As the first two verses told the story of the broken woman who had given up on love, and had decided to go on without it, he could hear the sniffles around him. His own eyes misted as well.

She stopped singing for a moment and the band played behind her, then she opened her eyes and looked straight out and he could see their shimmering brightness in the enticing oval of her face. He felt like she was looking straight into his soul.

The second verse spoke of how the woman had put her trust in a stranger and how he had offered her a promise so great that she was afraid. How she wanted to run, afraid to open her heart, afraid to be hurt again.

David ached with need. He knew the song was about Michele, and he knew the song was meant for him. He wanted to go to her right now and draw her to him. He wanted to erase the pain that she had felt and to join his voice to hers and bring her strength.

Finally, she got to the third verse. She sang about trust, about believing in love again. She sang about reaching out and embracing her fear and her sorrow to become complete. Her hands reached out as if she were drawing him close to her. She sang about commitment and being together forever. And the last line went directly to his heart.

"And we will share all our tomorrows together. Because now I know, I will always love you, Forever."

The audience rushed to its feet when the music stopped. They were clapping and stomping and crying as Michele stood in the spotlight, a slight smile on her lips and all the love completely comprehensible in her eyes. The stage lights came up and the band took their bows as the audience shouted for an encore. The spectators clapped and shouted so forcefully that the band came back and did two more songs—both toe tapping dance tunes and an easy sing along that kept everyone on their feet.

David pushed through the crowd, trying to make his way to the stage. He knew what that song meant. She was saying yes to him. She'd made up her mind. She'd finally realized how much he loved her. She'd finally realized they were meant to be together. He ran up the stairs and sneaked behind the curtains. A man immediately stopped him.

"Sorry, band only."

"Kurt?" David asked. He thought he recognized one of the guys from the security firm he'd hired.

"Yeah, who are you."

"David. David Blackstone. I hired you guys."

He saw the memory return to Kurt's face. He held out is hand and shook. "Sorry, now I remember. It's been a long day. Lot's of people to watch. I didn't know you were coming, David."

"Where's Michele? I have to see Michele."

Kurt looked around the stage. He could see everyone else moving instruments, packing up, but not Michele.

"I think I saw her go outside." He pointed to the far corner of the stage. "Take the backstage door and you might catch her."

"Thanks." He ran toward the door. He couldn't wait to get her into his arms.

Through the glass window in the door, he saw the back of her head, her long hair flowing freely down her back. Then he stopped short. A man bent down and brushed her lips. It was a quick kiss, but it was still a kiss. Then she embraced him and held tight.

David could feel the jealousy raise its ugly head. He grabbed onto the door, ready to bang it open then stopped short.

Wait a minute. Don't go off half-cocked. Wait and listen. He took a deep breath and slowly turned the knob.

"God, that was an amazing, Michele. I felt like you were singing it to me. Reminded me of old times."

Michele hugged him tight. "Oh Justin. I'm so happy right now. I can hardly talk. I just want to tell everyone about our love."

He held her against him. "I know just how you feel. You have to come home and see the kids. You have to come home and let everyone know."

"You're right," she answered. "I will. As soon as the tour's over I'll make a date. Thanks so much for coming, Justin. You've made my day." She rose on her toes to give him a quick peck goodbye and she heard the door behind her slam open so hard the glass shattered and spilled to the floor.

"The fuck you will!" David shouted as he stood towering behind her.

"David!" Michele looked up ready to introduce him, but then she saw the fury in his eyes, his fists pumping at his sides.

"So this is who you were singing to. I stupidly thought it was me. How long have you two been seeing each other? How long have you been jumping from my bed to his?"

"David, it's not what you think. This is Justin. You know Justin, from home."

"Yes, I know all about Justin…the guy you fell in love with in High School. Your brother told me all about him."

"Ah," Justin put out his hand toward David trying to make peace. "Really, David. We were just talking about you."

"I'll bet you were. Did she tell you how you were the only one who could make her feel this way? Did she tell you that you were the only one who could make her come? Did she tell you that she loved you in the heat of passion?"

"David," Justin tried again. "I think you need to calm down, man. You're saying things you'll regret later."

"I. Am. calm," David said through clenched teeth, his hands fisted close to his side. "I'm calm because I'm not killing you right now, which is what I want to do." Then he looked directly at Michele. "I believed all your lines. I believed all your stories. I believed that you meant what you said. That you loved me."

"I do. Oh, David I do." Tears were streaming down her face. She'd never seen him so angry. She'd never seen him so broken and hurt. She didn't know what else to say. What to do.

He refused to look at her. He pulled out his wallet and turned to Justin. "I don't want her anymore. You can have her. I hope you don't mind that I used her for a few weeks."

David slowly counted out ten one hundred dollar bills and threw them on the ground in front of Michele. When he looked up at her, his nostrils flared and he threw his shoulders back. "You were right. It's just sex. But it was good sex. I think you're worth more than twenty dollars now. I guess it's cheaper this way. No commitments. No regrets." Then he walked past both of them and headed down the alley, his legs eating up the asphalt.

Michele stooped to the ground and began to sob as Mary came around the corner.

"Sorry, guys I had to go to the bathroom. I …" She stopped, seeing Michele crumbled next to a bunch of money. "What's wrong? Justin, what's wrong?"

Justin pulled Michele up and drew her into his embrace. Deep, heaving sobs issued from her chest. He stroked her hair.

"It was David," he told Mary. "He found us hugging and saying goodbye and he misunderstood."

"Oh no. I'll go after him. I'll make him understand." Mary started down the alley.

"No," Michele raised her voice between sobs. "No. This was exactly what I feared. I saw this jealousy once before while on tour. But when I didn't see it again, I thought he trusted me. I thought he was different." Her voice shook and she swallowed hard to rein in control. "His jealousy reminds me of Jon. I can't live with that again. I won't. I'm glad I found out now, before…before we were married. Really…I'm… glad." Then she dissolved into tears again, her shoulders shaking.

Mary bent to the ground and gathered up the bills as Justin held their friend and let her cry it out.

CHAPTER 16

*T*heresa drove with Kat in the jump seat as the band headed out of North Carolina into Tennessee. Even the slow curves of the highway and the beautiful trees of the Great Smoky Mountains didn't soothe the band's mood. They had played gigs in Gatlinburg and Newport before heading to Knoxville. Michele had performed technically well, but everyone could tell her heart wasn't in it. They missed her optimism, her excitement to get from one gig to another. They now realized how much everyone had come to depend on Michele to keep them positive, to always be the one to overcome the drudgery of the road.

Kat turned in the cab. "Is she still in the back?"

Sarah nodded and rolled her eyes. "I think she's deleting all his emails from her computer."

"Oh no!" Kat stood. "Someone's got to stop her. This just won't do."

"Well, maybe she's better off without him," Rachel opined. "That was a shitty thing he did in Asheville. Doling out a thousand bucks. He had to know that would hurt."

Sarah's eyes looked down. "Yeah, that surprised me. I just didn't think he was the type to stoop that low—even if he was hurt and angry."

"What about a thousand bucks?" Kat asked, eyes wide.

"Nothing." Both Sarah and Rachel retorted.

"God, no one ever tells me anything."

"You've seen too much as it is, kiddo." Rachel smiled. "You saw me really screwed up and now you see what can happen if you love someone so much that your heart really does break."

"But it can't be over," Kat drew out the word dramatically. "They still love each other. It was just a misunderstanding. They can make up. They've made up before. We have a wedding in December."

"I don't think they'll make up very quickly from this one, honey." Sarah said, her voice quiet. "The wedding is definitely off—at least for now."

"Well, I don't believe it." Kat crossed her arms and flounced back into the seat. "They're just being stupid and I'm going to make sure they grow up." Then she turned back to the front to watch the road with her mother.

"I feel so bad," Rachel said. "I've never seen two people more in love. Even though I was heartbroken after Kavan left, it wasn't like this. I've never loved someone so openly and completely like Michele did. And when I saw what she and David had, I was so jealous. God, I was so rotten to her for so long."

Sarah reached over and patted her hand. "But you stopped, and that's what matters. Now it's time for you to be there for her."

"Yeah, I know." Rachel closed her eyes and took a deep breath. "The trouble is I don't know how to make the hurt go away. I didn't know what to do after Kavan. I didn't know what to do after Drake. And I still don't know. I'm getting better, but I still don't know how to make the hurt go away. Oh God, I don't want her to hurt anymore. I don't want any of us to hurt anymore."

"All we can do is be here for her. Just give her some time. She'll work through it. Deep wounds take time to heal."

"Yeah, I guess that's all we can do."

David walked naked into the kitchen. He reached into the cupboard and pulled out a bottle of Jack Daniels. He set it on the counter and stared at it. He broke the seal, tipped it back and took two long swallows, letting the burn work its way down his throat. He hoped it would burn away the misery in his heart. It didn't work. Ah hell, it had been worth a shot.

He'd already learned that drinking didn't make things better when he was younger. How old was he then? Twenty-five? Twenty-six? He wasn't sure. He just remembered getting shit-faced and passing out. The next day not only did he still feel like crap, but he was sick on top of it. He put the cap back on, twisted it tight and put it back in the cupboard.

He rummaged for the coffee beans, ran the grinder and then set up the coffee pot. He had to get back to work. He couldn't wallow for the rest of his life. He watched the coffee slowly fill the pot. Drip. Drip. Drip.

He walked away and went into the bathroom to take a piss. He couldn't remember what day it was. The only reason he knew it was day instead of night was because light drenched his loft.

As he washed his hands in the sink he saw his reflection in the mirror and groaned. How long had it been? Three days? Four? He practically had a full beard and his teeth looked yellow. He immediately brushed them until he could feel the enamel with his tongue again. There. Better. Now he wasn't a total slob.

After getting a full mug of coffee down, he was able to function— at least a little. He glanced toward the phone and saw his message light flashing. Was it possible she had called?

He checked the number. Same one each time, but from a number he didn't recognize. It was probably a new client. He hit play and turned up the volume as he headed back to the bathroom to shave. He might as well get back to work. There wasn't anything else for him to do.

"David, this is Mary. I'm Justin's wife. I was at the concert with Justin but had to step away for a moment. Justin and I have been best friends with Michele forever. Look, I know you were angry and you just misunderstood. Michele's really hurting and you have to make up with her. I can't stand to see her this way. I know you two really love each other. Please. Please find a way to apologize."

David groaned, burying his face in his hands. He'd really blown it this time.

He finally found the right woman for him and what did he do? He practically called her a whore to her face. Well, he didn't say it. But he knew actions really did speak louder than words. And he knew how much it would hurt when he did it too. He knew her past better than anyone, and he did it anyway. He wanted to hurt her and he did a great job. Even when he heard her sobbing and crying out his name, he kept walking.

Shit! What had he been thinking?

"That's the problem, you dumb fuck. You weren't thinking!" he said aloud. He grabbed a washcloth and rubbed at his face, hard. Then he lathered the shaving cream and picked up the razor, making careful long strokes first along his neck and jaw line, then along his cheeks as the same message played again two more times. Mary had wanted to be sure he got it.

It took about half an hour, and three nicks before he was clean-shaven again. Feeling a little more human, he stepped in the shower and turned the water on as hot as he could stand it.

David stood for a long time, his hands flat against the wall as the shower pounded heat into his back. He started to tremble and his breathing became rapid. He slowly lowered to the floor and let the tears fall.

Control, David thought. All these years he'd thought he had such control over himself, his emotions, over people. Then Michele walked into his life and his control went out the window. All because of some twisted sense of jealousy over a guy she dated in high school. God, he hadn't even given her a chance. She tried to tell him he was wrong, but he didn't listen—couldn't listen. All he could see was his parents and their strings of lovers. He picture Michele in Justin's arms, then Michele in Justin's bed, then Michele with Justin's child. And he snapped.

He turned his face up to the spray and levered himself back to standing. He felt like an old man, his body was so sore. He picked up a bar of soap and started lathering his shoulders and his arms.

Well, what are you going to do about it? Are you going to let her walk completely out of your life? What kind of commitment is that? He moved onto his chest and his back. Fine specimen of a man he was. First sign of trouble and he slinked into his cave and shut out the world.

His grandparents taught him better than this. He was going after her and he wasn't going to stop until they resolved this one way or another.

He moved more quickly to the rest of his body, scrubbing harder as he worked out the grime and pain. He hummed the final chorus of her acceptance song, and groaned. The pain was so deep his chest constricted, as if he could shut it down with his muscles. Then he took a deep breath and consciously relaxed. That damn song was written for me and I'm going back to claim it!

MICHELE LOOKED up from her book as she heard her cell phone ring. She glanced at the number, but didn't pick it up. She knew who it was. This was the fifth time today and he'd been calling for three days straight.

"Aren't you going to answer that?" Rachel asked.

Michele shook her head. She couldn't talk to him. She knew if she did, she'd probably forgive him and go running back. Oh God, how she missed him.

"Don't you think its time you two talked it out?"

"What's there to talk about?" Michele asked her chin in the air. "He just wasn't the man I thought he was."

"What do you mean by that?"

"He never really loved me."

"Come on, Michele, you know that's not true."

"Yes it is. No one who really loved me could have done that," she whispered. Then getting stronger, she added, "No one who really loved me would believe I'd cheat on him. No one who really loved me would walk away without waiting for an explanation."

"Don't you think you're being a little hard on him?"

"Hard on him? What should I do? Thank him for paying me off as his whore?"

Rachel winced.

Sarah raised her voice from the cab, her eyes still on the road. "You guys okay back there?"

"Were fine," Rachel answered. "Michele's just venting."

"Oh. Go ahead and vent Michele, it's about time you did."

Theresa was in the jump seat this time. She turned around to face them.

"Look, I know you think it's none of our business, but we all love you. We just want you to be happy. You need to at least give him a chance to apologize."

"And then what?" Michele challenged. "Go running back? Fall under his spell? Wait to get my heart broken again the next time he gets jealous? I can't take that. I can't live like that."

"I don't think he's going to do that again," Rachel said. "I think he's learned his lesson."

"How can you be sure? What about the next time someone approaches me after a gig and is flirting? Is he going to deck the guy instead of getting mad at me? What if I hug an old friend again, this time someone he doesn't know from my past? Will he trust me then? Will he listen? I'm in a band for God's sake. We see guys all the time. People flirt with us all the time and we have to be nice to them. It's part of the job. I can't be tied to someone who is going to worry every time I smile at another guy."

"I don't think it's like that," Rachel said. "I think this was a one-time deal. God, Michele, you'd just sung the most beautiful song you've ever written and you sang it to him and he knew it. He was coming backstage with stars in his eyes. He was coming back to gather you in his arms and take you off on his bright shiny white horse to his castle in the sky."

"Now you're really exaggerating."

"I know, but that's how he was feeling. I saw it in his eyes."

"Are you sure?" she asked, daring to hope. No! She wouldn't hope. She wouldn't listen. She couldn't.

"I'm positive. Believe me I know when a guy is just looking with lust and when it's something else. I've been waiting for that something else for years. His eyes were filled love and passion—all of it for you. They are so intertwined in his mind, he sees them completely together."

"That still doesn't make it okay."

"Your right, it doesn't. But it does explain how he easily misunderstood. Michele, he was running on pure hormones and emotion mixed together in about as volatile a combination as any guy could have. When he saw you with your arms around Justin, he just didn't think."

"You got that right."

"He probably went directly from his head with you in his bed to you being in Justin's bed. Without knowing it he transferred the feeling."

"Transferred? Jeez, are you sure you've never had any therapy? You're beginning to sound like a shrink."

Rachel chuckled. "Well, maybe I've been reading a few books. And they've kind of helped me, so I figure what the hell, maybe it will help you."

"I doubt it. I don't think there's anything in those books about complete assholes."

"Oh, I don't know," Rachel laughed again. "I think that's all these books are about—about screwed up people like you, and me, and David."

They sat in silence for a while. Then Michele's lower lip started to tremble. She clamped down on it hard.

"Anyway, you not answering his calls isn't going to help either one of you."

"I want him to hurt." Michele swallowed. She swore she wasn't going to cry another tear over him. She'd already cried far too many. "I want him to hurt as bad as I'm hurting."

Rachel reached her arms around her, pulling her head to her chest and rocked her back and forth as Michele cried softly, again. "I know, honey. I know."

~

KAT QUIETLY CLOSED the bedroom door. She had heard the whole thing and her own heart was breaking in two. She'd been counting on Michele getting over this. She'd been counting on this wedding. She just had to make it work. It seemed that no one around her could find happiness. This was the worst tour they'd ever had. First Rachel. Now Michele. And if something good didn't happen they would end the year on an awful note and that meant that the New Year would have an even more difficult time getting off to a good start.

She wasn't going to let that happen. Michele just had to get married. If Michele and David got married that would prove that love really does win in the end. Then Rachel would be able to see how a good man really could make your past hurt less, and that means she would be able to find someone to love her too. And then there was Sarah and Mom. God, Mom hadn't been happy ever since Dad left six years ago. And Mom just had to be happy, because there was no way Kat could ever leave home if she didn't find someone for Mom.

She just couldn't take all this angst. Yeah, that was a good word— angst. She'd just read that the other day in one of her books. Which one was that? Oh yeah, Sloppy Firsts. Now that girl knew how to take control. And Kat was just going to have to take control of this situation, too. Everything depended on Michele. If Michele and David couldn't work it out, Kat's life was going to end. That was just that.

She lifted her Mom's cell off the night table next to the bed and called up the menu. She punched OK for received call log. She knew David had called everyone else in the band too—except for Kat—and each one had said he'd have to work it out with Michele. She found his number then pushed Call, and held the phone to her ear.

One ring. Two rings. Three rings. "Come on, pick up. Pickup! Please."

Four rings.

"Hello?"

"Thank God. David?"

"Yeah, who is this?"

"It's Kat."

"Kat!" David grabbed the phone tight to his ear. "Is something wrong? Is Michele okay?"

"Yes, something's wrong, you dolt. And no she's not okay."

"Well, what is it? Is she hurt? Oh God, did Drake come back. Tell me. Tell me so I can help."

"No, it's not that. Not physical pain. It's worse, much worse."

David took a deep calming breath. He would do anything for Michele.

"What is it Kat?"

"It's you, you idiot!"

"I know," he swallowed and clamped down hard on his emotions. "I know I hurt her. I'd do anything to take it all back…to erase what happened. But I can't. And I can't go forward because she won't talk to me."

"Well I'm talking to you now and I'm all you got. Now we have to have a plan."

"I don't know Kat. I don't think you should get in the middle of this."

"Well, I am in the middle of this, and I'm the only one in this whole damn motorhome who can think straight. So, if you still love her you have to talk to me."

David paused. He didn't know what to do. What would Kat know about love and mature relationships? She was only fifteen and full of teenage hormones.

"Well, do you still love her? Do you?"

"I love her more than anything."

"Well? Do we have a deal?"

David didn't know if Kat could help, but he did know that no one else was willing to do anything. Hell, he'd agree to almost anything if it meant he could see Michele again.

"Yeah, we have a deal."

CHAPTER 17

*M*ichele looked at her cell phone before answering. It was her parent's number. She immediately pushed the talk button.

"Hello."

"Hi Honey. How are you?" Michele smiled at her mother's voice. It was always so warm and loving.

"I'm fine, considering."

"Well, it's that considering I want you to do."

"What do you mean?"

"Now, don't get mad at me."

"Mad? I'd never get mad at you, Mom."

"Well, you might after this, but I had to do it. I had to help my little girl be happy again."

"What do you mean? What are you talking about?"

"I just want you to listen. Promise you won't hang up."

"Hang up? I'd never hang up on you."

"Just promise."

"Okay. I promise."

"Just a minute." She heard her mother hand the phone off saying, "Now you talk to her."

"Michele? Don't hang up now. You promised your mother." She bit back an oath. She couldn't believe it. Her own mother was against her. Somehow David had gotten to her parents and forced them to let him make this call.

"I won't," she finally said. "I keep my promises, unlike some people."

"I guess I deserved that."

The silence hung in the air. She wasn't going to make it easy for him. She was already beyond her tolerance level by just agreeing to even listen.

"I need to see you. We need to talk."

"No," she said with finality.

"Then listen."

"I don't seem to have a choice, do I?"

"I was wrong. I misunderstood. Everything I did is unforgiveable. I know I hurt you and I'll do anything to make up for it."

He waited a long time and she said nothing. "Michele?"

"Yes?"

"Well?"

"Well what?"

"Can we try again?"

"No. I don't want to be with someone who can't trust me." He'd gotten her started now. "Do you think that just by saying your sorry I should take you back? You knew what you were doing. You knew how throwing that money at me would hurt? You're right, it is unforgiveable. I don't forgive you. I'll never forgive you!"

She struggled with the catch in her voice. She held the phone away from her, so he couldn't hear the sob escaping from her.

"Look, I have to go."

"Michele, I love you!"

"Don't you dare throw those words at me. You don't know what love is. You don't know what it means to truly open yourself completely and let someone in."

"You're wrong, Michele. I do know. I haven't been able to eat, to sleep, to work since I left you in Asheville. Even before I knew the truth, I wanted you back. Michele, I know you love me. You wouldn't hurt so much if you didn't love me."

"Yes, I love you, goddammit!" The sob escaped her and she couldn't get it back. She took several deep breaths before she could speak again.

"But that doesn't mean I have to take you back," she said quietly. "I can't, David. I can't go through it again. I can't open myself again. It's too hard. It hurts too much."

"Can you accept my apology? Can you at least do that?"

Michele searched her heart. She wanted to be able to put him behind her. She wanted to say goodbye, but not with anger—not with so much pain.

"All right. I accept your apology. But that doesn't mean I forgive you."

"I can live with that. For now."

She could hear his breathing was faster than normal. As she waited, it slowed.

"Thank you."

She didn't know how to end it. She didn't know how to say good-bye. She waited.

"If I call again will you answer the phone?"

"I don't know."

"I want a chance to work this out. A chance to see what's still there for us."

"David, there is no us anymore."

"I can't accept that. Yet."

She sighed. Would he always push her? Would she always let him? No. She would not let anyone control her every again.

"Will you at least agree to talk to me?"

"I don't know, David. I don't think it will matter."

"Just three times. That's all I ask. Will you agree to just three more times? If we aren't any closer to a resolution then I promise to leave you alone."

Could she do that? Could she allow herself to even listen to him? She knew she had to. She knew it was the only way to get over him.

"Okay. Three more times. But that's it, David. We're not getting back together. You might as well accept it. I have." Then she hung up.

MICHELE ZIPPED her bass back into the padded case and lugged it toward Annabelle. Once she got there, she helped Sarah first load boxes of promotional material into the storage underneath. Then, carefully, Michele slid the bass into the corner and strapped it down to keep it from shifting too much during the long trip the next day.

This past month they had done performances in Illinois, Indiana, Ohio, and Kentucky. Now they were heading back to Tennessee. It was the first week of October and they had a show in Murfreesboro, then a week with nothing until the next one outside of Nashville. It would have been better if these gigs had been scheduled when they were in Tennessee the first time, but that's just not how the calendar had worked out.

Much of their schedule was determined by summer and fall blue-grass and folk festival calendars, where bands were promoted as headliners or openers and paid accordingly. As this was Sweetwater Canyon's first big tour, it was important they play as many of those as they could schedule because that was where their primary fan base could be found.

They'd paid a festival booking agent, in the Midwest and South, a good portion of their fees to get a shot at most of the festivals this year. The rest of the schedule was on Theresa's shoulders. She sent out promo packs, music samples, and anything else she could find to convince people they should pay for Sweetwater Canyon to come to their location. It was a big job, but Theresa seemed to enjoy it most of the time. The rest of the band did help with assembling materials, and Kat had been a big help with getting the website put up through a kid she knew from her high school who loved computers.

Theresa stuck her head out the door of the motor home. Michele could see that she was tired. Her shoulders were bent forward and she held her head up like it weighed twice as much as usual. "We about ready to move?"

Michele looked at Sarah who nodded. "Yeah, just another minute. I'll make one last check." Michele went back one more time and scanned the stage area. The table to the right, where they had signed pictures and collected email addresses for fan marketing, was clear. She took a final look around the grounds. She didn't see anything they'd forgotten.

Then she saw something out of the corner of her eye, she snapped her head around and held her breath as she scanned slowly, her hands stiff beside her as she reviewed every Karate class she'd ever taken.

"Just me. Kurt." He stepped out of the shadows and waved.

She let her breath out with a whoosh. "Oh, Hi Kurt. You kind of scared me."

It seemed so long ago now that David had provided security for them. What was it now, two months since Rachel's problems with Drake? As the months wore on, one day started feel like the next and most of the time she just didn't notice Kurt following them anymore. She had to admit, in spite of her breakup with David, at least he still cared enough about their safety to continue to pay for Kurt.

"You shouldn't be walking around at night alone, ya know."

Michele let out a big sigh. "You're right."

She would give anything to return to those early days when all of them felt more innocent and free at their gigs. They'd been careful, but nothing like they were now. Now, Michele thought twice about the intentions of each guy who approached the table for an autograph, each one who flirted with her. She wasn't as easy in her patter with them, and she didn't feel as smooth with guiding the occasional drunk away from the table toward a show manager or park security.

Then there was poor Rachel. Sometimes she held up really well, talking and flirting almost like her old self. Other times, within five minutes she would whisper to Michele she had to leave and then she hightailed it back to Annabelle and holed up in the back bedroom, shaking. No one, including Rachel, was able to determine what would set her off.

Michele looked back toward Kurt once more. "Thanks for being here. Good night now." She walked back to the motor home knowing Kurt was following her and watching, and she felt a little more secure for tonight.

~

WHEN SHE NOTICED THE NUMBER, Michele stepped out of the motor home and walked toward the oak tree about ten feet away before answering. In the last two phone calls, she and David had come to a kind of truce. She'd begun to forgive him and she agreed that maybe they could be friends again. But she was still determined not to let him back into her heart. She couldn't be broken like that again.

On the fourth ring she finally answered.

"I want to see you," David started off without even a Hello.

"You're over 2,000 miles away," she said. "It's ridiculous for you to fly out here just to talk. We can talk just fine on the phone."

"Actually, I'm not that far away. I'm just outside Indianapolis. I can meet you at your next stop in Bowling Green. Just one night, Michele. That's all I ask."

Michele held her breath. He was too close. God no. She wasn't prepared for that. She wasn't prepared to actually face him. She had to put him off.

"What do you want from me, David? Seeing me face-to-face won't make a difference in how I feel."

"I think it will," he said softly.

She paused. The truth was she didn't want to have to face him. She wasn't sure if she could hold out against him if she actually saw him— saw his eyes pleading with her, professing his love.

"We'll work out a way to get together when we're back in Oregon," she finally said.

David wasn't willing to wait that long. He knew that the longer she could put off seeing him the more entrenched she would become.

"Please, Michele. I want to see you." What the hell had he been thinking? That he could just fly out and she would change her mind? Well, he had to try didn't he? "I'll come pick you up. We can talk."

"I don't want to be with you," she said flatly. "I want to be where it's safe. Where I can breathe."

"You can be safe with—"

She hung up.

He flung the phone away from him before he could beat it into small bits of plastic. Michele was driving him nuts. How the hell was he supposed to keep up with her? No matter what he tried, she kept sliding out of his reach before he had a real chance to grab hold. Now he was supposed to go chasing after her? Demand that she step to his tune for once?

Disgusted, he kicked back in the chair, stared at the ceiling. No, she didn't work that way. Michele had her own syncopation, her own timing to life. And the more he tried to control her, the less likely their music could work together. She knew how to write complex melodies, she just didn't want to live them.

There were details he needed to work out, more data he needed to accumulate, and some financial dealings he needed to put in place. He retrieved the phone and set it next to his laptop. He'd find a way to mesh their disparate melodies into an opus.

"It's pretty tight," Theresa said, her head next to Sarah as they huddled over a computer screen, trying to figure out the money situation.

"Sure is," Sarah agreed. "I can't believe those guys in Louisville stiffed us."

"We don't know if they stiffed us yet," Theresa corrected. "They said they'd put the check in the mail to us a month ago. You know we haven't been home to pick it up."

"Get real. They stiffed us. The contract said they were to have the check for us directly after the performance. There's no check in the mail and you know it."

"I don't know it. I hope they are telling the truth."

"What do you think Michele?" Sarah tossed the question forward.

"Yeah, I think they stiffed us," Michele said as she turned onto the Interstate once again. "You could tell by how that guy kept shuffling his feet and couldn't look us in the eye. I bet the next time we get an Internet connection and check the 'who to watch out for' listings you'll find some other bands have been stiffed too."

"Can't you get anyone else to commit between Murfreesboro and Nashville?" Sarah asked, turning back to Theresa and the computer screen.

"I've had more than six places on the hook, but no one will bite. I guess it's just getting too close to the holidays already and everyone's winding done their fall entertainment and planning for their Christmas concerts."

"What do we have after Nashville then?"

"Nothing until Tucson at the end of the month, unless we get some bites between now and then."

"I don't think we can make it on the money we have left," Sarah said. "We've been using our earnings from the first part of the tour to keep us in camping fees and food." Sarah looked around to make sure Rachel was still in the back bedroom; then she lowered her voice. "Also, the bills for Rachel really added up. I think all of us have tapped out our credit cards now."

"Yeah, that's the problem with no medical insurance," Theresa agreed matching the whisper as she worried at her bottom lip.

"Maybe we should cancel Tucson, and just head straight home after Memphis."

"I don't know about that," Theresa said. "We have a solid contract with them. They were one of the first people to book before we started our tour. We can't afford to get a reputation as a band that cancels contracts."

"Yeah, but I don't know if we can afford to live on the road for two weeks without a gig."

"I've got a thousand dollars," Michele offered, raising her voice above the sound of the engine.

Rachel and Theresa looked at each other and said nothing.

"It's blood money anyway," Michele continued when she didn't hear a question.

"I thought you sent that back to him," Rachel said quietly.

"I was planning on it, but it's cash and I just haven't had the time to get to the bank and convert it to a check." She paused. "I'll just think of it as a loan."

"I don't know, Michele." Theresa checked the numbers again. "Are you sure? We don't want to put you in a bad position with David."

Michele chuckled wryly. "It can't be much worse than it is now."

"I thought you guys were talking. I thought you were starting to make up," Theresa said.

"We are talking, sort of. I've accepted his apology, but … we have not made up. I'm not letting him back in to my life … at least not like before… not into my heart. Just think of it as my rainy day fund. It sure seems to me like its raining now."

Kat took the head phones off her ears and sat forward as she peered out the windows. "It's not raining."

"We're talking about money, Kat," her mother chided. "Not the weather. Go back to your music."

"Oh, you're talking about something important now and you don't need my opinion is that it?"

"No, that's not it. We'd love your opinion, Kat," Theresa said, sarcastic.

"Well, what do you need to know and I'll tell you the answer," Kat lifted her chin in a haughty tilt.

"We don't have enough bookings and we need to make more money. Any suggestions?" Sarah stepped in, her voice light, trying to keep Theresa and Kat from getting into their usual heated battle.

"Hmmm." Kat tapped at her lips as if the answer was there. "Have you tried calling Billy?"

"Yes," Theresa said, as if it were obvious she would think of that first. "He said he's done the best he could to get us around the

Midwest. You know he's not our permanent booking agent. He just helped us out, so we could get back to Branson and Asheville."

"Yes, I know that!" Kat raised her voice. "I'm not stupid, you know."

"No Kat, you're not stupid. You just don't always think before you butt into things." Theresa said.

"If you're talking about David, then you have another thing coming. None of you care about what's happening to Michele. None of you care about how the whole band is falling part. And you haven't helped anything, Mom. All you've done is make my life miserable. You…"

Michele tuned them out. Everyone was getting snippy, and Kat and her mother had a way of really getting on each other's nerves that drove everyone bonkers. Theresa could push all of Kat's buttons, and Kat knew how to push right back. Sarah and Rachel had told Michele early on in the tour that sometimes you had to just let them yell at each other and get it out of their system, and then things would eventually work back to normal.

Kat had been a part of the latest debacle with David too. He started first showing up to their gigs in Indiana. And, even though Michele refused to speak to him in person, he kept following them from place to place, always seeming to find a way to run into Michele.

Eventually Michele figured out that Kat kept contriving ways to get them alone together. Once she'd even locked them in a storeroom with some comment about "It worked in Parent Trap, so it can work here too." After an hour of David talking quietly and Michele yelling at Kat to open the door because she wasn't going to listen to anything David had to say, Kat finally let them out.

After that incident, Michele cornered Kat and wouldn't let her go until she got the full story. Kat had devised this plan over the phone with David—for him to follow her until she gave in. Michele couldn't believe David would even try it. It was so childish.

In the storeroom he'd told her he'd do anything to get her back. Michele remembered yelling at him, "Well, this is not the best strategy!"

"Then what is the best strategy?" he'd asked.

She didn't know what to say. The truth was she was putting up all her defenses to make sure there wasn't any strategy that would work to get her back.

Finally, after four nights and about 2,000 miles of David following them, she was tired of fighting—tired of dodging him. So she came up with the only answer she knew would make him go away. "Time, David. I need time."

Finally, he gave up and went home. Michele made Kat vow never to butt into what was between her and David again.

"Well, fine. You just figure it out without me then," Kat shouted and snapped her head back toward the front of the motor home and put the earphones back on. Then she exaggerated the tapping of her foot against the dashboard to make sure everyone knew she wasn't listening to them.

Michele smiled to herself. She could still remember being a teenager and how difficult that was. Of course, her experience had been completely different. She always had plenty of room to run and lots of work to do on the ranch. She had two parents who loved her dearly, always protected her, and was supportive of all the choices she'd made in her life—even the bad ones.

They'd been good at letting her make her own mistakes and learning from them; and they also freely and easily offered a shoulder to cry on anytime she needed it. But she did remember how every decision was life or death at age fifteen; and how, in spite of how much her parents cared and offered support, she had also thought they were really stupid and just didn't understand what it was like to be a teen in today's world. It wasn't until she was about twenty or twenty-one that she finally decided her parents were pretty smart after all.

She looked over at Kat again and noticed her foot wasn't tapping against the dashboard quite as hard now. But she was definitely still pouting.

"So, how bad is it?" Michele asked Theresa, now that Kat truly wasn't listening any longer.

"Were going to be broke before we get to Nashville," Theresa answered. "Your thousand dollars will make sure we don't starve, but if anything goes wrong with any of us...or with Annabelle here..." Theresa knocked on the table in front of her as if it would forestall any bad luck with the motor home. "We're sunk."

"That's the way it looks to me too," Sarah confirmed.

CHAPTER 18

David wished he could turn back the clock. He'd been wishing for a month now that he could go back to the way things had been before Asheville, but he knew that wasn't going to happen. Now he just wished he hadn't let Kat talk him into trying to confront Michele after a show, or that he hadn't followed her from town to town for four days like a lost puppy. It seemed he just couldn't do anything right with her. He'd handled the whole matter badly. Even when he'd tried to apologize he didn't do it right.

After an hour of trying to talk to her in that storeroom, trying to admit what an asshole he'd been, he'd reached out for her. At a loss for the right words to say, he thought if he could just kiss her she would know what he was feeling, how much he loved her, and maybe…just maybe…she would remember how much she'd love him.

Instead, as he put his arm around her waist to draw her close she'd stiffened straight as a board, unmoving. Her eyes had flashed in anger. Then she'd pulled his head toward her and whispered in his ear. "Do you have a thousand dollars? That's all I'm worth you know."

He'd dropped his arms immediately. The truth was she was priceless to him, but he could see telling her that would get him nowhere.

"Thought not," she answered. "All tapped out today are you? Now get out of my life, David Blackstone. I asked you to wait until we got back to Oregon. You didn't. I asked you to stop following us. You didn't. You've used poor Kat and played on her romanticism to try to get to me. Now, that's low. You proved to me you don't know what real commitment is.

"I want you out of my life. No lovers. No friendship. No Acquaintance. Nothing."

Then she'd started pounding on the door and yelling for Kat to let them out, with all kinds of threats as to what she would do to her if she didn't open the door that minute. He wasn't sure exactly how long they were in that storeroom together, but it was long enough for him to know there was nothing he could do to get Michele back. The best thing he could do was to return home, get on with his life, and let her get on with hers.

David continued to sit at his desk, staring morosely at the gray morning skyline. He used to love the rain and the gray as much as the sunshine. Now it just depressed him.

He heard the phone ring and picked it up without enthusiasm. "This is David Blackstone."

"David! How nice to finally find you at home." He recognized Danielle's purr and the invitation in her voice. God, he hadn't talked to her in more than six months. "How are you? I've missed you and I need a playmate."

"I'm fine, Danielle but I don't have time to play."

"Ah come on, baby, you know I can take your mind off all your troubles. I've heard via the grapevine that you're a little down about the mouth these days."

David frowned. He hadn't been talking to anyone. How could she know anything? One of his business associates? He didn't think it had been that obvious his emotional life was falling apart.

"You heard wrong. I'm just fine."

"Come on David," she whispered seductively. "You can tell me the truth. We've never had to lie to each other before."

David debated what to say. He didn't want to bring Michele into Danielle's sphere of friends. It just wasn't right. It would somehow make everything they'd had on the same par as all his other sexual exploits. He decided to say nothing.

"Poor baby," Danielle said. He could almost see her pouting. "You've finally fallen hard haven't you? What happened? Did she turn you down? Did she run away? Did you finally find out that love and sex just don't mix very well?"

"Nothing happened," he said angrily. "I didn't fall anywhere and no one's running away." He wasn't going to let Danielle know anything about his heart. Their relationship had always been about sex and a good time, he wasn't going to give her any more now.

"Well, good. I'm so glad to hear the rumors were wrong then." Her voice immediately returned to its quick, businesslike rhythm with just a hint of playfulness. "I wasn't sure I really had the energy for playing the comforter. You know me, David. All fun and games."

She paused for a moment and he could hear the clink of ice and the sound of stirring. It brought back memories of Danielle's favorite morning after sex drink—mimosas.

"I have a teeny tiny problem, I hope you can help me solve," she purred back into the phone again. In spite of himself, David could feel the warmth working its way down to his groin.

"Yeah, what's that?"

"You remember how I sometimes have a hard time with getting that key to work?"

The pictures in his mind were crystal clear. Danielle enjoyed playing the combination of Victorian virgin and high-class prostitute. This particular fantasy included the bustier that exposed all of her breasts except the nipple, the garter belt with complicated holders, and sometimes she even wore a chastity belt. It had always been his job to find the key and open the treasure.

"Yeah, I remember." His voice was gruff as he tried to put the picture of her spread before him out of his mind.

"It just so happens I'm lying in bed here at 10:00 in the morning and I was playing around with the thing, thinking of you and all our good times... and well... now I'm stuck. Can you please come over and help. It will only take a minute."

"Danielle," David said, remembering what had happened when he broke it off with her six months ago. "We'd agreed there wouldn't be any more of this. You were going off with, what's his name? Brad somebody?"

"I know, but Brad just wasn't any fun, David. He was smart and rich, and he treated me nice...but he just couldn't make me feel so well.... used....like you do. Let's face it, David, you really know how to spoil a girl in bed."

"You know my rule, Danielle. I only have one woman at a time and I demand the same."

"I know all about your rule, David. But you just said there's no one you're seeing right now. You wouldn't be lying to me, would you? You wouldn't be just trying to put me off if there was no one you were sleeping with, would you?

"There's no one I'm sleeping with," he affirmed. He wanted Michele. He wanted this to be Michele on the phone, not Danielle. But he knew Michele wasn't coming back.

"Being as you don't seem to be tied around anyone's finger right now and...well...I don't have a playmate either...I just thought..." She left it hanging. He could almost see her dipping her fingers into the Mimosa and trailing it up her long legs begging him to follow with his mouth.

Maybe this was just what he needed to get over Michele. Maybe going back to his old rules—sex just for pleasure with no emotions was the best way for him. He wasn't expected to put his cock in a closet for the rest of his life because his heart was broken, was he? No, he wasn't. That was one thing his father had made perfectly clear.

"I'll be right over. Don't move."

She sighed with obvious glee. "Oh, I'm right here, David. I'll make sure the door is unlocked. Don't dawdle now. I don't want to come without you." He heard her giggles as she hung up.

Over the past couple of months, David had thought he'd never be able to see another woman after Michele. But now, as he felt himself getting hard at the thought of Danielle waiting for him— offering simple, uncomplicated sexual pleasure—he knew he would recover. He checked his wallet for a condom. Finding none he searched the bathroom and finally found the box he'd stashed away in the back corner of the cupboard under the sink—the box he thought he'd never need to use again. He quickly stuffed two in his wallet.

On the drive over he kept telling himself how glad he was Danielle had called. How fortunate for him that he had someone like Danielle to help bring him back to the real world. A world he understood. A world where he could be in control again.

He parked and took the stairs two at a time. As promised, her doorknob easily turned and he let himself in. "Danielle?" he called, his voice a low growl of anticipation.

"Oh David. I'm so glad you hurried. I'm just getting so wet inside this thing. I really need to get it off."

He easily found her bedroom. When he walked in she was half sitting and half lying on the bright red silk sheets. He could smell the scent of jasmine in the air—her favorite perfume. She had one knee bent and one knee straight. She dipped a finger into her drink and then put it in her mouth and sucked suggestively.

David groaned and his cock hardened quickly. He quickly shucked his clothes and stood beside her, taking a moment to appreciate first her long legs that seemed to go on forever. His eyes then moved to the breasts pushed up by the bustier and he bent to them in the fantasy game they had always played.

"Come to me, wench," he said as his mouth caressed their tops.

She purred and slid down the pillow, arching to him as she held his head to her breasts. "Hurry my love. The King will be home at any moment." Then she pulled one of the strings at the top of the bustier and her breasts poured forth. "Oops," she giggled. Placing one hand under a breast, and guiding his mouth to the nipple she offered it to him. "Dinner, my lord?"

He sucked greedily at the light brown nipple. His hand moved between her thighs and began to stroke her legs close to the chastity belt as she moaned and called out his name, spurring him onward. Then her hands wrapped around his cock and she stroked quickly, bringing him close to the brink. "The key," she panted. "Quick, the key, it's under my pillow.

He reached under the pillow and held it in triumph. Her eyes flared in anticipation as she snatched it from him with her teeth, her hands continuing to work his cock.

He took the key from her mouth, and turned it in front of her face to tease her. "Faster, faster." She bucked against his hand at her thigh. "Open it and fuck me, David. Fuck me fast and hard."

Then she brought his lips to hers, kissing him thoroughly, alternately tonguing the inside of his mouth and biting his lower lip.

Suddenly David stopped and pushed himself away.

"Oh God. Oh God, no!" He buried his face in his hands.

"David, what is it? Did I hurt you? Did I bite you? I'm sorry, David. I thought you liked it a little rough. Did I hurt your lip?" She reached for him, trying to pull his head back to her breast, but he pushed himself off the bed and stood. "Please David. Let's try again. Tell me what's wrong. I'll go slow. You want it slow, baby? I can do that…just tell me."

It was the kiss. He was fine until they kissed. Then all he could think of was Michele and how this wasn't Michele. This was all wrong!

Sex by itself wasn't enough anymore. He wanted soul. He wanted heart. He wanted the promises of forever, of knowing that he could be fast or slow, funny or serious. That he could explore all the nuances of one woman and never know all the treasures within. Danielle knew all the tricks and she could obviously make him hard, but it just wasn't enough anymore.

"I'm sorry, Danielle." He looked down at her, taking in the invitation she had laid before him. He wished to hell he could take her up on it. "You are a beautiful woman and you are so sexy you make my cock stand straight up just looking at you."

"It doesn't seem to be standing now," she pouted. "Come back here. Look, I'll take this silly thing off." She easily inserted the key and slipped off the chastity belt. "See?" She pointed to the blonde thatch that was now in full view. "No work. OK?" She took his hand. "Let me do all the work this time, David. Let Dani make you feel good."

"It's not you Danielle. I just can't play anymore. You deserve someone who can match you. I can't."

"But David, you can. We've always been good together. No one can turn my body inside out like you can. Come on, I'll help you get over her." She placed his hand against her exposed breast. "Come play, David. Make them talk to you like you always did before."

David withdrew his hand, then bent and gave her a brotherly kiss on her forehead.

"You're sweet and kind, and I appreciate what you're trying to do. I wish I could take you up on it. I really do, but it wouldn't be any good."

Then he turned and stepped into his underwear and pants. He grabbed the shirt that had been thrown near the bedroom door, then paused and looked at her one final time.

"I'll lock your front door on the way out. Good bye Danielle."

CHAPTER 19

"Try it again," Theresa yelled.

Michele turned the ignition. Nothing. Nothing at all. She flopped back against the seat.

Annabelle had started spitting and rattling like an old lady about sixty miles outside of Nashville. In hindsight, they probably should have turned around then. But they'd been through this before, and the motor home had always settled in to the road eventually—usually after about twenty-five miles. Michele thought she could coax her along to Memphis then get her in a shop while they did their show. There was still five hundred dollars left of the thousand she'd put in the fund four days ago. She just hoped that would be enough to make some minor fixes to Annabelle and help them limp home.

But when she saw steam coming out from under the hood, she knew the water pump had gone and so she took the first exit she saw. That was for Only, Tennessee. Now they were stuck in a town that was true to its name. Only was a town with nothing in sight for miles.

Kurt had pulled up behind them in his black SUV when he saw the steam pouring out of the hood. But the hood was so hot they had to wait until it cooled down to even get a look.

Michele figured they could take water from the tanks and keep filling the radiator just to get them to Memphis. She just hoped that was all it was.

Finally, Kurt took a look under the hood.

"Yup. Definitely looks like the water pump is gone." He paused. "You better come look, though. I don't know much about engines, but I think it's a lot worse than just a water pump."

Michele climbed up the side of the motor home with Rachel and Theresa and they peered under the hood. She shook her head at what she saw. It looked like the belts were corroded or fried, and everything was covered with a sticky black mess. They weren't going anywhere.

Surrounded by farmland and forest, Only was barely a town at all. She'd seen a gas station off the Interstate, but no mechanical services, and they'd rolled past a couple houses and a flower shop. Other than that she didn't remember much. Someone was going to have to hike it.

She gave in and called the AAA 800 number. After waiting on the line a good fifteen minutes while they checked for any services, the customer service agent finally said a mechanic would meet them in two hours.

Three hours later, just as Michele was ready to dial again, a blue and white tow truck pulled up behind them. "Thank God." She crawled out of the cab to join Theresa and Rachel at the truck.

A slight young man, not much taller than Michele, stepped down from the big tow truck. Though he didn't look a day over sixteen, Michele immediately noticed his biceps and triceps were well defined, as if he'd worked around big rigs a long time. And his face and arms were tanned, liked he'd been in the sun all summer.

"So, ya'll broke down?"

"Yes," Theresa answered. "We think it was first the water pump, but now it's just stopped altogether. Won't even turn over."

"Let me take a look."

Now all five women and Kurt were outside the motor home, watching as the young man lithely climbed into the engine and tapped here and there, his butt sticking straight into the air, his legs dangling down the front. He mumbled to himself as he scooted from one side of the engine to the other along the large grill.

Kat kept giggling and pointing until Theresa sent her such a withering look that she stomped off and stood by Kurt's car to watch from a distance.

Then the mechanic jumped off and scooted on his back beneath the underbody. They could see a foot sticking out on occasion, and other times they couldn't see any part of him at all. After about ten minutes he worked his way back out from under the motor home and stood.

"You've got big problems, m'am."

"What?" Theresa asked, resignation clearly resonating in her voice.

"Well, first you probably need a new engine, it looks like this one is way past its prime."

"But I just bought this six years ago. It can't be that bad." Theresa said.

"Well m'am, you may have bought the rig six years ago but it's older than that. And this is the original engine. Most people are lucky to get them to last sixty to seventy thousand miles without a major break down. This baby has over a hundred thousand miles on it. And it looks to me like those were some hard miles too."

Theresa turned to the other women. "I didn't know. It was part of the divorce settlement. I thought he'd bought it new. It looked new when he first showed it to me. I never really paid attention to the mileage and all that."

"It's not your fault, Theresa." Michele hugged her first, but the others quickly gathered around her, giving her their support.

"It's possible they can re-bore the cylinders and fit new pistons and rings," the young man continued. "But it would cost more than buying a new engine or replacing it with a good used one. Then there's also the camshaft. It's about ready to go. You're lucky it didn't quit on you first. The water pump is the least of your problems."

"And, how much will all of this cost?"

"Problem is there's no one close who can handle a rig like this, which means you probably have to be towed to Nashville or

Memphis. That's probably about a thousand to fifteen hundred dollars just to get there. Then after repairs and all, depending on what you decide to do, I'd guess somewhere between eight and twelve thousand dollars."

Theresa leaned toward Michele for support. "We don't have that kind of money. We don't even have enough money for the tow."

"Well, I don't know what to tell ya, M'am. I can tow you now or you can call me back when you make up your mind. Least ways you're not in a bad place. Mrs. McVay's B&B is just three miles down that way." He pointed to the south "It's as nice a place as any to stay and she serves a pretty mean breakfast." Then he pointed behind them. "And back up by the Interstate they have some food and stuff you can buy." He looked toward Kurt. "Least you have another vehicle to help you get around."

Theresa looked at each of the band members. "I don't know what we can do. Memphis is two hours away. Even if we make it to Memphis for our gig, that will only bring us six hundred dollars. And to make it, we'd probably have to have Kurt here drive back and forth twice for all our gear. We can't fit all of us plus gear in his car."

Michele turned back to the mechanic. "If we did come up with the money, how long would it take to get it fixed?"

"Well, that's hard to say." He rubbed his chin between his thumb and forefinger. "Depending on when they could fit you in, and assumin' they had all the parts, I'd guess at least a week."

"Oh God." Sarah groaned. "This was exactly what I was so afraid would happen before we even started." She began to pace. "So either we're stuck here in Only, where we can't get any services, or we're stuck in Memphis and paying for a week of motel rooms and food which we can't afford. We won't even be able to live in the motor home to save money. Then, if we get it out of hock in a week, which is nearly impossible given our finances, we have only one week left to make it to Arizona for our final gig which pays only four hundred dollars because we were looking for exposure instead of money."

"That about sums it up," Theresa finally spoke. "Look, I don't know about the rest of you, but I think we need to think this through."

They all agreed.

Theresa held out her hand to the guy, but he sidestepped her handshake, showing he was pretty greasy and didn't want to get her dirty.

"Thanks for your help, sir," Theresa dug in her pocket for money to pay for his time.

"No need for that, m'am. It was a AAA call. I come out to look for free, just can't tow your motor home for free, being as the member has paid only for car coverage."

"Well, thank you," Theresa said again. "We need to make some phone calls and make some decisions. Can you leave us a card or something so we can call you for the tow when we're ready?"

"Sure, m'am." He fished a slightly bent card out of his wallet, leaving a grease-stained thumbprint on it and handed it to her. "That number on the bottom is my cell. You can call it day or night and I'll come on out."

"Thank you," Sarah and Rachel called out as he crawled back into his truck.

"Come on," Michele had her arms around Theresa and guided her back into the motor home. "Let's all sit down, have a nice cool drink and think about this."

Michele gestured toward Kurt and Kat standing and talking at his car. "You two want to come in too? Have a lemonade or something while we talk?"

"Nah. I gotta make a couple phone calls and check in," Kurt called back.

"I'll stay out here with Mr. Kurt," Kat called. "I'm sure Mom will tell you I don't have any opinions on this."

Michele looked at the two of them and wondered what they'd been talking and laughing about. But she knew Kurt was safe, and she didn't have time to worry about it now. She nodded toward them and then climbed into Annabelle along with the rest of the women.

They each talked about their personal finances and the group finances. They all knew there really wasn't any money. They'd been counting on the six hundred dollars from Memphis to get them to Tucson and then the four hundred dollars from Tucson to get them home. As it was they had already been living hand to mouth each day they'd been on the road the past two weeks.

After comparing notes about possibilities for loans from family, they all came up blank. Not one of them had parents who could or would chip in. Michele's parents lived very simply as it was. All their money went into the ranch. Not that they wouldn't get a loan for Michele if she really needed it, but she couldn't bring herself to ask them. They'd already sacrificed so much and accrued some debt just to help her get through college.

Theresa's father had died ten years ago, and her mother was in a retirement home on a fixed income. Definitely no help there. Rachel's mother had died of cancer when Rachel was only 19. The grief had probably been a factor in her being so anxious to marry Kavan and move to America. Her father ran a little Bed and Breakfast in Dunoon, but most of the profits were plowed back into the Inn to keep it running. Also, she didn't feel comfortable asking him for money on the first time she called since her divorce two years ago.

Sarah wasn't much help either. Her own mother had died when she was in middle-school, something she and Rachel shared was growing up without a mother in their teen years. Sarah's father fell apart in his grief, took up the bottle, and the small farm they owned in Oklahoma had come into disrepair, barely making enough to keep food on the table. Not to mention, she hadn't spoken to her father since she fled Oklahoma after high school six years ago.

It was clear no one was going to find the money from family. As Michele sat, morosely, she suddenly realized everyone was staring at her.

"What?"

They just kept staring, expectation clear in their eyes.

"What?" She raised her voice.

"You have to call him," Rachel said.

"Call who? I can't call my Dad or my brother. I've already explained they don't have this kind of money."

"You know who I mean."

Knowledge dawning, Michele immediately objected. "No way! Uh uh. There is no way I'm calling David. I'd rather die first. Put it out of your minds right now."

"We wouldn't ask you if we had another way out," Theresa said, her voice soft and coaxing. "He's the only one who has that kind of money that any of us know."

"None of us come from wealthy families." So, Sarah was ganging up on her too.

"No!" Michele shouted it. "There's got to be another way. I'll find it. I just have to think. I can't call him. I absolutely can't. You just don't know. You just don't know." Tears were threatening to spill but she held them back.

Rachel put her arms around her. "We know how hard it is, honey. We aren't doing this to hurt you. We just don't know another way. You said the thousand we already used was like a loan. Why can't this other money be a loan too?"

Michele pushed her away, stood and walked out the door.

She walked right past Kurt and Kat and kept on walking.

"Hey, where ya heading?" Kurt said, as he tried to catch up with her.

"Stay!" She said sharply. "I don't need a keeper. You can see for miles around, you don't need to follow me."

Kurt scanned the area and then backed away.

As she continued on her path, Michele overhead Kat say to Kurt. "Wow. What crawled up her butt?" She didn't hear any response.

They'd asked too much. She'd worked her heart out for this band. She would work night and day from now until doomsday if they asked her. But she couldn't do this. It was too much. They had to know that.

She picked up her pace, starting to jog. Running always helped her to think more clearly.

If she called David it would be like admitting to failure. She'd put all her eggs in this basket and she was bound and determined to prove to everyone that she could do it on her own. Even if it was just a loan —and there was no way she would accept anything else—he would have expectations. One of those expectations would be of getting to talk to her. It could be even worse—an expectation of seeing her again on a regular basis. And she simply couldn't allow that to happen.

In the past two weeks, she was just starting to feel like she could function again. She was just starting to feel the music moving through her without images of him or their time together. If she had to deal with him—negotiate with him—it would all fall apart. She just knew it.

Her shoes slapped the pavement as her full running form took over. She began to count her steps and concentrated on her breath. One, two, three, four…three hundred, three hundred one…four thousand fifteen…four thousand sixteen. When she started feeling the rain upon her face, she turned around. Then it really opened up and she was drenched in a good, old-fashioned southern thunderstorm.

She kept up her pace. She welcomed the rain. It was helping to wash away the pain, the pain that made her shut out everyone's needs but her own. She saw the black car drive by and then heard it turn around. Kurt came up beside her and rolled down the window, he slowed to match her pace.

"You're soaked, Michele."

"So?" She concentrated so as not to break her stride.

"Come on, get in. You'll catch pneumonia."

"I can't," she said, digging deep and picking up the pace.

"Yes, you can. Come on."

"Go away, Kurt. Go away or I'll start running across the field where you can't follow me."

She heard the window roll up and saw him head back to the motor home.

She started counting again. Six thousand seven, six thousand eight. She was OK. She could do this.

Michele walked in large circles near the motor home, cooling down, letting her breath calm to its normal rate. Her clothes now stuck to every curve. She was sure her bra was showing right through her t-shirt, and her shorts felt like they would be plastered to her thighs forever. She could feel the goosebumps forming along her arms and shoulders as the breeze kicked in. It was still raining, though not quite as hard.

Once her breathing regulated, she bent over and dangled her hands in front of her, then inched them to the ground. She pulled her head to her knees. Slowly she stacked her spine one vertebra at a time until she stood tall again. She took her time with the rest of the stretches, gathering more courage with each one. When she was confident she could face everyone again, she opened the door and stepped inside.

Rachel immediately wrapped a towel around her and hugged her tight. Sarah handed her another one for her hair.

"We all talked," Sarah said. "You're right, we can't ask you to do this."

"Just call him," Michele whispered.

"No. We'll find another way," Theresa said. "Even if we have to start singing in bars, we'll find another way."

"Look," Michele pushed away. "I said OK. So do it."

"You sure you want to call him?" Rachel asked.

"Not me, you." She pointed at Rachel.

"Me? But Michele, it's you he loves."

"That's the deal," Michele said, her tone brooking no exceptions. "You call him. He agrees to a loan. A loan only. The loan is between him and the band—not me, the band. There are no strings attached to me having any kind of relationship with him. I don't have to talk with him. I don't have to deal with him. I'll be a signatory to the loan only as a member of the band, just like each one of you."

She paused. No one was disagreeing. No one was talking.

"Well, get it over with," she pointed to one of the cell phones sitting on the table.

Rachel picked it up and holding Michele's eyes with hers she dialed.

Michele held her breath.

CHAPTER 20

"David?"

Michele wished there were a speakerphone. She wanted to know exactly what he was saying. She listened carefully to Rachel's side of the conversation.

"No. Everyone's fine…mostly."

"We'll we've got a bit of a problem. Annabelle died on us."

"Yup. The mechanic said at least eight to twelve grand."

"Yup. Believe me, you were our last resort."

"Yup. Her too."

"Nope. A loan. That's what we're asking for. A loan."

"Yup. Okay. No. I don't think she'd go for that. This is a loan to the band. The entire band."

"Yeah. I see."

"You have a point there."

"Yes, it makes sense."

"No. I could handle that. Hang on a minute. Let me ask."

Rachel put her hand over the phone. "He said he's glad to do it. He wanted to just give us a gift, but I told him no can do, it had to be a loan."

"And strings?" Michele asked.

"Well, there is a string, but it doesn't have to do with you—exactly."

"What is it?" Theresa asked.

"He'll loan us the entire amount under one condition. He becomes the booking agent and tour manager for the band for one year."

"No way! Absolutely not! He's just trying to get on the road with us so he can be near me. I can't do that. No. I say No!"

"Now wait a minute, Michele." Theresa put a hand on her arm to calm her down.

"This is not a bad idea. David has a great marketing background. He might actually be good for us."

"No." Michele repeated. "Rachel, you tell him no. You tell him he can up the interest rate, but he can't ask this."

Rachel put her mouth back to the phone.

"You heard huh?"

"Yeah, she's pretty adamant."

"OK, I'll tell her." She put her hand back over the phone. "He says that's the deal. Take it or leave it."

Michele grabbed for the phone. "Give it to me." Rachel handed it to her with a shrug.

"You bastard!" she yelled into the phone. "How dare you! How dare you put conditions. If you really cared about this band, you wouldn't do this. You're just trying to get back at me. Well, it won't work. Just forget it. You can keep your stupid loan and choke on it." Then she ended the call, shaking.

Everyone else was silent, eyes downcast.

"Well, I guess you told him," Kat finally broke the tension. "Not that it matters to him, mind you. He's not the one with the broken down motor home out in the middle of nowhere, with no money, and no food, and no way to get home."

Kat paused, then pointed an accusing finger at Michele and shook it at her dramatically. "You know what, I thought before you were like the princess bride. But I've changed my mind. You're more like the wicked stepsister. You think of no one but yourself." Then she marched past her to the back bedroom and slammed the door.

No one spoke for several seconds.

"I'm going to bed," Theresa announced. "This has been a tough day. I think it's better that we all sleep on it."

The next morning Michele woke up early and slipped out the door for a run. She felt pretty bad about how she'd handled David. He had to have known what her reaction would be. Why did he have to keep pushing her? Why couldn't he just accept that love wasn't enough?

She just wasn't sure she could stand having him around all the time and not be touching him, feeling him touch her. She'd never be able to get over him if she had to see him every day.

The rain had stopped, and everything smelled fresh. She looked across the road at the fields of cows grazing in rich green pastures and she felt a hard lump in her stomach. It reminded her of home. A lot more green than Montana, but still the same feeling.

She wished she were home now. She wished she were helping her Dad round up sheep, or helping her Mom get the morning breakfast on the table. She just wanted to feel innocent again. She wanted to feel warm and protected and not have to be faced with all these decisions. It seemed that, once again, she not only screwed herself but the band as well. She worked her way back to the motor home, her jog slowing to a walk as she approached.

She could see Theresa through the window, in profile, standing at the sink as if she were talking to someone further forward.

Michele opened the door and all conversation stopped.

"Talking about me, huh?"

For a minute no one spoke.

"Yes, we were." Sarah ended the silence. "Come sit down, Michele." She patted a place on the sofa next to her.

"I think I'd rather stand."

"All right." Sarah paused. "Here's the deal. We've all had a vote and we've decided. Right now, unless you've come up with something else during your run, David is the only hope we have of getting out of here and getting home. All of us are willing to accept his loan conditions."

"I'm not."

"We understand that," Sarah's voice softened. "So, we'll do it without you."

"You'll what? Are you kicking me out of the band?"

Rachel took over. "Honey, we're not kicking you out, you're taking yourself out. We know how hard it is for you to be with David and we wish there was another way. Truly we do. But there just isn't another option."

Then Theresa began. "I don't think David is going to fly out here and insist on riding with us back to Portland. In fact, we can try to negotiate that he doesn't ride with us until we get home. I have no idea what he has in mind for getting us all home or completing our contracts. But whatever it is, we have to go along with it. So, we'll agree to keep him away from you until we get home—if that's what you really want. But once we're home he's our manager. It's completely up to you then if you want to stay. If you can't find a way to live with him being involved with us, then we'll let you go your own way—as much as it hurts us, we don't want to hurt you."

Michele's eyes teared. She couldn't believe what they were saying. These women were like the sisters she never had. This had been her big break; the beginning of her career and now it was all going down the drain because of David Blackstone.

"We don't want you to go, Michele." Rachel reinforced, her voice choking. "We all love you, but we also don't want to see you hurting. And if it's going to hurt too much to be around David, then we're willing to let you go."

"I'll call him back myself." Determined, Michele held out her hand for the phone.

Rachel raised an eyebrow, then handed it to her and waited.

"I'd rather do this alone." Michele moved back to the door and opened it.

Michele looked up and down the road. She remembered passing a lone tree early in her run this morning. Resolute, she spotted it and headed toward it.

She slid her back down the trunk and sat. She drew her knees to her chest, placed the phone in front of her on one knee and waited.

She waited for her courage to return. Waited to make sure she could speak without her voice choking up or getting angry. Waited for the tears to stop falling.

When she finally felt ready, she dialed his number from memory.

She took a deep breath as she heard it ring.

"Hello?"

"Hi, David," Michele said softly.

"Michele." She could hear him choke at her name. Her heart screamed to escape, run and hide. She fought back the urge, taking several deep breaths.

"Look. I'm sorry," she began. "I just wasn't thinking straight. I just let my emotions take over."

"It's hard to let me back into your life, isn't it?"

"Yes." He knew her so well. He knew her thoughts, her yearnings, everything that made her tick.

"I'm not trying to take over."

"Well, it sounds to me like you are. Why can't you just give us the loan? Why can't you just pretend you're a bank."

"Even a bank needs collateral. What would be your collateral, Michele? No one in the band owns anything besides your instruments and Annabelle."

"We'd all be willing to put them up for collateral."

"Yes, but I don't know that it would be enough."

"My bass alone is probably worth two grand."

"I'm sure it is. And I'm sure that when you add up all of your instruments it more than covers the debt."

"Then why isn't that good collateral?"

"Because your instruments are meaningless to me without you to play them."

"They could be sold if we couldn't pay you back."

"Do you think I could do that, Michele? Do you think I could actually take away everyone's dream just like that?"

"Isn't that what you're trying to do to me? Stepping into the band, taking over?"

"No. I'm trying to help."

She couldn't find anything to say.

"What Sweetwater Canyon has needed all along is good promotion and distribution. I didn't step in before because I knew you didn't want me in your business—even when we were together I knew that."

"That hasn't changed. I don't want you in our business."

"But now there isn't a choice is there? Michele, I want to help and I'm very good at this. I've built a successful company from scratch. I've put contributors together for non-profits and for schools. I know distributors. I can get the right people in the right place at the right time. I just want to use my talents to help the band."

"I don't believe you. I can't…believe you."

"Then look at it this way. I want to guarantee my money. I figure the best way to do that is to be involved in the business. I do have a talent for making deals, for marketing concepts."

"But…"

"If a company declares bankruptcy and goes for reorganization, a judge has to approve your plan. The judge is in the middle of your business, checking your allocations, making sure you have enough money to go forward, double-checking that you are asking the right questions and getting the best deals you can. Sweetwater Canyon is declaring bankruptcy. All I want to do is make sure you get the best deals you can."

"So, you're going to be our judge."

"No, Michele, not your judge, your friend. That's all I want, to be a friend to Sweetwater Canyon. Is that too much to ask?"

She thought for a moment. It was too much ask. She wanted more than a friend from David Blackstone, but she couldn't tell him that either.

"No, that's not too much ask," she finally said.

"Thank you," he said. She heard his sigh of relief. "I'll get the tow truck set up, and I'll arrange for lodging in Nashville, and repairs."

Michele held the phone, unable to speak but unable to hang up.

"Michele?"

"Thank you, David," she finally said. "I have to go now."

She hung up and dropped the phone to the ground. She wrapped her arms around her middle and squeezed tight. She wished she could cry, but there were no more tears. She wouldn't have to face him until they got home. But then what? Was it worth giving up her dream just to avoid David Blackstone?

CHAPTER 21

Annabelle lumbered along the curves in the road as they made their way up highway 199 from Crescent City toward Grants Pass and then back to Portland. They'd gotten a late start. It was already noon, which meant they wouldn't get to Portland until at least. 8:00pm, if they were lucky. The motor home couldn't move as fast as a car.

Rain had poured non-stop for the past three days, which was typical of mid-November. Michele was in the jump seat. Her job was to watch for flooding while David drove. Once they got out of town, they'd be okay, but they couldn't afford to get stuck in the canyon. They had a gig scheduled in Portland for tomorrow night and everyone was looking forward to at least one night's rest in their own beds.

They'd been home for two months, and now they were doing gigs within a ten-hour drive from Portland. The fall rains and shorter days meant they were often driving at night. Michele had to admit, David had done a great job with bookings. When they got home from Tennessee, they had only two weeks rest and David had them booked at least four days a week through all of November and into the first two weeks of December—and for more than their usual asking price too. Sometimes a lot more.

He'd used his marketing skills and his money to hire a publicist, get professional pictures of the band, and get interviews with every major newspaper in the Pacific Northwest. He even had them scheduled to appear on Oregon Art Beat with PBS in February. His latest negotiation was to cut their first live album in just a couple of weeks. Their other CDs had been done in a small studio. David said doing one live would generate new interest and get the community involved.

The concert would be at Timberline Lodge. He'd already signed a contract with a local distributor who had national connections. They were looking at a first run of twenty-five thousand CDs, far more than the two thousand names they had collected on tear sheets during their tour.

With David's marketing push, in the past month they'd made enough money to almost pay off their credit cards, and they were beginning to make a big dent in the loan David had made to get Annabelle ready for the road again.. When he left the band next fall, as promised, she hoped they could get a full accounting and be able to pay back every cent.

David had kept his promise. He no longer tried to get Michele's attention. He didn't even try to be friends. The only problem was whenever they traveled overnight, he came with the band. They stayed in Annabelle and he stayed in a nearby hotel. Sometimes he splurged and they all stayed in a hotel. They'd kind of fallen into a way of dealing with each other—always cool, always polite, and whenever possible she tried to make sure one of the other band members was around.

She could see David's furrowed brow as he studied the road ahead. The windshield wipers were doing double time. They'd cleared Crescent City and were nearing the California border. Once out of California, all they had to do was get through that very windy section of canyon in the national forest and then they'd be home free. She had to admit, she was happy not to have to drive in this kind of weather.

She slid a glance toward him again, noticing the strong line of his jaw and the way his cheek muscle twitched as he concentrated on the road. She quickly looked away.

God! She still wanted him. No matter how hard she tried not to, she couldn't help herself. With the quiet way he'd been building up the band and making them solvent again, her heart had begun to melt. He had done so much for them without really asking much in return. She was beginning to see the David she fell in love with—the man who cared about people, who helped others. The man who built a successful computer business for the primary purpose of helping schools. Belatedly, she came to the realization that he had been that man all along but she was too hurt and too stubborn to see it. Despite all her promises to herself, he had pried her heart open again and she ached for him. David was the man she still loved and wanted.

The problem was she didn't think he loved her anymore. And she couldn't blame him. She'd been adamant when she told him to get lost two months ago. And it was only two weeks ago they'd fought again over him taking over too much of the band's business.

Of course, knowing he didn't love her anymore didn't make her love him any less. It just made her hurt. And being near him day after day, knowing their lives would never be shared in the marriage she had planned was sometimes more than she could bear.

She leaned back in the seat and closed her eyes. Three more weeks until the concert at Timberline Lodge. December. The month they were supposed to be married. It seemed so long ago that she had made those plans.

"You okay?" David asked.

"Fine. Just tired." She kept her eyes closed. "I didn't sleep well last night. I'll be glad to be home in my own bed tonight."

"Why don't you go lie down and get a little rest. I'm fine driving without you here. It's four lane until we pass Gasquet."

"Well..." Michele glanced back toward the women. There really wasn't a place to lie down. "I think I'll just close my eyes for a minute here. Just a couple minutes and I'll be refreshed."

He nodded. Michele sighed and let her lashes fall. She knew she wouldn't really sleep, but at least she didn't have to keep looking at him and wonder if there would ever be a chance at love again.

As she drifted in and out of semi-consciousness she remembered why she'd had such a rough night. It was her creeping jealousy. She was getting a taste of what David had feared with her before they broke up. He feared the men on the road—men who flirted and tempted. Well, now she knew about the women on the road, and David attracted them like wild dogs to a piece of raw meat.

It had been more than three months since she and David had last made love. She was sure he'd been with other women by now. A man like him couldn't help himself. After all, what was he supposed to do? Wait for her when she'd made it perfectly clear that wasn't going to happen between them?

The problem was she had to watch how women came onto him and she had no right to say anything about it. She'd seen it almost every night this past week. Inevitably, as he helped to set up the stage, someone would approach him and flirt.

One time she caught herself moving toward him to intercept. She had planned to put her arms around him, to stake her claim before anything could happen. But then she pulled herself back, knowing she had no right to take any more of David's happiness. That time she had to take a walk until just before the set started. It was the only way she could be sure she wouldn't deck the next woman that came sniffing at his door.

Last night, in Crescent City, it had been a tall, willowy redhead, with a model's thin figure and at least D-cup breasts. Michele first noticed her because she was almost as tall as David—she had to be close to six feet.

Michele had unzipped the case for her bass, her back to David who was checking cables and positioning monitors when she heard a sultry voice say, "Hi, I'm Jennifer. I'll be running the sound tonight."

Michele turned to the voice just in time to see the redhead holding her hand out for David to pull her up on stage. As he did she pushed him over and fell on top of him, her ample breasts practically falling out of her tank top into his face. Of all the times on tour that Michele had wished for a woman sound engineer instead of man, this was the one time she wished the opposite.

Then as they worked together to check the monitors and make sure the cabling was taped to the stage, the redhead kept placing her tight ass in front of David's face in obvious invitation. The worst part was when David began responding to the little come ons with a laugh or a smart remark.

She couldn't help but overhear some of the obvious lines from the harlot.

"Oooo, such big strong hands. I bet you have no problem carrying some weight up and down stairs."

"They can handle what they need to," David responded.

"Think they can handle me?"

"I 'spect so."

"You know, I really like tall men. It's hard to find someone who fits well with my height. The short guys are always down near my boobs or even lower."

"That's not necessarily a bad thing is it?"

The woman had giggled appreciatively and wiggled her hips in front of him again.

Then the woman had cleverly found a way to work her way around to having one leg trapping his thigh to hers as she reached across him to tape the last cable. "Is it really true the bigger the feet the bigger the…" She'd left it hanging and giggled.

David had laughed. "Well now, I can't say I've been comparing myself to other guys." Then he moved away and stood.

She stood too and sidled up to him and put her arms around his neck, pressing her breasts against his chest. "How 'bout giving me a peek later? I can give it a test run and tell you if it compares favorably."

David had laughed as he set her apart from him. "Hmmm. Definitely tempting. But I'll have to pass." Then he'd patted her behind and sent her on her way.

Later, when the band had finished packing and they retired for the night, Michele was lying in bed with the windows of the motor home open and she could hear David's laugh followed by some whispering and then a high feminine giggle. Then footsteps moving away. She wasn't sure if he'd left with her, but she suspected they were going back to his motel room. She tossed and turned all night as she imagined what they might be doing together.

Michele squinted through the windshield. They'd left the small town of Gasquet and were heading toward the canyon. Good. Only twenty-nine miles to the Oregon border. She closed her eyes again.

She jerked awake again as David came to a full stop. A few cars snaked ahead of them. God, she hoped there hadn't been an accident. She hoped no one was hurt. Then she saw cars turning around and heading back the other direction.

David continued to move the motor home forward, a foot at a time until they came to a police officer with a bright yellow umbrella. "Road's closed. Landslide. You can go about two more miles and see if there's a room left at Patrick's Creek or you can head to the campground."

"Do you think the road will open up again sometime tonight?" David asked.

"Doubt it. Slide's pretty bad. Crews are working on it now, but they'll have to stop once it gets dark and then start again in the morning. The rain's not helping."

"Any RV hookups at Patrick's Creek?"

"Nope, but you can park at the campground if you want. All the facilities are closed though."

"I guess we should head back to Crescent City then."

"Can't do that either," the policeman said. "The road below the campground is flooded and until the creek lowers no one get back." Everyone's stuck at the inn or the campground until that's fixed.

David turned back toward the back of the motor home. "What do you want to do? My vote is to go ahead to Patrick's Creek. At least that way we aren't backtracking. If they do open it up, I'm willing to drive through the night. But it's up to you. You're the ones who have to play that gig tomorrow night."

Everyone agreed to go ahead. David thanked the officer and

inched forward for the next two miles. When they finally got to Patrick's Creek, the parking lot was jammed with cars and there was no place to easily park Annabelle. David asked Michele to stay at the wheel while he inquired inside as to their options.

Michele watched the clock on the dashboard, hoping they didn't have to turn around and return to Crescent City. Fifteen minutes, twenty minutes, twenty-five minutes. Finally, she saw his tall frame loping from the building. He climbed into the passenger side, his clothes soaked from the downpour.

"I've managed to get us three and a half rooms."

"Hooray! Real beds, real food," Kat clapped.

"But why?" Michele asked. "We'll stay in the motor home. You just need one room for yourself. We don't need to spend the money."

"Well that's the problem. There isn't any more parking here and evidently the campground is full too. The owner said he'd be willing to take Annabelle back down to his place and park it next to his house. But he has no hook ups and he didn't want us staying out there, as he doesn't really know us and he has a wife and four kids to consider."

"What did you do, show him your bear face?" Rachel jibed.

David chuckled. "I promise I was on my best behavior." He paused. "Look, I got the last rooms he had. I figured Theresa and Kat wouldn't mind sharing a double bed. Sarah and Rachel, I was able to get one with two singles for you." He looked Michele straight in the eyes. "And we are together."

"Oh no." She looked away. "I'll sleep on the floor in one of the other rooms."

"Hold on," he said. "Hold on and let me finish. We're not exactly together, but sort of. There is a room with a double bed, and a second one adjoining it with a single bed. There's a wall and a door between them. There is a shared bath between the two. It was designed as a family suite, parents on one side, a kid on the other and a locking door at either end of the bath."

Michele looked desperately to each of the other women.

Rachel shrugged. "Come on, Michele, it won't be that bad. Like he said, you can lock the door to keep him out."

She looked to Theresa. "Don't look at me, girl. You don't expect me or Kat to share a bath with him do you?"

"Well?" David was waiting for Michele to agree.

"It's fine. You're right. I'm over reacting. Let's get our suitcases inside and let them park Annabelle wherever they can."

AFTER DINNER, Michele sat in the cozy lodge living room enjoying the roaring fire. She knew it was late, but she just couldn't bring herself to go up the stairs and get in bed. She didn't want to accidentally run into David in the shower, or have an opportunity to be tempted to his bed.

She stirred her third cup of hot chocolate. It seemed that no one else in the entire lodge was up anymore. Even the manager had left for the evening, after making sure she was OK. A clock bonged twelve times in another room. Surely David must be asleep by now. She climbed the stairs and let herself into her room, making sure she was very quiet.

She checked the bathroom to make sure the door was closed on his side. It was. She didn't even turn on the light over the sink as she brushed her teeth. She let the lamp from her room spill into the bath just enough so she could see. She ran the minimum amount of water, and hoped when she flushed the toilet that it didn't wake him. Feeling that she had successfully avoided seeing him in his sweats and bare chest, or worse yet naked, she crept back to her room and closed her door to the bathroom, sliding the bolt across.

She changed into a long t-shirt for sleeping, crawled under the sheets and comforter and switched off her lamp. She stared at the ceiling, thinking, and tears started filling her eyes.

Oh God. What was she going to do? Her head was spinning. How had she made such a mess of everything?

Everything was so complicated now. She didn't have David even though they loved each other. In order to get him back she'd have to sacrifice everything. The only way for them to get past the jealousy of life on the road was for both of them to leave the band. Then neither would have to worry about the temptations the other might face.

There was only one problem. Since being on tour with the band, and now seeing David every day and how hard he worked, how he helped promote them so well, she'd discovered she wanted it all—a career, David, a family, all of it.

And David? What about him? She thought about what he meant to her, how it felt knowing he didn't love her anymore. She could put all her energy into getting him back. She had to believe she could make him love her again. If she quit the band and showed him how much she was willing to sacrifice, he would fall in-love again, wouldn't he? At least then she could have love and children. But the thought of no music was devastating. She turned her face into her pillow, her shoulders shaking as she grieved for the career she had just started and the man she wanted to share it with.

DAVID LOOKED AT THE CEILING. He could hear her crying. He wanted to make it stop. He couldn't stand to hear those heartbreaking sobs. What could it possibly be? She'd seem to have found some type of equilibrium lately—not the one he'd hoped for but at least she was talking to him now.

Unable to stand it any longer, he pulled on his sweat pants and entered the bathroom. He turned on the light over the sink and tapped lightly on the thin door between the two rooms.

"Michele? Are you okay?"

He heard her choke back her tears, then a long pause.

"I'm trying to sleep," she called out.

"Sorry, I thought I heard you crying."

"Ah…no…I'm fine."

"Are you sure? It didn't sound like you were fine a minute ago.

Michele, no matter what's happened between us, I can still be a good listener."

He waited for what seemed like an hour and heard nothing.

MICHELE SAT on the edge of the bed, hugging herself in the dark, her pulse heavy and distinct. She could hear him breathing on the other side of the door. Then she heard him move away. She sighed, and stared into the dark. Alone.

"Dammit!" She heard a loud thump to the floor.

Without thinking, Michele jumped off the bed and ran to the door between them. "Are you all right?"

"Shit! I'm fine. Just hit my big toe on the corner of the damn bed frame. Damn it hurts."

She heard him limping back to the door again.

"Look, Michele," he whispered at the door. She could almost feel his breath through the small crack where she could see light from his room. "Will you open the door a second? There's something I'd like to say."

She stood stock still.

"You can say it right there, David."

"Come on, open up, I'm not going to attack you."

"Go back to bed, David."

"Okay, I'll talk through the door."

She held her breath and leaned against the door.

He expelled his breath on a sigh. "I just need to tell you I care when you're hurting. I care for the whole band. I want all of you to be a success."

"I know," she whispered.

"The last thing I want to do is make trouble for you. If it's too hard for you to have me here, I'll leave. As soon as we get back to Portland, I'll give everything back to Sweetwater Canyon. Okay?"

She thought a minute, trying to still the rapid thud in her chest. Leave? No she didn't want him to leave?

"Michele?"

She flipped the bolt between the two rooms and eased the door open a crack. His face was right there, his expression hidden in shadow from the dark of her room, but the light behind him haloed his dark hair.

"Come in a minute," she said, and she made her way to the lamp next to her bed, switching it on.

She turned back to him. "I'm still in love with you David," she began. He reached toward her, but she held up her hand to stop him. If he touched her, she would lose it completely.

"Michele?"

She couldn't meet his eyes as she spoke. "It's just that I know you don't love me anymore. I know that you've been seeing other women. And I just can't take it anymore. I know I have no right to tell you what to do with your life. I blew that chance. But I can't be with you every day and watch you walk off at night to be in another woman's arms. It's tearing open the wound again and again."

He listened, sitting on the edge of the bed with her. He took her hands in his. She didn't stop him.

"Michele, you don't know anything about what's been happening with me or what I've been doing."

"Wait. I have to finish this. I've made a decision. I'm quitting the band after we make the CD. Sweetwater Canyon will be on hiatus until February and that will give them enough time to find another bass player."

"Michele, no. You can't. You don't understand. You don't know what you're saying."

"I do know. I've been thinking about it for days now. It's the only answer. It's the only way I can survive." The tears started anew and she choked back a sob trying to erupt from deep in her chest.

"Come here," he said, so softly he thought she hadn't heard. And when she didn't move, couldn't even take a breath, he drew her in to his chest.

He didn't say another thing. He didn't have to. He reached under her chin and lifted it toward his face, his blue-green eyes searching hers for a heartbeat, and then his mouth covered hers, gently, lips barely touching.

She couldn't make her muscles respond to the message from her brain—no, Michele, no! She didn't move. Her knees softened, her hands laid against his chest but she didn't push him away. She just let him kiss her.

Then he moved back, his arm still around her, banking the passion in his eyes. "Michele, all you have to do is say yes. That's all," he said.

She started to shake. She knew this was wrong. She knew, if she let him touch her, the pain would be unbearable in the morning. But, the terrible truth was she wanted him, every facet of him. Run! Run! But she took no heed.

"Yes," she said. "Oh, God, yes." She closed her eyes and he was there again, his arms around her back, his mouth on hers, pulling her tightly to him, his lips parting hers, his tongue circling hers.

She responded with an abandon she'd thought she'd never see again, her arms snaking around his neck as they sagged onto the bed, David's hand skimming up her thigh beneath the long t-shirt she wore, cupping her hips in his hands as he moved her toward the center of the mattress.

He rose above her, slowly moving her t-shirt higher, his mouth following from her hips to her stomach to her breasts. Finally pulling the t-shirt over her head, he tossed it aside then crushed her mouth to him again, his hands sluicing up and down her sides and around to her bottom, sending darts of need so deep inside her she gasped.

He pushed his own pants off him and kicked them away, stretching his long length against her, easing her to him, kissing her mouth, her breasts again, his hands on her thighs, opening them.

Mouths, fingers, palms. They were all over her at once, so fast and so hot she couldn't keep track of them. Just as an orgasm would hit her hard and she thought she would die of pleasure, he was working her up again.

She found herself alternately begging for more and begging him to stop. Finally he moved inside her, and her breath came in catches. She drew her legs up, receiving him. Then, as she felt the wild rising of heat and exquisite release, he withdrew and rolled onto his back, bringing her with him. He coaxed her to straddle him, guiding her hips up and down his shaft.

She was panting, her skin slick on his. He positioned his hands on her breasts, kneading, circling. He sat up and feasted again, his hands holding tight to her bottom as she used her inner muscles to massage him. She arched her spine, her head falling back, hands finding his lean hipbones, fingers pressing against him. And she took him in deep, and he took her into oblivion.

Sometime before dawn she awoke and felt the sweet soreness between her legs. She smiled. She reached for him. The bed was empty.

CHAPTER 22

When Michele finally got home, she found it bereft of warmth. Everyone was tired as they made it to their corners of Theresa's house. All of Sweetwater Canyon was living with Theresa now. As they had all given up apartments to go on tour, and money was so tight, they'd agreed to move in with Theresa until they were making enough money to find places of their own again.

Michele's small space was a single bed in the far corner of the practice room. She laid her bass in the corner where it now lived with the other instruments, then opened her suitcase just enough to pull out her nightshirt. She wasn't sure she could go directly to bed, but she knew she didn't have the energy to talk to anyone.

The entire drive back to Portland had her wondering exactly what had happened last night. She knew she and David had sex. There was no doubt about that. But she thought, perhaps, there had been something more. She thought she had seen it in his eyes. Was it possible he did still love her?

No. It wasn't possible. She must have read more into it than he meant. He hadn't been in her bed in the morning and they'd barely said two words to each other during the eight-hour drive home. In fact, everyone had been amazingly quiet.

Unwilling to sleep yet, she got up and headed for the keyboard nearby. She hooked up the headphones to the back of the keyboard and put them over her ears, so she wouldn't disturb anyone. She pulled the bench out and began picking out a tune. I will love you forever. I will never let you go. / I give all my fears to you, because I will always know…

No! She slammed her fist onto the keys, and angrily took the headphones off. What was wrong with her? That was the one song she had vowed to never sing again.

She stood and marched to the kitchen. Finding no one else around, and all the lights off, she turned on the under-cabinet lights only. She scoured the fridge for something to eat. They'd been gone for a week this last time, and the pickings were pretty slim. In the freezer she found a box of Boca burgers and a bag of frozen peas. She pulled them out. Not gourmet, but it would do.

She cooked them both within minutes in the microwave then angrily marched back to her small space and her bed. She plopped herself down on the single bed, plate in front of her and a tall glass of water.

Michele grabbed the remote and turned on the twelve-inch television set she had taken out of storage when she'd moved in with Theresa. It had been a long time since she'd just wasted an evening on TV. She kept punching buttons until she finally settled on a rerun of a Simpson's episode. The volume down as low as possible, she was determined to enjoy it. It fit her mood perfectly. For the Simpson family, life was not only unfair, it was a ghastly mistake. She immediately started laughing.

EVEN HAD he not been forewarned by Kat, David would have known he was going to get the twenty questions treatment the instant he set foot inside Theresa's house. Rachel and Sarah were also there and regarded him with caution. Their greetings were polite, but distinctly cool. They were definitely withholding judgment, but one misstep on his part could easily swing the pendulum against him.

There were a few pleasantries exchanged before he was ushered into the kitchen and Theresa served her famous homemade lemonade and raspberries. They'd arranged him at the head of the table and the other four sat where they could all look at him. He gazed at each woman in turn.

He turned first to Rachel. "So, where's Michele?"

"We sent her out for groceries. With our big list, she had to drive all the way to the Fred Meyer's in Sandy, so she'll be gone at least two hours."

He nodded and took a breath. "So, what's this meeting all about?"

"Michele, of course," Rachel's eyes challenged him.

"What about Michele?" He didn't look away.

"That's right," Theresa drew his attention. "What are you going to do about Michele?"

"What do you think I should do?"

"Do you still love her?" Sarah asked.

His head was spinning as they asked questions one after the other, easily trading off and passing the baton like a well-choreographed dance. For the first time, he realized how much this band worked together, each one having a turn to be at the front and each one fading in the background for support or harmony. He smiled. They really did care, and he knew they would do anything for Michele.

"Yes, I still love her—with all my heart."

"Then why haven't you told her?" Kat finally chimed in. "She's so miserable. She doesn't think you love her anymore."

"She knows I love her."

"No she doesn't," Kat whined. "You have to do something. If you don't she's going to leave us after Christmas. You have to do something."

"Kat's right," Rachel took the lead again. "You were the one who hurt her. You were the one who let her down first."

"But we made up," he reminded them.

"Yes, you did," Theresa said. "And we thought you were getting somewhere with her. But whatever happened in Patrick's Creek has her in a tail spin."

How could there be any confusion after he and Michele had made love that evening. The ride home was quiet, but they were both tired and he had to leave town on a consulting job right away.

"What do you think happened in Patrick's Creek?" he asked.

"We don't know," they all said together. "She won't talk about it."

"Ah, I see."

"So what are you going to do?" Kat always came to the point.

"I'm going to marry her, of course."

"Yes!" Kat pumped her fist. "I knew it! I knew it!"

"Calm down, Kat," Theresa said. "We need to hear the details. I'm not sure Michele is aware of this yet."

SWEETWATER CANYON FINISHED the rehearsal with the last song they were considering for the live performance recording of their first CD.

"So how many is that?" Theresa asked.

"Twenty-eight," Michele answered as she set her bass back on its stand.

"Way too long," Rachel said, lowering her fiddle and opening her case. "We've got to pare way back. We agreed we would do somewhere around 15 to 17 at the most."

"It's so hard to choose what to cut," Sarah said. "We'll never agree. We have to have a play list that we can all agree on."

"I have an idea," Kat said. "Let's choose for each other."

"What do you mean, Kat?" Theresa winked at her.

"We all have our favorites that we like to play, and we all have our favorites that someone else does."

"Right," Rachel took over. "And since we are trying to concentrate on original tunes, so we don't have to pay so many royalties, it's only right that we choose which ones to do."

"Yes, but I know I'm my worst critic," Sarah said. "I always think something someone else has written is better than anything I've done."

"But your song, Paddling the Stream, is so beautiful," Michele said. "It's one of my favorites.

"Mine too," Kat echoed.

"As we have five of us and at least fifteen tracks, let's all pick two of our own favorites and then we will each choose one more that we didn't write. The one with the most votes wins. That will give us eleven original songs. We'll fill in the rest of the tracks with covers that help to keep the mix right," Theresa said.

"Good idea," Michele said.

Kat clapped her hands. "Perfect!" Then she ran through the sliding doors and down the hall.

When Kat returned she had bright yellow index cards that she passed out, along with pens. Each person wrote down the two original tunes of their own they wanted to record, and then their vote for the best one from someone else.

Michele chose Breaking the Bonds and Leave no Trace for her own compositions. She debated between a song from Rachel and one from Sarah as her final choice. She settled on Sarah's Paddling the Streams. She loved the melody and the harmonies, and it matched her feelings about life right now—a feeling of being in the middle of a search and unsure where she would end up.

Kat collected all the cards and began first reading the two selections each member had made for themselves. Theresa typed them into the spreadsheet on her laptop.

"Now we need to decide the order," Rachel suggested.

It went pretty quickly. They wanted to be sure to mix it up. A couple of upbeat or fun tunes and then a ballad. After about half an hour of haggling they finally had the initial order for the ten original songs, and they'd selected six covers to ensure the mix was good. The only question was what everyone had selected for the last original song and where it would best fit.

Kat stacked the cards again, dramatically drawing out the moment like she was going to read the Grammy winner for best song of the year. Michele giggled at her antics.

"Well, they are all ballads," Kat announced.

"Surprise, surprise," Sarah said, joining in the spirit of fun.

"And they are all by amazing talents in the Sweetwater Canyon band," Kat added.

"All right now, let's hear it," Michele reached toward Kat like she was going to snatch the cards from her and Kat danced back, giggling.

"Drum roll, please."

All four women began the rolling beat on their thighs.

"Paddling the Streams," Kat said first.

Sarah beamed and took an exaggerated bow.

"Accepting Love," Kat announced next.

Michele gasped. "No," she whispered. "I can't do that one."

Ignoring her, Kat picked up the next card. "Accepting Love."

"No," Michele said louder. "I can't. I just can't."

"Accepting Love," Kat read again.

"No, no, no."

"Accepting Love," Kat read the final one. "It's four to one, Michele. The last original song will have to be Accepting Love."

Everyone began to talk at once. No one was going to let her get out of it. Michele protested. She whined. She tried to bargain with them. No one would listen. They all said it was the best song she had ever written. They pointed out to her how it had always gotten standing ovations before she stopped singing it. They pointed out it was the perfect ending on the CD. Upbeat, and full of hope and promise.

Finally, worn down, she agreed. She even agreed it would be the final song on the album. God help her, she had no idea how she was going to pull it off.

DAVID LOOKED at his map again and then made the turn up the snow-packed drive. Things looked different in December. He'd only been here that one time, at the beginning of their summer tour, when Michele's parents had hosted the neighborhood in their barn for that benefit concert. Though he'd talked with her mother several times during their tour, he hadn't spoken with them since October.

Michele's mother had been very encouraging about getting them back together. In fact when he had come to her and confessed what an idiot he'd been—without going into all the grisly details of how he had hurt Michele—it had been her mother who had encouraged him to call from their phone. It had been her Mother who had extracted a promise from Michele not to hang up. He would be forever grateful for that.

He saw the house ahead of him and slowed to a crawl. He gathered his courage by remembering how much he had felt at home with them. He remembered how warmly they had embraced him, made him feel like part of the family. He hoped he still got the same warm reception. He had no idea how much Michele had shared her pain with her parents, either during the tour or more recently. When he had called to tell them he was coming, her mother had made no mention of it and had enthusiastically agreed to his visit.

He parked the four-wheel drive he had rented, and climbed out of the car. The plants that had been blooming so brightly in the late spring were now covered in snow. The white snow against the brown clapboards of the house provided a strong contrast. He noticed the stairs had been carefully swept, making sure there was no way to slip on the treads. He stubbed the toe of his boots against the bottom riser, shaking off as much snow as he could before climbing to the porch.

On the porch he noticed a boot scraper. Bending his right knee, he took the scraper in his left hand and worked the remaining snow out of the treads. Then he repeated the same process with his left shoe. He replaced the scraper in the holder beside the door, took a deep breath and knocked.

Mrs. Scott answered the door. She smiled broadly and embraced him like she would her own son.

"Come in. Come in out of the cold."

David stepped inside and she closed the door behind him. He

immediately removed his shoes and set them with the stack of others on a small square of carpet to one side.

"Can I get you something warm to drink? I have coffee and hot cocoa."

"Coffee would be wonderful, Mrs. Scott."

"Carol, please. I thought we agreed last time you would call me Carol."

"Thank you, Carol." He handed her his coat, and she scurried toward the kitchen.

His eyes began to adjust from the brightness outside to the cozy lamp-lit interior of the living room. He looked toward the ceiling and noticed the large exposed log that formed the ridge beam. One rarely saw logs that big anymore—especially in houses. The farmhouse had to be at least a hundred years old. He noticed there were few windows. He assumed that was to make sure the cold was kept out. In the center of the room was a large woodstove, and he could see the wood glowing bright red through the glass.

Michele's father slowly pushed himself off the sofa. David noticed he seemed a little tired, like he'd been working outside in the snow all day.

"Come in. Take a load off," Matt invited. "That's a rough drive from Butte when it's so white outside."

"Weather wasn't bad," David said as he shook Matt's hand. "At least it's not snowing."

Carol stepped quietly beside David and handed him his cup of coffee. "Black right? Did I remember right?"

"Why yes, you did. How do you do that? I don't even remember drinking coffee when I was here last time."

"For breakfast. I remember, Michele told me how you take it. All the girls were sleeping in the big motor home and you had taken Michele's old room. You all grabbed a little bit of breakfast and coffee before you took off down the road again."

Now David remembered. That seemed so long ago, when things had been so fresh and free with Michele, when it seemed nothing could ever mar their happiness.

"Please, sit." Carol pointed to the other chair facing the fire. Then she sat beside her husband.

Matt automatically took her hand in his, and David noticed how he stroked it lovingly as she snuggled closer. He wondered what it would be like to have that kind of relationship—the kind where you could count on your partner to always know exactly what to do and when. That was the kind of relationship he wanted with Michele.

"So, what's this all about, that you couldn't just tell us on the phone?" Carol asked. "This is a long way to come just to talk, David. Is everything OK?"

"Yes, everything's great."

"Then what is it?"

"I'm in love with Michele." He let it out on a big exhale of breath.

"Oh, we know that, honey. It was as plain as day when you came to visit last time."

David laughed. "I didn't know it was so obvious then."

Matt cleared his throat. "It was obvious Michele was happy. It was obvious Michele had some passion in her life."

David blushed. He still wasn't comfortable with them knowing he'd slept with their daughter.

"Oh, pshaw," Carol waved a hand at him.

"We know times aren't like they used to be. We know Michele's not a virgin. All that matters is that you know how to make her happy."

"That's all I want to do," David said. "And that's why I'm here, to ask your permission to marry her."

"You don't need our permission, son," Matt said, his voice gruff. "We like you fine. It's Michele's permission you need."

"Have you asked her, David?" Carol asked.

"Yes, I asked her before she left on tour."

"And did she say yes."

"Well, that's a bit complicated."

David described how she'd accepted his proposal, and when he went back to give her his grandmother's ring he'd found her with Justin, and then all the stupid things he'd done after that. It was an edited version, of course, but he didn't leave out how much responsibility he had in making things go wrong. He also tried to explain how he was trying to make things right, how hard he was working to make her realize how much he really did love her. He didn't exactly talk about what happened at Patrick's Creek, but he alluded to the fact that he thought he'd convinced her then as to his love. But nothing had been enough to completely turn the tide.

"I see," Carol said. "Well, she always was stubborn. But she knows what's right for herself in the end."

"So, my plan is to propose to her again at the CD concert. I would like you to be there. If she says yes, there will be a wedding—immediately—as soon as we can get a license and a preacher. I'm not giving her a chance to change her mind again this time." He paused. "And…if she says no…well…I…"

Carol stepped over to him and wrapped her arms around him. "She won't say no, David. She loves you. She won't say no."

CHAPTER 23

Michele looked out the windows of her room at Timberline Lodge. There was snow everywhere, blanketing evergreens that had already closed into themselves for the winter. Much as Michele loved spending time outside, she was ready for change. She was ready to step back and consider what to do next.

Winter meant staying indoors, with a blazing fire, hot mulled cider —cocooning. Her eyes misted briefly. It wasn't that long ago she had pictured herself settling in with David as husband and wife in December. In fact, today, Saturday was the date she and the rest of the band had tentatively chosen for the wedding.

She wrapped her arms around herself and looked out the windows again. Huge snowflakes were falling now. She wouldn't be surprised if by the time they closed the show tonight, there would be no access down the mountain.

It was okay. She had her family here. David had paid for the tickets for her parents as well as her brother and his family, and he'd picked them up at the airport and brought them here for the show. He also paid for their rooms at the lodge. She would have fought with him about spending the money, but he did the same thing for Sarah's parents and her brothers. He'd even flown Rachel's father here from Scotland. Rachel's mother couldn't come, but he'd offered. She evidently felt she couldn't leave England and her new family at Christmas time. David had said he was just so proud of the band that he wanted all the people special to them to be here and help celebrate their success.

Unfortunately, David's parents couldn't come, and Michele felt badly about that. Kat had told her that he'd invited them. He had wanted them to share in the band's success. When Michele tried to broach the subject with David, he had shrugged and said they'd stopped coming to important events in his life ever since he graduated from high school. She just couldn't imagine parents like that. Hers had made an effort to be at everything in her life, even when they couldn't afford it. And she knew they would keep coming as long as they could.

In the past month she and David had come to a kind of understanding. He really was good at the business end of things. They had more bookings for next year than ever in the history of the band. He'd already confirmed 150 shows and that was before their next tour. Though it still hurt for her to be around him, yet not with him, she had made her peace with it.

She'd also decided the band was too important to give up. As for David traveling with them next year, she figured she'd rather be with him as a friend than not at all.

She heard a knock at the door. It was only a few minutes before she needed to head downstairs. Maybe Kat or someone needed her help with a costume. "Who is it?"

"It's Kim, I've got to see you."

She threw the door open and her best friend rushed into the room, closing the door quickly behind her.

"Oh my God! You're here. I can't believe it," Michele babbled between tears and repeated hugs. "How did you know? How did you get time off? How did you..."

Kim hugged her tight then stood back to take a long look. "You look great. And if you do the whole concert in your underwear you'll get even more fans than you know what do with."

In her haste to greet her friend, she had completely forgotten she hadn't dressed yet. She blushed, then giggled, then blushed again. "How?"

"David of course. You don't think he'd let your most ardent supporter not be screaming from the audience for an encore do you? These live CDs need to sound like you're playing to a huge crowd. You know me, I can talk and scream enough for at least five people."

Michele laughed. She was already starting to relax.

"So, what are you supposed to be wearing? Can I help?"

Michele pointed to the dress on her bed. Kat had designed all of their costumes especially for tonight. Michele smiled with a tinge of sadness. The dress was very similar to the one they had planned for her wedding. When Michele had protested, everyone had insisted. They were all wearing the same dress, just in different colors. Rachel was wearing green to represent the evergreens of the forest. Sarah was wearing blue to symbolize the waterfalls in the gorge. Kat was wearing a deep chocolate to remind them of the fall leaves still clinging to trees. Theresa was wearing red to signify the winter berries on the holly. And Michele was wearing a pale gold to represent the fading sun of winter. It was all rather dramatic, and very Kat, but she had to admit it would be dashing on stage.

"Well, what are you waiting for?" Kim asked. "I'm here and you are going to look beautiful!"

Kim picked up the satin dress and slipped it over Michele's head, helping her to skim it along her arms and down her sides. It fit her curves perfectly. Kim helped with the zipper in the back and then reached for the evergreen wreath Michele was to wear on her head.

Michele looked in the mirror as she secured her hair around the wreath. Kim helped to weave the side strands between the branches of the wreath, while the rest of her hair fell freely to her waist.

"Wow!" Kim stepped back to admire her. "You look amazing! Like you just walked out of a fairy-tale forest."

"Kat's idea," Michele said. "She's been fixated on this story of the Princess Bride and she got a little carried away with all of us."

"Well, you're beautiful. I'm sure all of you will be radiant."

Michele took stock of herself in the mirror once again. Kat had done a great job. The dress was beautiful, Michele admitted. And with the wreath in her hair she even felt beautiful. Just the way Kat ordered.

~

MICHELE WAITED to one side for every one to be seated. Behind her was a thirty-foot Christmas tree, decorated in shades of cream and beige, against floor to ceiling windows that overlooked the snow-laden slopes of Mt. Hood. The grand stone fireplace dominated the back of the room, providing heat for all those seated for the concert. Deep wooden walls ran high into the cathedral ceiling, with hand-hewn, exposed beams telling their stories of true craftsmanship during the depression years. Iron sculpted chandeliers cast a warm glow upon the gathering of chairs and benches set upon sturdy, wide-planked floors. Woodcarvings, imaginative wrought-iron fixtures, and hand-hooked rugs completed the rustic picture softened by Christmas lights and decorations throughout the room.

Michele saw David and her head reeled. He looked amazing. He was wearing coal black pants with a matching dinner jacket. His shirt was the same pale gold as her dress. The tie around his neck was a deep gold silk that caught the light and reflected it back to his face when he turned.

She watched him greeting guests and making sure they were seated comfortably. David had found her parents a seat in the center of the front row, right next to Kim. Before she sat down, her Mom hugged him tightly then dabbed at her eyes with a hankie David retrieved from his breast pocket. Michele would have been worried, but her Mom was smiling so broadly she guessed David must have told an especially amusing joke or a touching story.

The house lights dimmed and the conversations in the audience ceased. Sweetwater Canyon took their places at the front of the room. There was no large stage this time, just a small square of floor—

enough to accommodate them and their equipment. Michele's bass was leaning upright on a stand so she wouldn't have to bend over in the dark to get it. All four women moved forward without their instruments and stood in front of the voice mikes.

The lights came up slowly and Theresa nodded as she picked up the cue from the recording engineer. The group began with an *a capella* ballad that spoke of the end of fall and the coming of winter, and the surprises a child discovers as she uncovers nature beneath the snow. It was one of the first songs Sarah had written and Michele felt it was the perfect beginning.

Michele sang as if in a trance. Their harmonies were blending effortlessly tonight. The combination of upbeat dance instrumentals with the meaningful ballads and stories each had composed touched her heart at every turn. It was if she was experiencing these songs for the first time.

The audience remained in the periphery of her consciousness, as she flowed in the continuous river of change from one song to the next. She felt the rapids that bounced them through rhythms that shifted and changed, sometimes making her feel like she had to just hang on to survive. Just as quickly, the next tune thrust them into an eddy that returned on itself as they sang a round four times through. Then they'd push off into a lazy, flowing stream of a ballad where she could rest and just fill-in and reinforce the strength of the foundation.

The final rapid propelled them into the last song, the one she had been dreading, yet promised to do—Love's Acceptance. She looked over to each of the women in Sweetwater Canyon and she could feel their hearts reaching out and supporting her. She nodded and stepped forward to the center mike where she would begin her solo. She heard the fiddle play the haunting introduction and Michele opened her mouth to sing. Instead, she found tears and her voice shook as she choked them back.

She looked back to Rachel with fear; but instead of compassion Rachel reflected back strength and love, then she improvised a longer melody line giving Michele a little more time. Michele stared into the front row searching for her parents. Her father had both his hands on her mother's as he held them tight in his lap. Her mother beamed. He looked at her mother with his heart on his sleeve. Such love and admiration reflected in his face that Michele knew she could sing it for them. She could sing it to celebrate their love of more than thirty years, and she would sing it loud and clear

Michele looked again to Rachel and nodded. Rachel played the opening segment again as Michele closed her eyes and let the tears fall freely. She recounted her love with David, from the young woman filled with fear and recrimination to the blossoming of her heart and soul. Michele sung with all the love she had held to herself so tight these past months, letting it spill over onto anyone who would dare to hear. On each chorus the rest of the band joined her in harmony, adding their strength to her acceptance of love.

Michele's voice quieted as she began the last chorus alone. Her mind imagined there was another voice singing her song, she stopped confused. David's voice picked up the melody as he walked to the microphone and stood next to her. Michele joined him, shifting to harmony, her eyes transfixed on his, afraid to move for fear it would be only a dream.

She felt him reaching toward her and pulling her closer as he peered straight into her soul. She saw all the love and passion they'd shared in the past and all the promise of the future. She was so awed by how willing he was to share his heart, to let her take it and do what she would, that she stopped her harmony and put her arms around his waist, burying her head against his chest where she could hear the vibrations of his music—where she could hear the counterpoint of their two hearts beating together again in harmony.

David held her like he would never let her go as he completed the last lines of her beautiful song in his rich baritone voice.

I will love you forever. I will never let you go.
I give all my fears to you, because I will always know,

you are mine and I am yours, never to be parted again.
You are mine, and I am yours, from now until then.
And we will share all our tomorrows together.
Because now I know, I will always love you.
Forever.

SNEAK PEAK AT HEALING NOTES: RACHEL'S STORY

Misty, grey clouds drizzled rain onto the blue-grey stucco of the small clinic and dotted the dirty, pock-marked sidewalk in front of Rachel Cullen's car. Even the doors on the nine small offices were grey. The lack of color matched her mood—no contrast, no feeling, just grey. It was her last time meeting with Dr. Patterson. She should be happy. She'd been fighting the counseling every step of the way during the last six months. Now she'd be free of these weekly visits.

Rachel was stronger now. She no longer jumped at shadows and her nightmares had stopped—well, maybe not stopped. Lessened. The dreams that used to haunt her every night now only appeared once every three or four weeks.

She took a deep breath and held it while she applied a gloss and rubbed her lips together. She let out her breath. Stuffing the tube back into her purse, she swore at the snap that wouldn't close. *You can do this! You're not going to let that bastard control your life any longer!* The snap finally caught. Now she just needed to get out of the car.

Her hands shook as she unlocked the door. She swung her legs from beneath the steering wheel and placed both feet on the ground with a splash, her shoes immediately drenched by the puddle she hadn't seen. *"Cach,"* she swore again. It must be a sign—a sign that this session was not going to go well.

Rachel stood tall, pressed down the lock, and slammed the car door shut. She stepped up to the building and followed the short path to suite 109, her shoes squishing with each step. Taking a deep breath she flipped her handbag over her right shoulder to bounce on her hip. She was ready to finally put the past behind her.

As she reached for the handle, the door opened and a little girl rushed out, maybe six or seven years old, with beautiful long blond hair caught up in a blue denim bow. She ran to a light blue sedan next to Rachel's and giggled as she skipped through puddles circling the car. Rachel couldn't help but smile at the child's carefree innocence.

After three circles, the girl stopped at the back end of the car, cocked her head and waved two fingers at her. "Hi."

"Um, hi." Rachel raised her hand and waved back. "Did you forget somebody? Your mommy maybe?"

"Claire, I told you to stay close."

At the sound of the tenor voice beside her, Rachel started. A man three to four inches taller than her had stepped out. In one hand he held several colorful ribbons attached to a bright pink, heart-shaped helium balloon that read *Happy Birthday*. He looked toward the car where the child was still giggling.

The little girl raced back. Skidding to a stop in front of Rachel, they bumped and Rachel teetered slightly toward the wall.

"Careful there." A weathered hand reached toward her and wrapped around her elbow. His touch was softer than she expected, but her knees still locked, ready to spring if she needed to move fast. He held her up with one hand. Deep brown eyes, emphasized by his full head of short, wavy blonde hair, looked at her then turned toward the girl."

"Apologize, Claire. You almost knocked her over."

"I'm sorry." A small hand lifted to touch her other arm.

"That's okay. Really. I should have been paying more attention." Rachel smiled and pointed to the balloon. *"Latha breith."*

"Excuse me?"

"Oh, I…" She had lapsed into Gaelic. Something she hadn't done in public since Kavan left her almost three years ago. "I said 'Happy Birthday.'"

The man looked at his daughter and his smile reached his eyes, sending a tingle along Rachel's spine. What she would give for a man to smile like that when he thought of her.

She bent to the little girl dancing in circles near the door. "How old are you?"

"Six. I get to go to first grade this year." The little girl looked up as Rachel straightened again. "You're pretty, like my mommy. But you talk funny."

Rachel laughed. You could always count on children to be straight.

"Scottish or Irish?" the man asked.

"Scottish. Dunoon. It's a little town on the Firth of Clyde." Rachel concentrated on not moving, avoiding the continued squish of her shoes.

"I thought I detected a slight accent, but it's not a full brogue."

"I've worked hard to lose it. To make myself understood."

The little girl pulled on her father's hand. "Can we go now? I'm ready for my cake." She jumped off the curb, making a big splash and then stood next to the passenger door of the car, her eyes wide. The man laughed and waggled a finger in his daughter's direction.

"She's darling." Rachel said to the back of his head. She didn't want them to leave. She'd much rather go celebrate a birthday with this happy family than walk into that office one more time.

"Daddy, hurry. I'm starving." The little girl's tiny hand rubbed at her stomach dramatically.

With another laugh, the man turned to Rachel. "I can't keep a starving child waiting now, can I?" He took a step away then turned back. "Dr. Patterson is really good. Don't be afraid."

"I, uh…" Rachel flushed that a stranger would know the purpose of her visit. Of course, they must have just left Dr. Patterson's office. Was it the child or the man who needed help? Or both?

She watched the man all the way to his car. She liked the way he walked, his stride confident, purposeful. He thumbed the lock on a keychain and opened the car door. The little girl jumped into the seat and said something that made him laugh. He pointed inside and the girl immediately grabbed the seat belt to secure it. He turned his head toward Rachel as he closed the passenger door. "Have a nice day." He threw the words over his shoulder as he rounded the car to the driver's side, the balloon gaily swaying above his head, adding the only bright spot of color to the grey day.

She watched them drive away until their bright happiness had disappeared from view. Her eyes misted. She angrily rubbed the back of her hand across them. For a moment she'd imagined herself as part of that happy family—a woman out to enjoy a birthday celebration with her daughter and the man who loved her. Evidently, even this happy family had problems.

Resolute, she turned back to the door in front of her and entered. After Kavan had divorced her, she had rid herself of loyalty to any man. Now she needed to rid herself of one last nightmare.

♬

Rachel crossed her arms in front of her and looked down. Why was this still so damn hard?

Dr. Patterson waited patiently for an answer.

"I try not to think about it much. I'm tired of this hanging over my head. I'm ready for it to just go away and forget about it."

"Is that why you've seen me every week for six months? Because forgetting is so easy?"

Rachel clenched her teeth and stared, unblinking, at the therapist. "It might have been easy if you hadn't forced me to talk about it every week, relive every moment, talk about how I felt. I wanted to just forget it and get on with my life, but you made me think about it all the time. I'm glad this is the last session."

"You're using anger as a shield."

Her fist hit the arms of her chair. "Well, it's a hell of a lot better than crying all the time."

Dr. Patterson leaned forward. "Every emotion is viable as part of your healing. If you want to be angry on our last day, that's fine with me."

Rachel shifted uncomfortably in her seat. Dr. Patterson always saw through her attempts not to deal with her feelings. But she was scared. Really scared.

Not scared to talk about the rape. She'd done that a million times too many already. No. She was scared that this was the last time she could count on her once a week visits. Though she'd fought the revealed intimacies every week, she had also come to rely on them. Sometimes the only thing that got her through a week of walking on eggshells with her friends, or avoiding every man who looked at her, was knowing that Tuesday would come and Dr. Patterson would be there to debrief. Now she was supposed to have the skills to handle it on her own.

Rachel sighed. Fear never got her anywhere. "I'm fine. It'll be hard, but I'll be fine. When things get bad, I always have my music."

"Speaking of your music, it's interesting that you've let your relationship with Michele lapse, and have withdrawn from the other two adults in your band. Kat is the only one you've let inside your heart."

Rachel shrugged. "I'm just not comfortable with the looks all the time."

"Looks?"

"Yeah, like I have an incurable disease and they have to be careful around me because they might catch it."

"Do you think being a rape victim is a disease?"

"No. Yes. I don't know. I just get tired of being the one everyone feels sorry for. It's like I burst the bubble of a world filled with love, and they still want to hang onto it and I don't. So…"

"And Kat doesn't make you feel this way?"

"She's just a teenager. She truly believes that love will heal everything, and she never looks at me like it won't happen for me."

"Do you believe it will happen for you?"

Rachel remained silent. Dr. Patterson had maneuvered her back to the painful subject—the one she would probably never resolve. Maybe it was that Kat still believed in true love for everyone that made her hang on. She wasn't sure, but she didn't want her last session to dwell on this.

Dr. Patterson continued, "Michele was married at the end of your tour last year, right? Only a couple of months after you were out of the hospital."

"Don't." Rachel curled her fingers into her palms until her nails bit into the flesh. Even a small physical pain helped keep the tears at bay.

Dr. Patterson's gaze remained steady and she leaned forward. "Don't shut down, Rachel. Accepting Michele's marriage is the only way to re-establish the relationship you want with your friends. You can do this."

"No. I don't want to talk about this. I do accept her marriage. I'm happy for her. Really, I am."

"You accept her marriage in your head, Rachel, but not in your heart. Your heart is still hurting."

Rachel flinched and backed into her chair as her breathing accelerated. She raised her chin. How dare Dr. Patterson assume she knew what was in her heart. Did she think just because she'd been talking for six months she could presume…

"My heart is just fine. It's my head that's screwed up. That's what you were supposed to fix." Rachel stood. "And now our time is up and it's still not fixed. What does that say about your counseling abilities, Dr. Patterson?"

Dr. Patterson sat back in her chair and sighed. "Back to anger? Or can you admit to fear?"

Rachel willed her heart to slow as she paced behind her chair. Yes, it was fear. Fear that Kat's belief was based in the naiveté of youth, fear that she'd never regain her strong friendship with her other band mates, fear that she would always be jealous of Michele and her happy married life, and fear of not having Dr. Patterson to force her to talk about all this stuff.

In the face of all that fear, anger was her only defense. Maybe that wasn't so bad. At least she could function. At least she would be able to walk out of here with her head high. She grasped the back of the chair and leaned on it.

"Look, I'm thirty-four, divorced, probably can't ever have kids. Is it any wonder I don't believe in true love? So what? Not everyone finds somebody to spend the rest of her life with. I'm okay with it. Really. It's time to move on."

Dr. Patterson was noticeably silent. Rachel itched to fill the void.

She gestured with her palms out to the side and facing upward. "Look, I'm fine." She walked to the front of the chair. "You've really helped me. I can see that. I'm good. Really." She held out her hand to Dr. Patterson, ready to shake and say good-bye.

Dr. Patterson leaned back in her chair and crossed one leg over the other, relaxed. "We still have ten minutes, Rachel. No need to rush out."

Undecided, Rachel held her breath. She fiddled with the strap of her purse and glanced toward the closed door. She looked back to Dr. Patterson, still undisturbed in her chair, acting as if it didn't matter what Rachel chose at this moment. Was it really up to her to end this?

Rachel held out her hand again, "No. I'm good. Thanks for all your help."

Dr. Patterson smiled and rose. She took her hand and then pulled her in for a hug. "You'll make it, Rachel. There will be some bad times and some good times, but you'll make it. You're strong. Just don't give up on your dreams."

Rachel's eyes misted. That was the problem. She'd already given up.

Dr. Patterson stepped back. "If you find yourself giving up, or something new comes up…like a man in your life…and the fear is overwhelming, you can always come back to see me."

Rachel snorted, but a soft laugh filled with trust followed. "Yeah, like I'd let you into my sex life too."

Dr. Patterson smiled. "Yes, your sex life *and* your love life."

Rachel frowned. Some people just never believed her. Love was not in the cards for her. She'd accepted it even before the rape. That's one thing that hadn't changed.

"Strong women face their fears," Dr. Patterson said. "They accept the choices they've made and use them to gather more strength."

Rachel flinched. "Well, yeah. I'll work on that. Thanks."

She left the office as quickly as possible. It took all her concentration not to run to her car.

Outside, the rain had cleared and it was a gloriously bright and crisp February day. Typical Oregon as spring approached—mostly rain, but then when you least expected it the sun shined clear and bright, bathing the landscape with sparkles of light and shadow. She shielded her eyes as she looked up at the sky and saw a rainbow in the distance. Rachel laughed as she skirted the puddle next to her car and climbed in. So much for believing in the weather signs. It was as if the whole world was trying to change her mind.

ACKNOWLEDGMENTS

No book is created alone and this is no exception. First, I have to thank the members of the Misty River Band in Oregon. They allowed me to travel with them to several gigs, and it was through them I learned what it is like to be a small local band and the process for building a following. Their music captured my heart, and their kindness will be forever remembered.

Second, I must acknowledge the editing of Babe King. Her extensive knowledge of music and its nuances helped to shape the scenes where the band is playing specific types of songs. Her careful reading and editing of those scenes made them so much stronger.

Finally, thanks to my critique partners, the Crit-Wits, who always kept me writing and ignored every excuse I made; and to my husband who continues to be my greatest cheerleader and an amazing cook. He keeps me fed when I'm on deadline, laughs when I'm forgetful, and still loves me even when I ignore him. I know I am so very fortunate to have him.

ABOUT THE AUTHOR

Maggie Lynch is the author of 26+ published books, as well as numerous short stories and non-fiction articles. Her fiction tells stories of men and women making heroic choices one messy moment at a time. Her nonfiction focuses on helping indie authors be successful in their careers. Maggie is also the founder of Windtree Press, an independent publishing cooperative with over 300 titles among 24 authors.

Maggie and her musician husband live in the beautiful Pacific Northwest, and are ruled by two demanding cats. In 2013, after careers in counseling, the software industry, academia, and worldwide educational consulting, Maggie chose to become a full time author. Her fiction spans romance, suspense, fantasy and science fiction titles. Her non-fiction focuses on guiding authors to success in planning, distributing, and marketing their completed work.